REDEEMED

ALSO BY MARGARET PETERSON HADDIX

<— THE MISSING: BOOK 8 —>

REDEEMED

MARGARET PETERSON
HADDIX

SIMON & SCHUSTER BOOKS FOR YOUNG READERS

NEW YORK LONDON TORONTO SYDNEY NEW DELHI

SIMON & SCHUSTER BOOKS FOR YOUNG READERS

An imprint of Simon & Schuster Children's Publishing Division

1230 Avenue of the Americas, New York, New York 10020

SIMON & SCHUSTER BOOKS FOR YOUNG READERS is a trademark of Simon & Schuster, Inc.

For information about special discounts for bulk purchases,

please contact Simon & Schuster Special Sales at 1-866-506-1949 or

business@simonandschuster.com.

The Simon & Schuster Speakers Bureau can bring authors to your live event.

For more information or to book an event, contact the Simon & Schuster Speakers Bureau at

1-866-248-3049 or visit our website at www.simonspeakers.com.

Also available in a Simon & Schuster Books for Young Readers hardcover edition

Interior design by Hilary Zarycky

Cover design by Dan Potash

The text for this book was set in Weiss.

Manufactured in the United States of America

0617 OFF

First Simon & Schuster Books for Young Readers paperback edition September 2016

2 4 6 8 10 9 7 5 3

The Library of Congress has cataloged the hardcover edition as follows:

Haddix, Margaret Peterson.

Redeemed / Margaret Peterson Haddix.—First edition.

pages cm.—(The missing ; [8])

Summary: Jonah was able to save all of time from collapsing but in doing so gained a twin brother, Jordan, who must learn what has happened and do his own part to save time—and his parents.

ISBN 978-1-4424-9756-6 (hardcover)

ISBN 978-1-4424-9758-0 (pbk)

ISBN 978-1-4424-9759-7 (eBook)

[1. Time travel—Fiction. 2. Space and time—Fiction. 3. Twins—Fiction. 4. Brothers and sisters—Fiction. 5. Family life—Fiction. 6. Science fiction.] I. Title.

PZ7.H1164Rd 2015

[Fic]—dc23

2014014609

For Meredith and Connor
At least your middle-school years were not *this* crazy

ONE

When Jordan Skidmore came down the stairs that morning, he didn't expect to see a strange kid sitting in his family's living room.

He *really* didn't expect to see a strange kid who looked exactly like Jordan himself.

Jordan instantly forgot that he'd been running downstairs to tell his sister, Katherine, that he had dibs on the biggest TV in the house. He forgot that, until a moment earlier, he'd been happy to be staying home sick from school, and to have nothing ahead of him all day except taking it easy.

He skidded to a stop on the wooden floor. "Who— who are you?" he blurted.

It felt like a stupid question. Jordan might as well have skipped ahead to *What evil scientist stole my DNA and secretly cloned me?* That was how much he and the other kid looked alike. The other kid had Jordan's exact same shade of light brown hair, the exact same shape and shade of dark blue eyes, even the exact same stupid chin dimple, positioned just enough off center to make his whole face look slightly askew.

No, wait—that kid's dimple is a little to the right, and mine's a little to the left, Jordan thought.

Which meant that looking at this kid was like looking into a mirror. Only this was a mirror image that could sit while Jordan was standing; he could shove back his messy hair while Jordan let both arms dangle uselessly—and he could raise his eyebrows and blink even as Jordan felt his own face stuck in a mask of shocked astonishment.

And it was a mirror image that could wear totally different clothes. Jordan had on a basketball camp T-shirt and gray sweatpants. This kid was wearing the nerdiest clothes ever: a sweater vest and short pants that buttoned at his knees and the same kind of stiff, ugly shoes Jordan's dad wore to work.

Jordan also noticed that this mirror-image kid didn't answer. But Katherine did. For the first time Jordan realized that his sister was sprawled on the floor by the other kid's feet.

"Jordan, Jonah—the two of you have *got* to stop acting like the other one doesn't exist!" she said.

Huh? Jordan thought.

Katherine was Jordan's younger sister, eleven years old to Jordan's thirteen. Still, she usually acted like it was her job to boss him around. Usually Jordan just ignored her. But what was she even talking about now?

"You're exactly alike!" Katherine went on lecturing him. And . . . was she lecturing the other boy too? Did *she* know who he was and why he looked so much like Jordan? "You're practically the same person! *That's* why you're not getting along!"

Jordan got the "exactly alike" part. But the rest of it made no sense. How could he and this other kid have ever gotten along or not gotten along—or acted like the other person did or did not exist—when they'd never seen each other before in their lives?

Jordan saw something like understanding slide over the other boy's face. Did *he* know what Katherine meant?

Is this just some really, really good prank? Jordan wondered. *And the other boy's in on it?*

The truth was, Jordan was more likely to try to prank Katherine than the other way around. And even if this was a Katherine prank, how could she have made someone look so much like Jordan? Even the best Hollywood makeup artist couldn't do that, not even with makeup and a prosthetic nose and chin.

This kid wasn't wearing makeup. His nose and chin looked as real as the nose and chin on Jordan's own face.

So, then . . . Jordan scrambled for other explanations that didn't involve impossible pranks or evil scientists and secret cloning.

Something truly awful occurred to him.

Jordan was adopted. He'd never known anything about his birth family. Though he never bothered thinking about it much, it was possible that dozens of people out there in the world looked like him. He might have all sorts of blood relatives—brothers, sisters, cousins, even— that he'd never met.

Brothers and cousins wouldn't look exactly *like me*, Jordan argued with himself. *Sisters definitely wouldn't.*

But the idea that this kid might have something to do with Jordan's adoption made him feel even more unsettled. His mind blanked out for a moment. He barely noticed Katherine and the strange kid—Jonah? Was his name Jonah?—snapping their heads to the left, to gaze out the front window toward the driveway. He barely noticed the sound of a strange car speeding into the driveway and slamming on the brakes with such a screech that the car must have just barely missed smashing into the garage.

So it was even more of a jolt when the front door beside Jordan swung open and banged against the wall.

He turned just in time to see three strange kids sweep in through the door. They all looked to be about thirteen too. Two were girls and one was a boy; one of the girls was super tall.

"I thought—I thought you were going to change back," strange mirror-image boy stammered behind Jordan.

Jordan was kind of relieved to hear the other boy sounding shocked too. But was he talking about changing clothes? These kids' clothes looked normal: T-shirts and jeans like anyone would wear.

Except . . . is that one of my shirts the boy is wearing? And one of Katherine's shirts the shorter girl is wearing? Jordan wondered.

"We couldn't wait," the shorter girl said breathlessly. Her voice sounded kind of familiar, but Jordan couldn't figure out why. "We had to make sure all three of you were safe first. Oh, Jonah . . . Jordan . . . Katherine . . ."

How does she know me and Katherine? Jordan wondered. *And—does this prove mirror-image boy is named Jonah?*

"We were so afraid we'd lose all three of you forever," stolen-shirt boy wailed behind her.

Why would some kid Jordan had never seen before worry about losing Jordan and Katherine?

And does nobody else notice that this Jonah kid looks just like me? Jordan wondered.

Before he could ask any of these questions out loud,

the shorter girl slammed into him, with stolen-shirt boy hitting him a split second later. It wasn't a tackle. It was more like a running hug. The two of them pulled Jordan along, dragging him toward Katherine and Jonah. The kids yanked Katherine up from the floor and Jonah up from the chair into some weird group hug. Jordan didn't even know any of these people except Katherine—and he and she had stopped hugging each other about the time Katherine started kindergarten.

Mom and Dad would probably like us to keep doing Skidmore family hugs all the time, but . . . ugh, Jordan thought. *Not going to happen.*

Maybe Katherine was thinking along the same lines, because as the two running huggers crushed them all closer together, she began stuttering, "M-mom? D-dad?"

Sarcasm, Jordan thought. *Way to call those two out on how weird they're being. They're acting like parents!*

But Katherine's face looked deadly serious. And worried.

She was such a drama queen.

"What happened to you?" she asked the newly arrived trio of strange kids. "I mean, I can *see* what happened to you—you're, like, kids. But why? Or—did you travel from the past? How much did Jonah mess up time after I left?"

"I didn't mess up time!" Jonah protested hotly. "I fixed it!"

"Katherine, it's true," the taller girl said, hovering behind the weirdo group-hug scene. "You missed a lot. Jonah saved everyone."

Jordan grimaced. None of this made sense. *Travel from the past? Messed-up time? Huh?* But he felt something like a stab of jealousy. Had Jordan ever accomplished anything that made people say *his* name with such reverence and pride?

Short answer: No, Jordan thought. His parents were the type who made a big deal when he got good grades or scored a soccer goal or did some Boy Scout service project. But even they would never say that Jordan had "saved everyone."

Somehow this made Jordan feel even weirder about the fact that identical-boy Jonah had his arm wrapped around Jordan's right side, even as Katherine hugged him from the left. Jordan jerked back, breaking everyone's hold on him.

"I don't know what any of you are talking about," Jordan said, and it annoyed him that his voice came out squeaky and childish instead of strong and forceful. "But Katherine, you're going to get in trouble for inviting all these people over when we're both home sick."

He sounded like a five-year-old threatening to tattle.

The short girl wearing Katherine's clothes reached for

Jordan again. "Oh, honey," she said, patting his shoulder. "I can see where this would feel very strange to you."

Her voice *was* familiar. So was the way she was patting his shoulder.

It was exactly what his mother would say and do.

Jordan stared into this strange girl's face. And now that he was focused, he recognized her. This girl looked exactly like his mother did in old pictures—the ones from thirty years ago, when she was a teenager.

Jordan shifted his gaze to stolen-shirt boy's face, and it matched Jordan's memory of his father's old pictures too.

How could these two kids who were standing in Jordan's own living room right now, in the twenty-first century, look so much like pictures from the past?

Jordan could think of only one explanation.

Because suddenly he saw the real reason Katherine had stammered, *M-mom? D-dad?* She wasn't being sarcastic. Just stunned. These really were his and Katherine's parents. Only somehow they'd turned back into kids again.

Jordan collapsed to the floor.

TWO

"Jordan? Jordan?"

Katherine's voice seemed to come at him from a million miles away. Jordan felt like he was surfacing in a pool after a really deep dive—or maybe like he was coming to after passing out.

"I didn't . . . faint," he murmured defensively. "Don't tell anyone . . . I blacked out . . . like a wuss. It's just because . . . I'm sick. I have a fever. Mom gave me cold medicine this morning . . ."

Jordan could barely squeeze out the word "Mom." But talking about the medicine gave him an idea.

"Can cold medicine . . . make someone hallucinate?" he asked.

He liked this explanation. Probably he'd just had a weird medicine-induced hallucination—that was all.

Thinking that gave him the courage to open his eyelids just a crack, just enough to see Katherine hovering over him, her blond ponytail dangling down toward his face. He braced himself for her to make fun of him, as usual. But she seemed to be squinting at him with a look of concern.

"Did you hit your head or anything, falling?" she asked.

Since when would Katherine care? Jordan wondered.

"I'm fine," Jordan lied, struggling to prove it by sitting up. But his vision swung out of focus again, and the best he could do was prop himself up on his elbows.

"It's okay," Katherine said, sounding much kinder than Jordan would have expected. The type of response he was used to would have been more like *Don't you ever dare do anything like that at school! You'd embarrass me!*

"This is weird for me, too," Katherine continued, wrinkling up her nose in a wry expression. "And I've gotten used to weird things the past few months."

Why would Katherine be any more used to weirdness than Jordan was? Was this a setup for her to say, *After all, I've had to live with weirdo you my whole life?*

Katherine just sat there staring at him, a look of deep worry in her blue eyes. This made her look like Mom. And . . . like the girl who'd called Jordan "honey" a few moments ago.

Was that girl maybe Katherine's mirror image in the

same way that that Jonah kid was Jordan's? She didn't look as much like Katherine as Jonah looked like Jordan, but . . .

Jordan winced, and resisted the urge to look around for all the strange kids, to see if they were still around. He was going to stick to his hallucination theory, and as long as he didn't see those kids again, he could still believe it.

"The others went into the kitchen so they wouldn't freak you out even more when you woke up," Katherine said, almost as if she knew what he was thinking. Her voice was steady and calm and strangely more mature-sounding than her usual sixth-grade-girl squealing. "I guess you had already blacked out when Jonah explained things. But . . . is it true? You really don't remember having an identical twin your whole life?"

Jordan was so indignant he shoved himself the rest of the way up on his arms, so he was almost nose to nose with Katherine.

"Why would I remember having an identical twin my whole life?" he demanded. "I *don't* have an identical twin! I've never had an identical twin! It's just you and me and Mom and Dad—"

The thought of the Mom-like girl and the Dad-like boy he'd seen—or thought he'd seen—made his voice lose some of its certainty. And his traitorous brain was offering qualifiers: *You know, you can't really be sure about never having had an identical twin. You're adopted. And there have been cases of identical twins being separated at birth and raised apart, neither one knowing about the other . . .*

Katherine nodded slowly, still maddeningly calm.

"The thing is, *I* remember it being you and me and Jonah my whole life. I remember having both of you around from the very beginning," she said. "But my brain kind of . . . hiccups or something every time I try to think of you and Jonah together. Jonah says that's because the two of you grew up in different dimensions of time, and when Jonah fixed time, that smashed the dimensions back together again."

Jordan waited for Katherine to laugh and squeal, *Ha! Ha! Fooled you! You actually looked like you believed me there for a minute! You thought I would actually talk about different dimensions of time like they were real!*

Katherine's face stayed serious.

"Oh, right, and I guess *you* got to be in both our dimensions," Jordan said, in a way that left two possibilities open. If she was joking, he could claim he was being sarcastic. But if she was telling the truth—or what she believed was the truth—well, he did want to know if she'd been in both dimensions.

"Exactly," Katherine said. She smiled, almost as if she was proud of him. "You're catching on to this stuff a lot faster than Jonah and I did."

Huh? Jordan thought. *I'm not catching on to anything.*

But he wasn't about to let Katherine see that.

"Of course you'd get to be in both dimensions," Jordan taunted, still in a way that could be taken as serious. Or not. "Because you're so special."

"That's not the reason," Katherine said solemnly. It wasn't like her to pass up the opportunity to say she was better than Jordan. "Just about everybody was in both dimensions. And a third dimension, too, that I don't even know much about yet. But you and Jonah and, I guess, the other thirty-five kids from the plane—you were the only people who were in just one of the dimensions."

She'd totally lost him now. He really didn't like thinking about alternate dimensions or identical twins. This was childish, but he wanted to crawl back into bed and have Mom feel his feverish forehead and tell him, *You're just having a bad dream because of being sick and taking medicine. None of this is real.*

"If I go back to my regular dimension of time, will Mom and Dad be their right ages?" he asked crankily.

Katherine bit her lip.

"Um . . . I don't think you *can* go back," she said. "And Mom and Dad being grown-ups again, that was supposed to be fixed already. But, I don't know, I guess there's some extra problem—"

She broke off as a sudden banging sound began at the

front door. Someone outside screamed, "Jonah? Katherine? *Kath-er-iiiine?*"

Katherine scrambled up, ran to the door, and yanked it open.

"Chip!" she cried.

A boy with blond curly hair stumbled across the threshold and swept Katherine into the kind of embrace Jordan could never stand to watch in movies.

Who do they think they are? Jordan wondered. *Romeo and Juliet?*

Jordan had never seen this Chip kid before in his life. But Katherine was acting like she had. She and Chip were acting like they were in love, and they'd been separated for years by some horrible war, or some deadly epidemic no one was supposed to survive, or something else even more tragic and melodramatic.

Jordan had seen kids at school—mostly eighth graders—act like this over boyfriends or girlfriends just because they hadn't seen each other overnight. But not Katherine. As far as Jordan knew, Katherine didn't even have a boyfriend.

Katherine was *eleven.*

Now she and this Chip kid were kissing.

As Katherine's older brother, shouldn't Jordan say something like, *Hey! Hey! Break it up, you two!?*

Before Jordan could say anything, someone else—a dark-haired man—stepped past Katherine and Chip and into the house. He rushed over and crouched down to clap his hand on Jordan's shoulder.

"Jonah—you made it back safely!" the man said. He winced slightly. "Have you . . . have you met Jordan yet?"

"I am Jordan," Jordan protested.

The man winced again.

"Sorry," he said. "I'm still getting used to this too."

He seemed to be looking Jordan up and down. Defiantly, Jordan stared right back at him. Jordan guessed that Katherine or some of the other girls he knew would think this man was really handsome. But behind his chiseled good looks, the man had an air of exhaustion, or maybe even desperation, as if he'd just survived something traumatic.

Or maybe was still in the middle of something traumatic.

"I can see now that you're not Jonah," the man said, very seriously. Somehow Jordan could tell that the man was talking about more than just the placement of a chin dimple. Jordan felt almost insulted, as if the man were saying Jordan didn't measure up. "It's just . . . the last time I saw *you*, you were a year and a half old."

Jordan realized that, on top of all the other oddities

going on this morning, it was also strange that this man Jordan had never seen before—or didn't remember ever seeing before—had just walked into Jordan's house.

"Uh, do my parents know you?" Jordan asked.

"Jonah and Katherine do," the man said. He stuck out his hand. "I'm JB."

Jordan was saved from having to shake JB's hand because Katherine came bouncing over just then, pulling Chip along behind her.

"It's good to see you, too, JB!" she exclaimed, dipping down to give him a rough hug, as if he were some favorite uncle. Which, of course, he wasn't. "I'm so glad Chip and the other kids are okay. Are you here to help Mom and Dad and Angela?"

JB cut his gaze back and forth between Jordan and Katherine and Chip.

"That situation is . . . complicated," he said. "Maybe we should leave that subject for later?"

Jordan felt like he did when Mom and Dad spoke in code language because they didn't want him and Katherine to know something. They'd kind of stopped doing that once he and Katherine hit middle school, because it mostly stopped working.

But now this guy is acting like he's got secrets I'm not allowed to know about but Katherine is? Jordan thought indignantly.

"Oh, hey, Jordan," Katherine said. "Aren't you sick?"

"Um—" Jordan began.

"And, like, hallucinating or something?" Katherine continued. "And didn't you black out a minute ago? Don't you think you should just go back to bed?"

"And then everything will be fine when you wake up again," JB said, too heartily.

"Oh, right," Chip agreed. "That's how these things work. When you're sick, I mean."

JB was still crouched in front of Jordan. Katherine stood right behind the man, her hand still on his shoulder, her arm still linked through Chip's. It was like the three of them were a team—a team united against Jordan.

Jordan wanted to say, *You're sick too, Katherine. Don't you think you should go back to bed? After you send these strangers away? Don't you think Mom would be mad that you let them into the house?*

But his mind kept . . . what had Katherine called it? "Hiccupping"? Jumping around, anyway . . . over certain details. Before he'd come downstairs, hadn't he believed that Katherine was home sick too? Before he saw the oddly young versions of his parents, hadn't he thought that Mom was working from home today, to take care of him and his sister? Why couldn't he remember, one way or the other?

Jordan rubbed his forehead.

"Why do I feel like . . . ," he began. But he saw how JB, Katherine, and Chip instantly drew closer, instantly began darting glances at one another, as if they needed to work together to handle whatever Jordan was going to ask.

How could I believe anything any of them might tell me? Jordan wondered.

"Maybe I will go back to bed," Jordan said. "I feel kind of weird."

"Great idea!" JB said in a totally fake voice, acting like Jordan was some kind of genius just for repeating the same plan Katherine had suggested.

Hadn't she just suggested that? Or was Jordan a lot sicker and more confused than he thought?

Jordan turned and walked toward the stairs. He kept his head down as he climbed them, and acted like he felt too awful to ask any more questions.

He had to act like that. He had to pretend he wasn't curious.

Because he was totally going to sneak back downstairs and listen to everything the others said as soon as they thought he was gone.

THREE

Coward, Jordan accused himself.

He was pretty sure a braver kid would have stayed downstairs, would have kept asking questions, would have demanded answers—and gotten them. Jordan should have been like some of the guys at school who were so sure of themselves they sometimes managed to talk teachers into postponing or even canceling tests. Any of those guys would have done *something* about the too-young Mom and Dad and the weird mirror-image kid, Jonah.

Jordan wasn't like that.

Something had happened at the start of this school year: It was like suddenly all the seventh graders just *knew* that some of them were cool kids and some of them were not-so-cool kids and some of them were total losers. It wasn't like elementary school, or even sixth grade, where pretty much everybody was goofy and nobody cared. (Or, at least, Jordan hadn't cared.) Now, most days Jordan just hoped he counted as one of the not-so-cool kids and hadn't slipped down into the category of total loser.

You're acting like a loser, he told himself as he stepped into his room. His little charade would work only if Katherine heard him shut his bedroom door but didn't hear him reopen it.

Jordan was just reaching back for the doorknob when his gaze swept his room, and—it wasn't his room.

Or, rather, it was and it wasn't, all at once. His Ohio State basketball poster was still angled above his desk, but it shared space with a Lego robotics poster he'd never seen before—though it looked a little like one he'd had when he was younger. He'd taken his own Lego poster down, actually, at the start of seventh grade. Several of the other posters around the room were strange too: one practically on top of another, as if someone blind had tried to decorate the room twice, once with Jordan's actual posters and once with ones that were just a little different or a little like ones he used to have.

Jordan blinked, and for a moment he thought he saw a completely different room—a home office, maybe, with the kind of inspirational wall hangings his mom favored.

Oh, now I'm totally hallucinating, he thought.

He blinked again, and the weird version of his room was back. He forced himself to look at the furniture.

His desk and dresser were still there, but maybe Jordan was suffering from double vision or something, because now there seemed to be a second desk and a second dresser crowded beside each of Jordan's. The new ones looked practically as much like the originals as Jordan looked like that Jonah kid downstairs.

Jordan glanced toward the bed, braced for the same kind of double-vision problem. But the bed was even more different: Somehow it had turned into bunk beds.

Jordan had never had bunk beds in his life.

And double vision wouldn't make him see bunks.

How could someone have taken away my bed and replaced it with bunk beds just in the few minutes I was downstairs? Jordan wondered.

Somehow this change was even scarier than all the strange people downstairs, because Jordan *could* have an identical twin; there *could* be kids who looked like his parents' childhood pictures.

The bunk beds were impossible.

Jordan got his hand around the doorknob. He spun out of the room and *then* he slammed the door, shutting himself off from the view of the strange posters and the extra desk and dresser and the preposterous bunk beds. He stood in the hallway for a moment, panting.

Just a hallucination, just a reaction to being sick, just . . .

He wasn't convincing himself of anything.

Don't be a loser. Don't be a coward. There's got to be some explanation for all this . . .

He began tiptoeing back down the hallway, back toward the stairs. Mom and Dad were the type of parents who liked having family pictures all over the house, and Jordan felt better seeing the old familiar photos: There was the picture of Jordan standing by his tent at his first Cub Scout campout . . . Katherine at five with a gymnastics trophy . . . both of them playing basketball when they were maybe seven and eight . . . Jordan proudly holding up the first fish he ever caught, a tiny sunfish . . . Er, no—was that a giant catfish? And why was he suddenly wearing a blue shirt in that picture, instead of a red one?

It couldn't be a picture of that Jonah kid instead of me. Couldn't be, couldn't be, couldn't be . . .

Jordan stopped looking at the pictures. He put his head down—there were school pictures hung along the stairway, and he kept his gaze away from any of them as he cautiously eased down one step at a time. He concentrated on avoiding squeaky spots on the stairs. When he reached the point where he could almost see into the living room, he stood on tiptoes and peeked around the corner—that room was empty. But he could hear voices coming from the kitchen at the back of the house.

Jordan tiptoed away from the living room and into the dining room the family almost never used. He crouched down beside the china cabinet, and practically under one part of it. This had been one of his favorite hiding places back when he and Katherine were little and they thought hide-and-seek was a thrilling game.

The buzz of voices in the kitchen broke out into distinguishable words.

"—feel sorry for him," Katherine was saying. "He's so confused. Is it really going to make any difference if he hears everything?"

"We have to contain the damage!"

That was JB's voice, wasn't it? JB's voice, completely tense now that he wasn't playacting for Jordan's benefit?

"But if Jordan's going to have to live with the—what did you call it? Blended dimensions?—for the rest of his life, shouldn't he—"

Jordan thought this was the tall girl speaking now. She'd hung back so much while everybody else was running and hugging that he hadn't noticed much about her. Was she maybe somebody else that he might have recognized if he'd looked a little closer? She was tall and pretty and African-American and . . .

And, really, that was all that had registered with him.

He didn't think she was anybody he'd ever seen before—at any age—but he couldn't be sure.

"Angela, I'm not talking about the dimension challenges," JB said, sounding impatient. "Those will work themselves out. I'm sure of it. It's you and the two Skidmores being the wrong ages—and Chip's parents too, and God know how many other adults around here—"

"Angela said that was going to be fixed. Right after we got to see our kids." Was that Dad sounding so pathetic? He'd always been a little nerdy, but somehow that made him lovable as a grown-up.

Jordan was embarrassed for him now.

That whiny voice would get him labeled a total loser at school, Jordan thought.

"The time agency is working as fast as they can," JB said, and Jordan had the feeling he was speaking through gritted teeth.

Time agency? Jordan thought. *As in time travel, like Katherine was talking about before?*

It didn't make sense to Jordan. Even if time travel were possible, couldn't someone spend years figuring out what to do—and then come back in time to make the fix? And to everyone else it would look like no time had passed at all?

"You're saying we can't do anything but wait?" This

was the young version of Mom, sounding dismayed. The real, grown-up Mom didn't like waiting or not having anything to do. Normally, if she saw Jordan or Katherine just lying around—when they weren't sick—she'd be like, "Oh, could you help me fold this laundry?" or "Would you stir the soup in the Crock-Pot?" or "Want me to quiz you for your social studies test tomorrow?"

Jordan could hear Mom clearing her throat, the way she always did when she was annoyed.

"And you're saying we have to keep our own son confined to his room and in the dark about everything until we're adults again?" Mom asked. Jordan wanted to cheer. She may have been the wrong age, but at least she was on his side.

"That is what I'm saying." This was JB again. "All of you need to sit tight and let the experts do their jobs."

"JB, I thought you'd eased up on thinking experts are the only ones who can solve problems," Jonah said—it had to be identical-boy Jonah. Except he sounded so calm and authoritative. Jordan could never in a million years imagine his own voice sounding this way. "These are my parents, remember? And they've just met you. Be nice."

"I know, I know," JB said, as if Jonah had every right to scold him. "I'm sorry. There's just a lot at stake."

"Isn't there always?" Katherine asked. Was she *teasing* JB? "But if two totally different dimensions can smash together, and that's working out, then can't the age problems be okay too?"

Silence. Jordan had a feeling that JB might just be standing there in the kitchen with a look of panic on his face.

"The time agency was able to solve all *your* problems, JB," Jonah said encouragingly.

What does that mean? Jordan wondered.

The only thing he could think of was that JB might have had his age messed up too. But how could he have changed back when nobody else did? Anyhow, it was hard to imagine JB as a teenager, so Jordan decided he was probably wrong. He listened even more intently.

"They only risked changing me because the alternative was worse," JB said.

This was another mysterious statement that didn't help Jordan in the least.

In the kitchen JB let out a heavy sigh.

"What happened with all the un-aging—it was unprecedented," JB said. "We've got dozens of adults within a one-mile radius who went back to being thirteen-year-olds. An entire middle-school staff is now the same age as the students."

Does he mean Harris—my school? Jordan wondered.

It should have been funny to imagine all Jordan's

teachers as thirteen-year-olds. But Jordan didn't feel the least bit like laughing. The way JB was talking, none of this sounded like a joke.

"With every second that ticks by, the likelihood of permanent damage increases," JB said grimly.

"But why—" Katherine began.

"We don't know!" JB exploded. He seemed to be struggling to control his voice. He continued in a softer tone. "All we can think is that there was something seriously wrong with the Elucidator Charles Lindbergh was using."

"Elucidator—that's the device that lets people travel through time, right?" Mom asked.

Now even Mom was talking about time travel like it was real.

"Hold on—who's Charles Lindbergh?" Chip asked. "What's he got to do with anything? I thought this was all Gary and Hodge's fault."

"It was." This was Jonah again. "But they manipulated Charles Lindbergh into doing some of their dirty work. Lindbergh was a famous pilot from, like, eighty or ninety years ago."

"He was the one who kidnapped me and turned me back into a baby," Katherine added.

Why wasn't everyone laughing? None of them were actually taking her seriously, were they? Someone from eighty or ninety years ago couldn't have kidnapped Katherine. As for turning her into a baby—

That's not any crazier than Mom and Dad looking like teenagers again, Jordan thought.

He felt dizzy again. He leaned his head against the side of the china cabinet.

Maybe this was all just a dream? Maybe after Mom agreed to let him stay home from school, he'd fallen back asleep—in his normal bed, in his normal room, in his normal life—and everything since then had just been a particularly vivid nightmare?

He missed whatever was said next in the kitchen. Something rang, and JB groaned, "Noooo . . ." Then he muttered, "I'll take care of it."

Nobody answered him. Had JB maybe been speaking on a cell phone, instead of to the others in the kitchen?

"JB, what's going on?" Angela asked. "They *are* going to be able to fix this, aren't they?"

Jordan strained his ears to hear JB's reply, but there wasn't even a whisper. Jordan turned his head so he could press his ear tightly against the wall.

And then someone grabbed his arm and yanked him out from beside the china cabinet. It was JB.

"Get out from there!" JB snarled. "How much did you hear?"

FOUR

"Elucidator," Jordan babbled, as JB's fingers dug into his arm. "Charles Lindbergh. Time travel. And . . . there are bunk beds in my room."

"Bunk beds? Really?" Katherine said, coming into the dining room behind JB. The others were right behind her.

"Haven't our sons always had bunk beds?" Dad asked. But he was squinting like he really just wanted someone to agree with him, to talk him into the notion.

"Did the time agency put them there, or did it just happen?" Angela asked.

"Is my room his room now too?" Jonah asked. His tone was the opposite of Dad's: He seemed to want someone to tell him no.

"Can we all please just stop talking about beds and rooms and—" JB seemed to be making a visible effort not to explode completely. He kept a firm grip on Jordan's arm and began angling him back toward the stairs. "I know this is a difficult time for you, Jordan, but remember, you're sick. You're going to go back to sleep, and later you'll just remember that you were delirious, and—"

"Don't do that to my son," Mom said. She stepped forward and jerked JB's hand away from Jordan's arm.

Whoa, Mom, Jordan thought. She looked like a middle-school cheerleader—especially since she was wearing a baby-blue sweatshirt of Katherine's that said CHEER! in sparkly letters. But she sounded *fierce.*

Mom crossed her arms and faced JB directly.

"You may think you're in charge here, because you're the only one who's an adult right now, and you know more about time travel than the rest of us," Mom said. "But this is still our house—my, uh, husband's and mine—and there are house rules. It's not fair for you to lie to Jordan like that and make him think he's just imagining things. I won't allow it."

The kid version of Dad stumbled over beside Mom and clumsily crossed his arms too.

"Yeah," he agreed. "What she said."

"Nobody messes with the Skidmore family," Katherine said, giggling. She sidled up alongside Dad and Mom. "And Jordan probably already heard so much that you might as well tell him everything. And the rest of us too."

Jordan locked eyes with Jonah, who was still standing on the other side of the dining room table.

See, this is my family. Not yours, Jordan wanted to say.

Why did he feel mad at Jonah, when JB was the one who'd grabbed him and tried to trick him and send him back to his room?

"JB, maybe some damage just can't be contained," the tall girl—Angela?—said softly. "Maybe it's not even damage."

"Sometimes when your troops complain against you, it's not because they're insubordinate," Chip said. "It's because you're wrong." He leaned close, as if he were some old man imparting wisdom, not just another teenager. "Ruler to ruler, I'll tell you, sometimes you have to give the people *some* of what they're asking for, lest they seize power for themselves."

Was he *trying* to sound like some old king from a Shakespeare play or something? And what did he mean by "ruler to ruler"?

JB let out an exasperated-sounding sigh.

"Okay, okay," he said. "Jordan can come back into the kitchen with us. But there are some questions I'm not answering from anybody."

Everyone trooped back to the kitchen. Jordan noticed that there were five chairs around the kitchen table rather than the usual four—had someone pulled over an extra one just this morning, or was that another bizarre change that happened when the mysterious bunk beds appeared?

JB glowered at him, and Jordan decided he should stick to important questions, because there was no telling how long he'd be allowed to stay in the kitchen.

"How did you know I was in the dining room?" Jordan asked. "I didn't make any noise."

Mom and Dad looked as puzzled as Jordan felt. Katherine, Jonah, Chip, and Angela exchanged knowing glances.

"That's something you should know about time travel," Katherine said. "People from the future can see pretty much anything we do. Anytime."

"That's creepy," Mom said, hunching up her shoulders and shivering. "Why isn't that illegal?"

"It typically is in connection with the recent past," JB said in a soothing tone. "But—"

"I'm confused," Dad complained, his voice whiny again. "JB wasn't in the future. He was standing right here with the rest of us. I didn't hear Jordan make any noise. How *did* JB know he was out of his room?"

"His Elucidator told him," Katherine explained. "That thing that looks like a cell phone. He got a message from the future."

Seriously? Jordan thought. *Katherine thinks we're going to fall for that?*

Nobody laughed or even smirked. The other kids all looked grim. JB frowned and put his hand over the pocket in his shirt where he'd evidently put his cell phone. Or his "Elucidator." Whatever.

"Maybe we can limit the explanations to only the information that Jordan—and, for that matter, Linda and Michael—absolutely need," JB muttered, sweeping his hand toward Mom and Dad, lumping them in with Jordan. "They're not going to travel through time ever again, so they won't need to know about Elucidators."

"But it sounds like Elucidators and time travel shaped our lives—and our family," Mom said in a steely voice. "Don't we need to know about them to understand our past? What's the saying? 'Those who cannot remember the past are condemned to repeat it'?"

Trust Mom, even as a teenager, to come up with something like that.

JB stopped beside the island in the middle of the kitchen. Jordan would have preferred to sit down—he still felt a little dizzy—but everyone else seemed too keyed up for that. They all stood around the island, almost as if they were squaring off and choosing sides for an argument.

"You can't expect the Skidmores not to have questions,"

Chip said. It sounded like he was trying to be a peace-maker. "I mean, even I'm confused, and I've been to other centuries! The separate dimensions with Jonah and Jordan—how did that work? They were both in the same dimension back in the nineteen thirties, right?"

The nineteen thirties? Jordan thought. *What?*

But once again, everyone else seemed to accept this with absolute calm.

JB sighed and leaned against the island. "Jonah and Jordan, like typical identical twins, were born in the same dimension," he began. "There *was* only one dimension when they were born, more than eighty years ago. Time split when they were kidnapped from history and—"

"No, no, no, no, no," Jordan interrupted, because he couldn't stand it any longer. "I don't know about that Jonah kid, but I was *not* born more than eighty years ago. I'm thirteen! I'm not like them"—he gestured wildly at the kid versions of Mom and Dad—"I've never been any older than this! I've never been kidnapped, and I wasn't ever in 'history,' and, and . . . I do *not* have an identical twin!"

Everyone looked back and forth between Jonah and Jordan. Jordan didn't have to be a mind reader or have any of those time-travel Elucidator hocus-pocus skills to be able to tell: Every single person in the room was thinking some variation of *Dude, scream all you want. But you two are identical.*

"I mean, I'm not *supposed* to have a twin!" Jordan said. "It's not right! It's never been this way before!"

JB looked around at the whole crowd. "And you thought knowing more would make things *easier* for him?" he asked.

"This is hard no matter what," Jonah said, and for some reason everyone turned to him respectfully, as though he were some wise person who knew more than anybody else.

"Maybe *he* really is eighty-some years old, and he got turned back into a kid, just like Mom and Dad," Jordan said frantically, trying out a new theory. "But me—I'm thirteen. I was born *thirteen* years ago! I—"

"Quit embarrassing yourself," Katherine muttered, digging her elbow into Jordan's ribs. And this was so much like the normal Katherine, the one he was used to, that Jordan managed to bite down on his lip and keep from screaming anything else.

"The two of us are both thirteen, but we were both born more than eighty years ago," Jonah said, still in that freakishly calm voice. But Jordan thought maybe the other kid wasn't as calm as he sounded: He wouldn't quite meet Jordan's eyes. "The reason you don't remember the nineteen thirties, Jordan, is because our enemies kidnapped you when you were only a year and a half old. And then they un-aged you and brought you to this time period. They kidnapped me, too. And a bunch of other kids."

Jordan jerked his gaze accusingly toward JB—hadn't JB said that he'd last seen Jordan when Jordan was only a year and a half old?

"It wasn't me!" JB protested. "It was two men named Gary and Hodge."

"They were collecting famous missing children from history, to take far into the future to be adopted by families who would pay them a lot of money," Angela added.

"I'm famous?" Jordan asked incredulously. He turned to his parents and squinted at them in confusion. "And you paid time-traveling *kidnappers* to get me?"

"We didn't know anything about the time travel or the kidnapping until . . ." Mom glanced at the kitchen clock. "Until about an hour ago."

"But—this is weird—it's like I can't remember exactly how your adoption worked," Dad said, wrinkling up his nose in a confused squint. "It's like we went through one procedure with Jordan, and a different procedure with Jonah, but it was all at the same time. . . . Why would we have done the adoptions separately?"

"Because the two of us were in different dimensions, and you remember both of them," Jonah said.

"Your brain is probably trying to fuse the memories from both dimensions together," JB said. "It's only because you're in the midst of other oddities that you can see the discrepancy."

He pulled out his phone—*no, Elucidator,* Jordan corrected himself—and glanced at it anxiously, as if hoping
he'd gotten a message, maybe about Dad's memory. JB
grimaced. Did that mean he'd gotten bad news, or just
no news at all? Jordan slid a little closer to JB and craned
his neck, but he couldn't see anything on the phone/
Elucidator screen.

JB raised his head and glanced suspiciously toward
Jordan. To cover for his spying, Jordan quickly blurted,
"Let's go back to . . . am I famous?"

"Oh yeah, that's right—Jonah, if you went back to the
nineteen thirties, did you find out your original identity?"
Chip asked curiously. "Yours *and* Jordan's, I guess, if you're
twins. Are you royalty, like me and Alex and Daniella and
Gavin? The secret children of someone famous, like Emily?
Or someone who only became famous in the future, like
Brendan and Antonio? Or—"

"We're nobodies," Jonah said, and for the first time he
didn't sound calm. His voice was tight. "We were just fakes
Gary and Hodge used to try to fool people. To fool Charles
Lindbergh and to fool the people who wanted to adopt
famous kids from history and"—he darted a quick glance at
Jordan and then, just as quickly, looked away—"to fool *me.*"

Somehow he said the last part as though it were
Jordan's fault. Jordan wanted to protest: *I didn't do anything*

to try to fool you! I'd never even seen you before this morning! Believe me, I would have been happy never to have met you at all!

"But all the kids on the plane were famous!" Chip protested.

"Not me," Jonah said, his face rigid. "Not Jordan, either."

"What plane?" Jordan asked.

"The one that brought you to this time period," Angela said, picking up the explanation. "Well, it was actually a time-travel device, but it *looked* like an ordinary plane. Gary and Hodge were trying to escape some time agents who were chasing them, and so they crash-landed the plane in this time period. Thirteen years ago, I mean. I was working at the airport then, and that's how I got involved. I saw the plane appear out of nowhere, carrying only babies . . ."

She stopped and squinted toward JB.

"Wait," she said. "Now the different dimensions are confusing me, too. Did Jordan's plane crash-land, too? Or did Gary and Hodge send him here on purpose, just to confuse Jonah and make everything work with Charles Lindbergh?"

"Hard to say exactly at this point," JB said distractedly, glancing down at his phone/Elucidator again. "Everything's a little muddy right now, until . . . Ugh! Why can't anyone locate that Lindbergh Elucidator at a moment that a qualified time agent can sneak into, so we can steal it?"

He slapped his hand against the granite counter.

"How about sending someone who isn't a qualified time agent?" Jonah asked. "If you need that defective Elucidator so you can make Mom and Dad and Angela the right age again, then—"

"We would never send anyone except a qualified time agent after that Elucidator," JB said, with a tight smile that seemed neither happy nor friendly. "So it doesn't matter whether anyone else could sneak after it or not."

He made time travel sound almost like hide-and-seek or capture the flag or some other spylike game—only with higher stakes and greater consequences. The minute JB's gaze dropped to his phone/Elucidator again, Jordan saw all the other kids besides Mom and Dad exchanging significant glances.

Dad seemed oblivious. But Mom caught Jordan looking at her and she raised an eyebrow questioningly.

"Send me to get that Elucidator," Mom said abruptly, pointing right at the sparkliest *E* of the word CHEER! on her sweatshirt.

"What?" JB exclaimed, dropping his hand so his phone/Elucidator almost hit the counter.

"It makes sense," Mom said. "I don't belong in this time period anyhow, as a teenager. So I'm out of place to begin with. And that Elucidator would either be in the nineteen thirties or the far-off future, and I haven't been in either of those time periods before, so there wouldn't be any chance that I'd mess up time by being in the same place twice. And this would help my family."

She looked around beseechingly, her gaze lingering on Jordan and Jonah and Katherine.

"Oh!" Dad said, as if he were just catching on. "Send me, too!"

"Right, because the two of you have the least amount of time-travel experience of anyone in the room," JB said scornfully. "Even *Jordan's* done more time travel than you!"

Why did he have to use Jordan as the example of someone stupid and inexperienced?

"You could send me," Katherine said. "Or Chip or Jonah or Angela. If it's against time-agency regulations, you could do what you did when we were dealing with 1918 and you kind of accidentally on purpose set your Elucidator for voice commands. How were you supposed to know that some eleven-year-old girl like me would grab the Elucidator and zip off to the past in front of a bunch of assassins?"

Did Katherine actually do that? Jordan wondered. His stomach felt queasy.

"Because if you tell me to do something 'accidentally on purpose,' the time agency would never suspect me of faking a mistake," JB muttered sarcastically.

Did he mean that he would have tried something like

that if Katherine hadn't just ruined his plan by suggesting it?

Is the time agency still spying on all of us? Jordan wondered.

There was an awkward silence that reminded Jordan of the school play last year, when one of his friends forgot his lines and none of the other actors knew how to cover for the mistake.

"Hey—Venn diagrams," Katherine said.

"*What* are you talking about?" Jordan and Jonah both said. And it was horrible how identical their voices sounded, blending together. Their voices even cracked on the same word.

Katherine smiled sweetly at both of them, turning her head side to side.

"I think I figured out the best way to make sense of the different dimensions," she said. "It's like those Venn diagrams they have us draw at school."

She turned around and grabbed the pad of paper Mom kept by the phone for messages. Then she rifled through the junk drawer for a pen. While everyone watched, she put the paper down flat on the island and drew two interlocking circles.

"See, these are the two separate dimensions Jonah and Jordan were in," she said. "Everybody except the kids who came from the past lived in both dimensions, and remembers things from both dimensions."

In the center, where the circles overlapped, she wrote, *Just about everybody.*

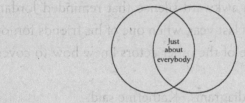

"I see where you're going with this, but there should really be three circles," Jonah said. "Because there was a third dimension too, where no kids from the past ended up in this time period. So I guess you got to be an only child there, Katherine."

He grabbed the pen and drew a third interlocking circle around the *Just about everybody.*

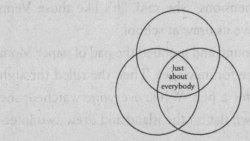

Jordan expected Katherine to yell and grab the pen back, but she didn't. She just tilted her head to the side and said, "I did? Shouldn't I remember that, too?"

Is that what I saw in that one moment when my room looked like Mom's personal home office? Jordan wondered uncomfortably.

Some dimension where Katherine was the only Skidmore kid?

"It's easier for time to overwrite an absence than a presence," JB said distractedly. He was looking at his phone/Elucidator, not Katherine's drawing. "So it makes sense that you've already forgotten that dimension. It's harder to forget either Jordan or Jonah when they're standing right in front of you."

"Too bad for you, Katherine," Jordan blurted, because this whole topic was making him feel weirder than ever. Teasing Katherine, at least, was normal. "I bet you *loved* being an only child. Having all the attention to yourself . . ."

Katherine kept her headed tilted thoughtfully.

"No," she said. "I think I do kind of remember. I was . . . lonely."

"I still don't understand, and that diagram doesn't help at all," Dad complained. "It looks like all the dimensions are the same."

"That's because I'm not finished," Katherine said. "Watch."

She took the pen back and wrote *Nobody extra from the past* in the open space of the circle Jonah had drawn.

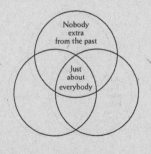

Then she pointed to one of the other circles.

"In this dimension," she said, "Jonah, Chip, and the other thirty-four kids who came off the plane from the past remember only their own dimension."

She wrote, *Jonah, Chip, other kids from plane,* in the part of the first circle that didn't overlap with anything else.

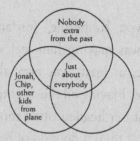

Jordan still wasn't ready to believe the story about any kids coming from the past—or, for that matter, about extra dimensions of time—but he saw Chip, Jonah, and Angela nod.

"And this is Jordan's dimension," Katherine said, pointing at the third circle and writing *Jordan* in the only open space left that didn't overlap with any other circle.

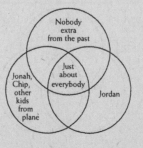

Then she put the pen down.

"Wait—you're saying I'm the only person in that category?" Jordan asked.

"That's right," Jonah agreed.

"But why? Weren't there other kids on the plane in my dimension too?" Jordan asked. And it was ridiculous how hard he had to work to keep the panic out of his voice.

"In your dimension, you were the only baby taken off the plane thirteen years ago," Jonah said. "All the other babies in your dimension stayed on the plane and—well, then it gets complicated. All you need to know is that you're the only person who remembers only your dimension and nothing else."

As he spoke, Jonah stayed on the other side of Katherine, his hands flat on the island counter. But Jordan felt as though Jonah had punched him. Jordan had as much trouble pulling air into his lungs as if he'd gotten a solid jab in the gut.

"Then . . . I'm all alone?" Jordan asked, and this time he couldn't disguise how forlorn he felt.

"Of course not, honey," Mom said, circling the island to pat his back. She pointed at Katherine's drawing. "Remember that 'just about everybody' is in your dimension, too. You're not alone at all."

Somehow it wasn't very comforting to have Mom pat his back when she looked like she was the same age as him. It was just weird.

"And anyhow, those circles just show what happened in the past, what we lived through before the three dimensions merged," Chip said. He seemed to be trying for a soothing, conciliatory tone. But he ruined it by adding admiringly, "Right, Jonah? We're all in the same circle now. That's how you saved time, isn't it?"

Chip touched Katherine's drawing and then squeezed his fingers together, as if to show the three circles coming together into one.

Jordan also squeezed his fingers together. Into fists.

But before he could say or do anything else, JB started shaking his phone/Elucidator.

"How could the Elucidator malfunction at a time like this?" he said disgustedly. "Hadley, listen, I'm not getting your transmission. I'm going to have to put this on voice commands and reset. Hold on."

Voice commands! Jordan thought. Wasn't that what Katherine had said JB had set his Elucidator on when he'd wanted her to grab it and go to the past? Even though he'd said it wasn't allowed, was he setting up a way for Katherine or Jonah or Chip to go to the future and snatch the Lindbergh Elucidator and fix everything?

Jordan glanced around at Katherine, Jonah, and Chip. All of them were watching JB run his fingers across the phone/Elucidator's screen.

"Okay, now try to retransmit," JB said, holding the phone/Elucidator in front of his mouth.

Katherine rose up on her tiptoes. If she stretched out her arm, would she be able to grab the phone/Elucidator out of JB's hands?

Jonah leaned in. He was farther away, but his arms were longer.

Chip was on the other side of the island from JB. He'd have to dive across the countertop to get his hands on the phone/Elucidator.

Whoever grabs JB's Elucidator and goes to the future and fixes things for Mom and Dad will be the biggest hero of all, Jordan thought. *He or she will be alone in a good way.*

And I'm the one who's standing closest.

Jordan reached out and snatched the phone/Elucidator from JB's hands.

"Take me to the future!" he screamed. "Take me where I can get that Elucidator we need to help Mom and Dad!"

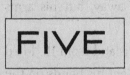

FIVE

Everything happened fast.

Mom still had her hand on Jordan's back, and she grabbed hold of his T-shirt even as she screamed, "Jordan, no!"

Katherine clamped her hands around Jordan's arm and screamed, "You're crazy! Give that to me!"

Jonah screamed, "Katherine? Mom?"

And, distantly, Jordan heard Dad yelling, "Wait for me . . ."

And then the kitchen disappeared, and everything went dark.

Apparently there was such a thing as time travel, after all.

Jordan seemed to be zooming through a great void. In the darkness it took him a moment to realize that Katherine still had a death grip on his left arm—she was probably cutting off his circulation. And Jordan's T-shirt was oddly tight, with something pulling it backward.

Mom's hand, Jordan thought, with a sense of relief he'd never want to admit to anyone. *Mom's still with me too.*

So however this time-travel stuff worked, Mom and Katherine grabbing him evidently meant they got to speed off toward the future with him.

That's all right, Jordan thought. *They can be heroes with me.*

And, though he'd never tell *her,* it might actually be helpful to have Katherine along, if she really did have time-travel experience.

Now was the time for Jordan to make some joke to show how calm and confident he was, like action heroes did in movies. But before he had a chance to speak, he heard another voice, low and angry.

"You're risking all of our lives, and the fate of the entire space-time continuum." It was Jonah. And Jonah was . . . Jordan squinted. Jonah was on the other side of Katherine, clinging just as tightly to her arm as Katherine clung to Jordan's.

"Be careful. Hand the Elucidator to Katherine or me, and we'll send Mom and Dad and you back to safety," Jonah continued. He sounded like someone talking to a dangerous wild animal he didn't want to spook.

Jordan ignored Jonah's request and asked, "Dad's here with us, too?"

From the other side of Jonah, Dad moaned, "Ooohh.

Is it possible to get seasick from traveling through time?"

"It's called timesickness, Dad," Katherine said sympathetically. "I get it too. You'll feel okay after you land. Well, eventually."

Jordan's eyes adjusted enough that he could see Katherine turning back to face him.

"Really, Jordan," she said, in the same kind of measured, cautious tone Jonah had used. "This is dangerous. At least send Mom and Dad back home so they'll be safe."

What? Jordan thought. *And lose having them here to protect me if I need it?*

Jordan couldn't say that out loud without sounding like a total baby. And he couldn't think of any excuse that would sound better. Reluctantly he lifted the phone/Elucidator toward his mouth and muttered, "Send Mom and Dad back home where they'll be safe."

Nothing happened. He could still feel Mom's hand clutching the back of his shirt. He could still hear Dad off to the side moaning, "Ooohhh. What happens if you throw up out here?"

"Why didn't that work?" Katherine asked, whipping her head toward Jonah.

"I don't know," Jonah admitted. "Jordan, *please*. We're running out of time."

Katherine snatched the phone/Elucidator from Jordan's hand.

"Here, Jonah," she said, passing it on as if they were playing a simple game of keep-away. Keep-away from Jordan.

"Hey!" Jordan protested, swiping his arm toward Jonah and missing by a mile. "Give that back!"

He waited for Mom or Dad to tell Katherine and Jonah it wasn't polite to grab things—which was ridiculous when they were all floating through this dark nothingness because of Jordan grabbing the phone/Elucidator to begin with.

Mom and Dad didn't scold anyone. Jonah did.

"Katherine, that was *so* dangerous," he complained, even as he hunched his back and turned away so there was no way Jordan could grab the phone/Elucidator back. "What if the two of you had dropped the Elucidator, like what we thought happened that time with Andrea? Then we really would have been in a mess!"

"Well, I didn't drop it, did I?" Katherine asked, a bit of her usual sassiness back in her voice. "And I knew Jordan would never *give* it to me. Or you. So I had to grab it. Just . . . do what you have to do! The lights are getting close!"

Lights on the horizon zoomed toward them, faster and faster and faster. What did that mean?

Jonah bent his head toward the phone/Elucidator and spoke firmly: "Elucidator, send Jordan, Mom, and Dad home to safety."

Jordan braced himself to be sucked backward. But once again, nothing happened.

"Jonah?" Katherine cried, her voice edgy with fear. "What's going on?"

Jonah didn't answer her. He was muttering into the phone/Elucidator, "I said, send them home! Home! Mom, Dad, and Jordan! Send! Them! Home!"

"Jonah!" Katherine cried. Even in the near-complete darkness, Jordan could see that the color had drained from her face. "We're almost *to* the lights! We don't even know where we're going in the future! *Do* something!"

Jonah looked up from the phone/Elucidator.

"I can't," he whispered. "JB wasn't just pretending that this Elucidator was messed up. It really is broken!"

SIX

Jordan began spinning. He felt like every cell in his body—or maybe every molecule? Every atom?—was being torn apart.

"Don't worry!" Katherine screamed. "This part doesn't last long! We'll land soon!"

Jordan wasn't sure how he could hear her, because it felt as though his ears—like every other part of his body—had been broken down into individual atoms. Or maybe individual electrons, protons, and neutrons.

If this really is just some hallucination caused by cold medicine, I am never doing any actual serious drugs, Jordan thought. *This is what they should do to kids in DARE class, instead of giving all those stupid lectures. . . .*

And then he couldn't think anything else. Maybe his body really had been torn to bits.

The next thing Jordan knew, he was lying on some sort of flat, motionless surface—a floor? The ground?

Probably floor, he decided. *Something indoors, because it's so smooth. . . .*

He knew from camping in Scouts that no matter how carefully you tried to pick a flat space for your sleeping bag outdoors, there were always tiny pebbles and twigs and clumps of dirt that would poke into your back in the middle of the night.

And how could he be thinking about Scouts and sleeping bags and dirt at a time like this?

Think about . . . finding that other Elucidator thing to fix Mom and Dad, he reminded himself. *And maybe that will make it so I'm back in my normal dimension, or whatever gives me back my normal family and my normal life. . . .*

Finding anything was going to be hard, because he felt both blind and deaf. He couldn't see or hear anything. He tried blinking a few times, and feebly lifted one hand to hit the side of his head, to try to clear his ears. He couldn't even feel his own hand. Had he lost all his senses?

Even as he started gasping in panic, he began hearing Jonah whispering nearby, "Elucidator, don't make any noise. And please make us invisible. Please, please, please, Elucidator, let that function still be working. . . ."

Invisible? Jordan thought. *Is that why I can't see?*

Somehow he knew that wasn't right, but it took his brain a moment to figure out why: *Oh, yeah. Invisible is when other people can't see you, not that you can't see anything. . . .*

"What was in that cold medicine?" Jordan tried to say. But it came out more like "Unh ah inh . . ." because his tongue felt as thick and uncooperative as a slab of meat.

Also, something slapped against his face and covered his mouth.

Katherine's hand? he thought. *Oh—I can feel things now!*

"Shh!" Katherine hissed in his ear. "Don't make any noise until we know where we are, and if we're safe. . . ."

Was there some reason they wouldn't be safe? And . . . hadn't they been going to the future?

It was so weird, how his brain couldn't seem to hang on to a detail like that.

"Mom, Dad, Jordan—if you're feeling sick, it's just because you're in a new time, and it takes a little while to adjust," Katherine whispered. "You'll feel better in a little bit. Just stay hidden and be quiet until you can think and hear and see straight. . . ."

Jordan wanted to ask, *Are we hidden now?* But getting his tongue and mouth to form those words seemed about as likely as climbing Mount Everest at the moment.

And, oh, yeah, she said to stay quiet. . . .

"*Are* we invisible?" Katherine hissed, probably to Jonah.

Wasn't it crazy that she'd ask a question like that? And sound serious about it?

Jordan squeezed his eyes shut and opened them a second time, and finally they started working again. He could see Katherine and Jonah and Dad lying beside him. He turned his head the other direction, and there was Mom. All four Skidmores—five, if you counted Jonah—were lined up on some hard floor.

Like corpses, Jordan's brain told him, and he felt himself start to shiver.

Belatedly, his brain also told him that Jonah had been shaking his head no. Every single Skidmore was completely visible, the red of Dad's T-shirt and the purple and pink of Katherine's sweater as bright as neon.

The Elucidator in Jonah's hand hadn't been able to turn any of them invisible.

"Is there, like, crazy-strong air-conditioning in the future, or are we someplace really cold, like Hudson's ship in 1611?" Katherine asked, still in a whisper.

Was she talking about the year 1611 like it was a time she'd actually lived through?

"Shh," Jonah replied. "You have to be quiet, too."

"Unhhh . . ." That was Dad.

"Do you think Mom and Dad are having even worse

timesickness because of that whole un-aging thing?" Katherine asked anxiously.

Jonah shrugged and drew his fingers across his lips. Evidently that meant *zip it!* in all dimensions.

And then Jordan saw Jonah struggle up into a sitting position. If Jonah could sit up, Jordan could too.

Jordan started pushing himself up on his wobbly arms. The vague shapes above and around him swung in and out of focus. Sterile-looking tables . . . colorful projections that glowed like a computer or TV but without any sort of actual screen or wall behind them . . .

Jordan's best guess was that they were in some sort of futuristic lab.

Maybe it's empty, he thought. *Maybe it won't matter that the Elucidator couldn't make us invisible, or that our whispering might have been too loud. . . .*

At the edge of Jordan's range of vision, Jonah had not only managed to sit up, but was now twisted around and peeking over the top of the nearest lab table.

"What do you think an Elucidator might look like in the future?" Jonah whispered, turning his head toward Katherine. "Maybe . . . like the thinnest credit card ever?"

Jordan watched as Jonah glanced around, then slipped his hand over the edge of the table and picked up something.

Just then Jordan's elbows buckled and his chest slammed down against the floor. Pain shot through his body, and he screamed, "Ahhhh!"

The sound echoed in the silent lab.

A moment later, a strange face loomed over him.

SEVEN

"Get us out of here!" Jonah hollered. "Take us all . . . someplace safe! Like—the nearest time hollow?"

In the next instant, the face disappeared from Jordan's view. So did the tables and the colorful screenlike projections and everything else about the sterile lab. Everything went dark and spinny.

Time traveling again? Jordan thought.

But the sensation of spinning and zooming through darkness ended as quickly as it had started. In what seemed like the blink of an eye, Jordan was on solid ground again—or, actually, solid floor. He could see a room around him now. But when he looked around for any identifying features or clues about where he was, there weren't any. The room was just empty and bland, with nothing-colored walls and a nothing-colored floor and lighting that didn't seem to come from anywhere—it just *was*.

The bright colors of Dad's red shirt and Katherine's pink-and-purple sweater were even more jarring here.

So Jonah brought us to a place where there's nowhere to hide? Jordan thought anxiously.

Before he could point that out, Dad sat up and said in an amazed voice, "I don't feel sick anymore."

Katherine giggled. "That's how time hollows work," she said. "As long as we're here, you also won't get hungry and you won't get thirsty and you won't ever have to go to the bathroom. It's like we're totally outside of time. Nothing changes in a time hollow. Jonah and I were stuck in a time hollow for decades once, and we never got hungry or thirsty that entire time."

She had to be making that up. Didn't she?

Jordan saw Mom raise one eyebrow questioningly—having her do that with a kid's face didn't work as well as when she was a grown-up. Katherine and Jonah ignored her. Dad just patted his stomach.

"You're right," he said thoughtfully. "I don't feel hungry, and I seem to remember that when I was thirteen the first time around, I was *always* hungry. It's so strange—I don't feel like I need anything at all."

"I'd take being an adult again," Mom said, practically in

the same annoyed and annoying tone that Katherine so often had in her voice. Then Mom grimaced. "I guess that's what both of you, Jordan and Jonah, were trying to accomplish. I *do* appreciate the effort. But maybe this time around we could take things slow and you could *think* before you act?"

Jordan realized that everyone else was already sitting up. He pulled himself up and glared at Jonah.

"I *might* have taken us to the right time period—Jonah didn't exactly give us much of a chance to look around," Jordan complained. "So some man saw us. So what? Maybe he could have helped us. Maybe we could have made up some really convincing story and . . ."

Jonah and Katherine were both shaking their heads.

"Jordan—I recognized that man," Jonah said. "He's our worst enemy."

"Gary? Hodge?" Dad asked. "Was it one of them?" He clenched his fists like he was ready to punch someone.

Jonah and Katherine looked at each other.

"This guy's even worse," Katherine said. "That was Second."

Maybe it wasn't possible to be hungry or thirsty or sick in a time hollow, but Jordan could have sworn he felt his stomach start churning, just at the grimness of Katherine's voice. She wasn't joking about any of this. She was terrified.

But Jordan couldn't let anyone see that he was scared too.

"You're afraid of some guy who's named for a number?" Jordan asked. "What—is he that proud of coming in second place?"

By the standards of wisecracking movie heroes, that was pretty lame. But Jordan was proud he could joke at all.

Nobody laughed.

"Second's real name is Sam Chase," Jonah said, frowning. "He used to work for JB—JB *trusted* him. He told us Sam Chase was his best projectionist."

"And a projectionist is . . . ," Dad prompted.

"Someone who makes predictions for time travelers," Katherine answered. "So they can see how their trip might affect time. Usually you don't want to change anything about the past, because it could mess up everything."

"But Sam Chase got sick of things not changing." Jonah took up the story. He crossed his arms in a way that made him look furious. "He tricked JB—and, well, me and Katherine and our friend Andrea, too—and he decided to rearrange history. He started calling himself Second Chance."

"And he shifted and split time, just for the fun of it," Katherine finished. "He almost destroyed it completely."

Jonah and Katherine were just talking. They were just *kids*. And there was nothing remotely dangerous anywhere in sight. Even the face Jordan had seen back in the lab hadn't seemed that menacing—the guy had mostly just looked like a computer nerd with messy hair.

But Jordan still found himself having to fight the urge to shiver in fear.

"JB thinks Second is the one who taught Gary and Hodge how to make their split dimensions," Jonah said.

"Really?" Katherine said. Evidently this was news to her, too. "So you and Jordan growing up in different dimensions—that all traces back to him too?"

"How is he at re-aging people who already lived through their teen years once and would rather just be adults again?" Mom asked, and at least she managed to sound *slightly* humorous about the whole thing.

"I don't know," Jonah said, shrugging helplessly. It was still strange how much looking at Jonah was like looking into a mirror. But Jordan had never seen his own face look so miserable. "I don't know if that was Second when he was still Sam Chase and still loyal to JB. I don't know if he's told the whole time agency we were there, and now we've gotten JB into serious, serious trouble. I don't know if we somehow managed to cross over into the new dimension Second created, and maybe he'd try to follow us if we went back home. I don't even know if this plastic thing I grabbed is an Elucidator or not!"

He held up the thin sliver of plastic he'd swiped from the table back at the lab.

"Okay. Okay," Mom said. She took a deep breath, just like she always did when she was trying to talk Katherine down from some stupid sixth-grade drama with her friends. "Let's just look at this logically. *Something* got us out of that lab and into this . . . what did you call it? A time hollow? And we know the other Elucidator Jordan took from JB wasn't working. . . ."

"*Do* we know that?" Jonah asked. "That Elucidator took us from our kitchen into the lab in what must have been the future. I was thinking the Elucidator was broken the same way as the light switch in our bathroom last summer, where sometimes it worked and sometimes it didn't, and it was impossible to predict. Remember, Dad, you had me help you fix that?"

"Ummm . . . ," Dad said.

"No, *I* helped Dad fix the bathroom light switch!" Jordan said hotly. It'd been, like, a five-minute job, and Jordan had complained the whole time. But he still didn't want Jonah taking credit.

Dad scrunched up his face.

"I . . . can't really remember which of you helped me," he said. "It might have even been Katherine. . . . Sorry, guys."

Katherine was squinting too.

"I guess it was probably both of you, just in the different dimensions," she said. "I don't remember doing it."

"Anyhow," Mom said, waving her hand as if trying to shove away any possible arguments. "Let's get back to the Elucidator. This is all new to me, but . . . is it like an iPhone? Does it have something like Siri? Could you just ask it if you could make your dad and me the right age again? Safely, I mean?"

"Elucidators are like . . . you know that story about the Sphinx?" Jonah asked. "How it's tricky and full of riddles? You can never get a straight answer from an Elucidator. At least, *I* can't. Charles Lindbergh told me he could."

Mom's jaw dropped.

"You *talked* to Charles Lindbergh?" she asked, sounding awestruck.

"Hey, Mom, remember, Charles Lindbergh kidnapped me and turned me into a baby?" Katherine chimed in. "*Not* my favorite person. Just because you like history, don't go acting like he's Justin Bieber or something."

"A lot of history is pretty awful," Jonah said, and again he had that *Be grateful that I am sharing some of my vast wisdom with you* tone in his voice.

Dad shook his head impatiently.

"I never liked history," he said. "I hated it in school. Bor-ing. Like school in general."

"Michael!" Mom said, sounding horrified. "Don't say that in front of the kids!"

Dad got a stricken look on his face. He leaned toward Jordan, Jonah, and Katherine.

"I think your mom is way more grown-up as a thirteen-year-old than I am," he whispered, as if he were sharing a big secret. "I keep forgetting I'm supposed to be acting like a dad."

Mom shot Dad a disgusted look. It was a lot like the looks Katherine usually gave Jordan.

"Can we get back to the task at hand?" Mom asked. "Jonah, it's possible that you're holding two Elucidators right now, though we're not sure if either of them works, or works right. Even if you're afraid that going home right now might create problems, couldn't you call JB and ask him what to do? If he was using an Elucidator to communicate with people in the future, couldn't we communicate with him?"

"Except *he* doesn't have an Elucidator right now, Mom, because Jordan took it," Katherine reminded her. And it was amazing: She didn't sound snarky or mean like she normally would, saying, *Mom, you're wrong!*

What had happened to Katherine in all her time travels, to change her so much?

Mom made a face.

"I guess I was still thinking Elucidators were like cell phones, and even if JB doesn't have his Elucidator anymore, we could still call him on the landline. . . ." She sounded ashamed of herself for not having figured out more.

"Anyhow, our house could be swarming with time agents right now," Katherine continued.

She made them sound like storm troopers.

"Maybe we *could* get these Elucidators to show us what's going on at our house right now—I mean, right after the five of us left," Jonah said, as if he'd just thought of that. His voice shifted into an authoritative tone: "Elucidator, show us that scene. Project it on the wall, so we can all see."

The wall in front of them turned into a screen of sorts, though the picture was even sharper than the highest-definition TV screen Jordan had ever seen. It was even more intense than being back in the kitchen: He could see each individual hair on Angela's head, each whorl of the granite countertop Chip was leaning against, each line on JB's face as he called out, "Jonah? Katherine? Jonah?"

What are Mom and Dad and me? Jordan wondered jealously. *Chopped liver? Doesn't he care that the three of us disappeared too?*

"So there aren't a million time agents there and JB hasn't gotten a replacement Elucidator," Jonah muttered.

"Yet," Katherine reminded him.

The scene on the wall froze.

"At least one of you is thinking of grabbing an Elucidator and zooming back there to arrive in the next instant, so we cannot project the next seconds with any confidence or accuracy," a disembodied voice said.

"*That's* how this works?" Dad marveled.

"Who was thinking of going back?" Katherine asked accusingly.

"Me," Mom said meekly.

"Well, stop, and then we'll see what happens next," Jordan suggested.

He kept watching the screen. Nothing happened.

"Do you know how hard it is to keep yourself from thinking about something?" Mom asked.

Jonah ran his hand over his face.

"Let's try this instead," he suggested. "Elucidator, show us the room where we saw Second—er, Sam Chase, whatever he's calling himself now—in the second after all of us Skidmores left."

The scene on the wall changed to a crystal-clear scene of a futuristic lab. Jordan guessed it was the same place he'd seen before in a blur. But it was totally empty. Neither Second nor anyone else stood in its broad aisles.

"Um . . . show us where Second went in the instant

after all of us Skidmores left," Jonah said. He sounded stricken—why was he frightened by the sight of an empty lab?

Something weird happened with the wall. It was almost like the projection was replaced with a trick mirror, because it seemed to return an image of the same nothing-colored walls that surrounded his family (and Jonah). Jordan could see his family and Jonah reflected on the wall, too, but the view was twisted around somehow, so it showed their backs instead of the images head-on, like a regular mirror would show. There was Katherine's ponytail, knocked off center and coming out of its rubber band. There was the back of Dad's head, which should be balding but was so improbably covered with thick, frizzy hair. There was the back of Jonah's nerdy sweater vest with its argyle design. There was . . .

Wait, is there a sixth person crouching down and hiding behind me and Mom? Jordan wondered. *And he's been quiet and out of sight because none of us has turned around and looked behind us since we arrived in this time hollow?*

Jordan whirled around, looking behind him. Everyone else seemed to notice and turn at the same time.

Except as Katherine and Jonah whirled around, they also screamed, "Second followed us!"

EIGHT

The man crouched behind Jordan burst into a wide grin.

"Guilty as charged!" he cried. His voice didn't match his words—he sounded as gleeful as if he were accepting a prize. "I thought you were going to take forever, deciding to look for me."

Jonah tugged on Dad's arm to shove him back; Katherine did the same thing to Mom and Jordan.

They're trying to shield us, Jordan thought numbly. *What do they think this man's going to do?*

In the next moment Jordan felt his body freeze. He could still move his head and neck, but everything below his neck seemed immobile. He had no control over his arms or legs or torso, and his limbs were stuck in the most awkward positions. Katherine had only halfway succeeded in shoving him behind her, so Jordan was balanced improbably on his right knee and his left fingertips.

"Once again, your primitive instincts have failed you," Second taunted them. "Jonah, you're under the impression that you're holding two Elucidators, correct? Why didn't you just immobilize me before I had the chance to do the same to you? Were your instincts to protect your family that overpowering? That's actually kind of sweet."

"Stop making fun of us," Jonah muttered.

Katherine went for a more direct approach: "What do you want?" she demanded.

"What do you think I want?" Second asked. His eyes danced merrily. Combined with his messy hair, this made him look a little crazy. "I would be so interested in hearing your theories. We've just had such a fascinating turn of events! So much is in flux right now. . . ."

Jordan decided to use the same strategy he adopted when teachers asked hard questions in class: As far as he was concerned, somebody else could do all the talking. He turned his head toward Mom, but she looked white-faced and speechless. Katherine was biting her lip, a sign that she was spitting mad, maybe even too mad to speak. Dad kept opening and closing his mouth, but no sound came out.

That left Jonah. And of course wise, calm Jonah was up to the task.

"You promised," Jonah said, his eyes burning into Second's. "After Katherine and I saved time back in the sixteen hundreds, you said you would stay in your dimension of time and stay out of ours. But then you *helped* Gary and Hodge. You taught them how to ruin everything, how to ruin my life . . ."

Why did he turn his head and glare at Jordan just then? Why was he acting like Jordan, not Second, had ruined "everything"?

Second held up his hands, palms out, in one of those *Hey, man, don't blame me* gestures of innocence.

"To use a phrase that has echoed through recorded history—in all dimensions—'Am I my brother's keeper?'" Second asked. "And I say: No. I am not."

Katherine gasped.

"You mean—you're related to Gary? Or Hodge?" she asked. "Is that why—"

Second sighed. "I keep forgetting that I am dealing with children," he muttered. "And children from a more primitive time . . . I only meant that figuratively. I claim no kinship with either of those bumblers."

"You're quoting the Bible," Mom said. "That's what Cain said after he killed his own brother, and he tried to pretend he didn't know where his brother was. But he *was* responsible. He was guilty." She whipped her head side to side, gazing frantically at Jonah and Katherine and Jordan. "Is this man a murderer? Do we have to worry about that, too?"

It was really scary to hear Mom say words like "killed" and "murderer." Those weren't things Jordan was used to hearing either of his parents fret about.

It was even scarier that neither Katherine nor Jonah answered Mom.

Second pressed his lips into a thin line of annoyance.

"You're getting off track," he said. "Let me clarify: Neither Gary nor Hodge was ever my protégé. I made no effort to teach them anything. I was just as stunned as anyone else that they were able to enter my separate time and learn from my examples. And . . . everything I desire is just as endangered by the potential results of their actions as you are. So I think I am justified in breaking my promise. You don't know this yet, but you need me to."

For a moment everyone was silent. Then Katherine whispered, "So you want us to help you again? You want to work together?"

Second smiled. But it was just a matter of moving the corners of his mouth. The smile didn't make him look happy or pleasant.

"That would be one way of looking at this," he said in a tight voice. "But . . . that's not how any of you are going to view things a moment from now."

"Why? What are you going to do?" Mom asked frantically. "Please—can't we just talk things out before anyone does anything?"

"Don't make me have to beat you up!" Dad said.

And then both of them vanished.

So did Second.

NINE

Jordan toppled over. He was so caught off guard at being unfrozen that he didn't even think about putting his hands out to catch himself. His shoulder smashed into the floor. He would have hit even harder if it hadn't been for Katherine being partly in front of him. She mostly broke his fall.

Now she's going to yell at me for chipping her fingernail or something, Jordan thought, even though *her* elbow stabbed *his* stomach.

It didn't actually hurt. Was pain something else being in a time hollow could prevent?

Why hadn't the time hollow prevented Mom and Dad from vanishing? What could Jordan do to make sure Katherine didn't vanish too?

Before Jordan could say or do anything, Jonah jerked

back on Katherine's arm, pulling her toward him and away from Jordan.

Jonah didn't seem to care about helping Jordan up.

"You're just trying to trick us into panicking and doing something stupid," Jonah called out, addressing the blank space where Second had been only a moment before. "You're just trying to manipulate us into doing what you want!"

"Jonah, he took our parents," Katherine said. "Whatever he's trying to manipulate us to do—it's going to work."

"Mom? Dad?" Jordan called. The words came out garbled. Probably the other two thought he was just whimpering.

"We're not going to do anything to help you until you bring Mom and Dad back!" Jonah threatened. He was still talking to empty air.

Katherine sighed. Jordan was slightly relieved to see her push herself away from Jonah.

"You're both acting like idiots," she said. "Duh. It looks like he left us with both of the Elucidators. Elucidators, show us where Second took Mom and Dad."

"Or just take us there," Jordan suggested.

Instantly the bland room around them vanished.

"Jordan!" Katherine screamed. "It's doing what you said!"

"I didn't mean—" Jordan began.

"Stop! Turn us back around! Take us back to the time hollow!" Jonah screamed.

They were in darkness now, but Jordan could see words glowing in red lights just above Jonah's hands. Was one of the Elucidators projecting those words somehow? Was that because the Elucidator had obeyed Jonah's command for silence back in the lab, even if it hadn't made them invisible?

Or did this just mean that only the Elucidator Jonah had picked up in the lab was working now?

Jordan decided he didn't care about those exact questions right now. In the spinning darkness he craned his neck so he could read the glowing words. They said OVERLOAD OF COMMANDS. WILL NEED TO RECONFIGURE BEFORE ANY CHANGES ACCEPTED. NO CHANGE IN DESTINATION ALLOWED AT THIS TIME.

Did that mean they couldn't go back?

"Please," Jordan moaned.

"If you can't take us back, can you just freeze us here until you reconfigure?" Jonah asked.

"Guys, shut up!" Katherine screamed. "We're about to land! Don't confuse the Elucidator by telling it anything el—"

Then Jordan couldn't hear her or Jonah, because he

had the sensation once again that his body was being torn in all directions.

If people are going to be smart enough to invent time travel, can't they invent an easier way to do it? Jordan wondered, in the split second before his brain stopped working.

The next thing he knew, he was on a solid floor once more. As he began to regain his senses, he realized that Katherine had her hand pressed tightly over his mouth.

"Don't make any noise until we know where we are," she whispered in his ear. "Promise?"

Jordan nodded, and she slid her hand away.

Smooth, flat floor, Jordan thought. *Sterile-looking tables. Glow of TV-light projections overhead . . .*

"We're back in a lab," Jonah whispered from beside Katherine. He was sitting up already, peeking over one of the tabletops. "I think it's the same lab as before. But—"

"It's empty. I don't see Mom and Dad," Katherine said dejectedly, as she joined Jonah in cautiously sitting up and looking around.

Jordan didn't quite trust himself to move yet. So he was at the perfect angle to see the words projected into the air above Jonah's right hand: YOU DIDN'T SAY YOU WANTED TO BE WHERE YOUR PARENTS WENT WHILE THEY WERE STILL THERE.

Was that what Jonah meant about Elucidators being tricky? Jordan had said, *Or just take us there.* Who would have ever expected that he also needed to say, *Take us to that exact moment?*

"Hey, guys," Jordan whispered, wanting to point out the words to Jonah and Katherine.

Just then, Katherine and Jonah both slammed back to the floor. Katherine's hand went back over Jordan's mouth.

"Someone's coming!" she hissed into his ear. "Don't say anything else!"

All three of them cowered, hidden behind a desk. Jordan heard a door opening at the other side of the room. He heard footsteps—had two people just entered the room? Or three or four? He almost missed the sound of the door shutting. Was it being eased together by someone who didn't want to be overheard?

"Are you *sure* this is a protected space?" a man's voice asked. Did he have a strange accent, or was it just anxiety that made him clip his words off so abruptly? "You're certain no one can detect our presence here?"

"This is where Gary and Hodge came when they escaped from time prison," a woman's voice responded. "And the time agency never knew. So yes, we're safe here."

"You have news of those two? Our top performers?" This was a different man. His deeper voice was harder to understand, but Jordan was pretty sure he was being sarcastic. "I've been so worried about them."

Was he talking about Gary and Hodge, the same men who had supposedly kidnapped Jordan and Jonah and other kids? Were these people kidnappers too? So were they maybe on the same side as that guy Second, who had taken away Jordan's parents?

This was even harder than figuring out what made people not-so-cool kids or losers at school.

Jordan heard a thumping sound—maybe the woman had hit the deep-voiced man on the arm. "Stop it," she said. "You know Interchronological Rescue would have gone bankrupt years ago if it hadn't been for Gary and Hodge."

"We're going bankrupt anyhow, if the time agency has its way," the first man muttered.

Jordan wasn't going to worry about some company he'd never heard of going bankrupt. As far as he was concerned, that was one of those grown-up problems that didn't affect him.

"Yeah, they hate us, but do you think the time agency would actually resort to murder?" the woman asked.

That got Jordan's attention. It evidently stunned the two men, too—he heard one of them gasp.

"No one from the time agency would do that," Deep Voice argued. "It'd ruin their sense of their own perfection. And they'd have to file a lifetime's worth of paperwork to justify it."

"Why are you making these wild accusations?" the first man asked. "What have you heard?"

"Gary and Hodge have gone missing," the woman said. "I haven't been able to reach them in any point of time, in any dimension. They vanished completely from August fifteenth, 1932."

Jordan snapped his head toward Jonah. Hadn't Jonah said that Gary and Hodge kidnapped them both from the nineteen thirties? Had Gary and Hodge vanished at the same time?

Jonah had his brow wrinkled, like he was thinking hard. But he didn't look nearly as worried as the woman sounded.

"But . . . but . . . ," This was Deep Voice again, and he was stammering. "Everything they set in motion is still progressing, right?"

"Right," the woman said. "Time is going to end. Soon. And unless we find Gary and Hodge, none of us have anywhere safe to escape to."

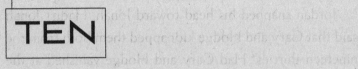

TEN

Katherine's fingers dug into Jordan's face, the palm of her hand smashing down harder against his mouth.

Okay, Katherine, okay! Jordan thought. *I get it! You really don't want me talking or doing anything else to give away that we're here!*

But if the three people who worked with Gary and Hodge didn't want all of time to end—wasn't that something that Jordan and Katherine would agree with? If Katherine was willing to work with that Second guy to get Mom and Dad back, wouldn't she be willing to help other bad guys save time?

Jordan saw that Katherine was also holding Jonah's arm, as if she didn't trust him to keep still and silent either.

"I'll cover your tracks if you want to go to your source at the time agency," Deep Voice was saying. "Do you have *any* theories? Any leads?"

"The Skidmore incident has to be the key," the woman replied. "Gary and Hodge despised those two kids."

The "Skidmore incident"—something connected to my family? Jordan wondered, with chills traveling down his spine. Too many strange things had happened for him to guess which "incident" they might mean. *And the "two kids" they're talking about . . . Are they Katherine and me? Jonah and me? Jonah and Katherine?*

Why would two men Jordan had never heard of until this morning hate him?

It looked like Katherine was about to claw through Jonah's arm. Jordan felt as though she was trying to smash his mouth down into the floor. Along with the rest of his head.

"All right," the first man said. "Let's all see what we can find out, and then meet here again this afternoon. Does five o'clock work for both of you?"

Maybe the other two just nodded. Jordan couldn't hear any replies.

"We're not telling Curtis Rathbone about any of this, right?" the woman asked.

"Very funny," Deep Voice said.

And then the door opened and shut again, and Jordan was sure that all three adults had left.

"Would you let go before you tear my face to shreds?" he hissed to Katherine. Though it sounded more like

"Unh, unh, unh . . . sssss . . ." because she had such a tight grip on his mouth.

Katherine looked down at the hand she had digging into Jordan's face, and then the one digging into Jonah's arm.

"Oh, sorry," she muttered, pulling away. But then she shot her gaze back to Jonah, as though he mattered a lot more.

"If they were telling the truth, we've got to do something," she said. "We've got to tell JB, or, or—"

"Don't you think JB already knows?" Jonah snapped. "Don't you think that's why he was so tense and stressed out back at our house?"

"Wasn't it enough to stress anyone out that Mom and Dad were the wrong ages?" Jordan asked. "And that two—no, three—dimensions were squished together?" He really wanted to say, *And that this whole goofy time mess gave me a twin brother I don't even want?* But he managed to hold back that question. "Look. Why don't we just find Mom and Dad and let them figure out what to do and who to tell?"

For a moment it seemed like Jonah and Katherine were the identical ones: They shot Jordan the same look of utter disbelief.

"Mom and Dad don't know *anything* about time travel or Gary and Hodge or how to save time," Katherine said.

"But don't you still want to save them?" Jordan asked. He hated the way he sounded: like a little kid whining, *I want my mommy and daddy! Give me back my mommy and daddy!*

"Sure, but what good will it do to save them if all of time ends right after that?" Jonah asked. "We've got to fix everything."

Don't let him make you panic, Jordan told himself. *There's no way the three of us could fix everything. Nobody could expect that. He's just messing with you.*

Wasn't he?

Katherine shoved a stray strand of hair out of her eyes.

"Why would Gary and Hodge want to end all of time?" she asked. "How does that help them? I thought they just wanted to get rich! What's the point of being rich if everything's just going to end?"

"Gary and Hodge expected *our* dimension of time to end," Jonah said. He cut his eyes toward Jordan, then back to Katherine. "I mean, the dimension I was in and Jordan wasn't. Hodge told me that was going to happen regardless, because things changed too much with the plane crashing and thirty-six babies staying in a different time. And Gary and Hodge were going to escape to the dimension where nothing changed. Or nothing important, anyway."

He'd better not be talking about my dimension! Jordan thought. *Making it sound like I'm not important . . .*

"But then you smashed all the dimensions together," Jordan said accusingly. He hadn't quite followed all the time-travel hocus-pocus the others had explained to him, and he still wasn't sure he believed any of it. Even witnessing it himself wasn't entirely convincing. (What if this wasn't actually the future he was sitting in right this moment? What if this was just some huge, elaborate trick?) But it kind of felt good to blame Jonah.

Jonah shook his head. "JB said putting the dimensions back together *saved* time," he insisted. "He said everything was fixed. Except for Mom and Dad and Angela and some other adults still being kids."

"Could that change things enough to end time forever, in all dimensions?" Katherine asked. "Could Gary and Hodge have changed their ages on purpose, trying to make sure the one dimension ended and then . . . then what they did turned out to be more powerful than they expected? So it's going to ruin everything?"

"Okay," Jordan said, starting to stand up. His legs were getting stiff. "Let's find Mom and Dad, and then let's find those guys Gary and Hodge, and we'll just tell them they have to make Mom and Dad the right ages again or they'll ruin time. . . . This is easy!"

Katherine grabbed Jordan's arm and tugged him back down.

"Stop being so stupid," she said. "This isn't easy. You don't know where Gary and Hodge are. You don't know what's out there. You don't even know where we are!"

"I'm guessing we're at some office building for Interchronological Rescue," Jonah said. He sounded almost like that JB guy back home. His voice was just as tense. "Remember, Katherine? That's the company Gary and Hodge worked for. And those people said something about Curtis Rathbone—remember, he was the head of the company, the one we saw talking on the video way back at the cave, the day we all found out the truth. . . ."

"Oh, no. You're right," Katherine said, slumping back against the side of the lab desk. "That means . . ."

"Right," Jonah said. "We're in enemy territory. And Second's got to be around here somewhere too. And I bet he has Mom and Dad stashed somewhere we can't get to."

"And there's something about this room that would keep the time agency from seeing what happens here . . . so we can't count on them for any help . . . ," Katherine whispered.

They were practically finishing each other's sentences. For all Jordan could tell, maybe they were practically reading each other's minds. It was like they were some time-traveling duo who'd worked together for years.

And it was like they'd both forgotten Jordan was even there.

Hello? Jordan wanted to say. *Katherine's* my *sister. It's* my *parents we need to rescue.*

And for all their talk, what were these two even figuring out? As far as Jordan could tell, he was the only one who'd suggested actually *doing* anything.

"Fine," Jordan said, his voice a little too loud for someone who was supposed to be hiding. "If you two want to be cowards about everything, let's just ask those magic Elucidators to show us where Gary and Hodge are right now, and where Second and Mom and Dad are. And then—"

Both Jonah and Katherine were frowning at him.

"I'm not sure we should trust either of these Elucidators," Jonah said. "We know the one you took from JB wasn't working right to begin with, and the other one has some connection to Second, so—"

Jordan ignored him.

"Elucidators, where are Mom and Dad right now?" he asked, dipping his head toward the cell phone–like object and the plastic card Jonah was holding. Strangely, the cell phone looked sleeker and more futuristic than it had the last time Jonah had looked at it, but that had to be his imagination.

Words glowed in the air once more: I CAN'T ANSWER THAT.

Jonah shot Jordan an *I told you so* look. Jordan ignored that, too.

"Elucidator, where are Gary and Hodge right now?" he tried again.

At least the words changed this time: GARY AND HODGE ARE NOT PRESENT IN THIS TIME PERIOD.

Okay. Maybe Jordan should have expected that. He'd heard their coworkers say they'd vanished. And with time travel, that probably meant that they'd vanished from this time.

But he wasn't going to give up, not with Jonah glowering at him.

"Then where—I mean, 'when'—are they?" Jordan asked. HERE IS A TIMELINE SHOWING ALL MOMENTS THOSE TWO HAVE ENTERED the words glowed back at him.

Jordan saw a glowing line in the air with dots all over the place.

"Shut that down!" Jonah ordered. "That's so bright someone could see it from outside!"

The glowing line obligingly disappeared.

"We're wasting time," Jonah hissed. "I already know why Gary and Hodge aren't answering their coworkers! Charles Lindbergh used an Elucidator I gave him and turned them into babies again, so they couldn't cause any more trouble. So—"

"Why didn't you tell us that before?" Jordan challenged.

Jonah ran his hand across his forehead. Jordan

recognized that motion: It was what Jordan himself did when he was frustrated.

Except for their clothes, Jonah already looked exactly like Jordan. Having him act like Jordan too made things even creepier.

"There hasn't been time for me *to* tell!" Jonah protested. "I mean, with you grabbing things and sending us the wrong places . . . And there's, like, more than five hundred years of stuff that happened to Katherine and me and Chip and the other missing kids that you don't know about, so where was I supposed to start?"

"I didn't know about Gary and Hodge turning back into babies either," Katherine said quietly. And this was not like her. Katherine was never quiet. "Did you leave them in 1932? Or—"

"I don't know!" Jonah said, as if he were annoyed with Katherine, too. "JB took care of them. All I was thinking about was getting home and getting my normal life back. . . ."

The look he shot Jordan then was so disgusted he might as well have said out loud, *I wanted to get back to my life where you didn't exist.*

"So for all you know, JB might have killed those two babies," Jordan said, jumping to the most extreme example to get back at Jonah.

"JB wouldn't have done that," Jonah protested.

"How do you know?" Jordan asked. "What if you're not even right about who the good guys are and who the bad guys are?"

"Stop it!" Katherine interrupted. "You two are, like, almost shouting at each other. Someone's going to find us!"

For some reason, Jordan felt angry with her right now too.

"You know, if I weren't here, I bet the two of you would just sit around saying, 'Ooh, we're so scared, we're so scared, what will we do if someone finds us?'" Jordan accused. He tried making his voice a little quieter, but it rose as he went on. "You think you know so much more than me—what good is all that knowledge if it just makes you scared? What are you ever going to do?"

"We're going to . . . to . . . ," Katherine sputtered.

"We're going to skip ahead in time to five o'clock today, so we can hear what Gary and Hodge's coworkers say when they get back together," Jonah finished for her.

"Could you do *that* for us, Elucidators?" Jordan asked mockingly.

He expected the Elucidators to tell him all over again what they couldn't do. But only one word glowed beside Jonah's hands:

YES.

ELEVEN

Jordan's anger evaporated.

"Oh, wow," he breathed. "That's so cool. Think how time travel could work with school—you could skip the whole boring day . . ."

"People would notice you were missing," Katherine said. "You wouldn't get away with it."

But she sounded more amused than annoyed now. Then she ruined it by turning to Jonah.

"Remember how amazed we were the first time we traveled through time?" she asked. "We made so many mistakes back in the fourteen hundreds . . . Jordan, just wait until the first time you turn invisible. That's really bizarre too!"

"Shouldn't we turn invisible before we skip ahead in time?" Jordan asked. He was proud of himself for thinking of this.

And Jonah and Katherine think I don't know anything. . . .

Neither of them looked impressed.

"I guess so, but it probably won't do any good," Katherine said. "I bet everyone at Interchronological Rescue has traveled through time. That means they'd be able to see us anyhow."

Jordan squinted at her blankly. Had he just then accidentally skipped ahead in time, and missed hearing something about traveling through time and being able to see invisible people?

"Katherine, remember, he doesn't know anything about the rules of time travel," Jonah said impatiently. He turned toward Jordan, and slowed down his voice like he was talking to a little kid. A really stupid little kid. "See, Jordan, invisibility only fools time natives. Anyone who's ever traveled through time can see invisible people. It looks like they're made out of glass or something, but they're still visible."

Jordan was not going to ask what a "time native" was. He could guess that one. Wouldn't it be someone native to a particular time? Someone who belonged in that moment?

"You'll see," Katherine said. "It really is freaky. Elucidator, make us invisible."

Nothing changed about Jonah, Katherine, or—Jordan looked down—Jordan himself. But when Jordan glanced back up, he saw glowing words again near the Elucidators in Jonah's hands: INVISIBILITY IS NOT A FUNCTION I CAN ACCOMPLISH AT THIS TIME AND IN THIS PLACE.

Jonah winced. "There is something really weird going on with these Elucidators," he said. "Maybe we shouldn't use them anymore until we know what it is."

"What, you want to just sit around waiting until five o'clock?" Jordan complained. He had no idea what time it was now, or how far away five o'clock was. Gary and Hodge's coworkers had made it sound like it might be hours before they met again—enough time to contact "sources" at the time agency and cover for someone's spying. But even if it was just five minutes, Jordan didn't want to wait. He could feel himself getting antsy, like he did during the last five minutes of science class, when it seemed like time stopped and the boring teacher was going to ramble on forever.

"Jordan, you don't know all the dangers possible," Jonah said.

"Not that it's your fault," Katherine added quickly.

That didn't help. Jordan shot both of them a defiant look, then bent down toward the Elucidators in Jonah's hands.

"Elucidators, send us ahead in time to five p.m. today," he said.

Jordan didn't feel any of the spinning dizziness of his last few trips through time. But maybe he wouldn't, when he wasn't even moving ahead a full day?

Then he saw words glowing near Jonah's hands: MY ACTIONS ARE BLOCKED BY THE TIME-DEADENING PROPERTIES OF THIS ROOM. YOU MUST LEAVE THIS ROOM TO TRAVEL THROUGH TIME.

"Okay, that's suspicious," Jonah said. "Why could we get *into* this room with time travel, but not out of it?"

"Gary and Hodge's coworkers said it's a protected space," Katherine reminded him. She cupped her chin in her hand, as if she planned to think for a long time. "Hmm . . ."

"Are you two going to do nothing but talk about this until five o'clock?" Jordan asked incredulously.

"We've got to figure out what's going on," Jonah said. "I don't trust Second, he's using Mom and Dad as bait, we don't even know what year this is—we've got to be careful!"

What was it about Jonah that made Jordan feel so much like punching him?

"Right—Mom and Dad are missing, so *I'm* not going to just sit here doing nothing!" Jordan said.

He reached over and grabbed both the cell phone and the plastic card from Jonah's hands. Then he stood up.

"Jordan, wait!" Katherine cried.

"You're not thinking this through!" Jonah argued.

Both of them reached toward Jordan, trying to grab the two Elucidators back. But Jordan was a step ahead of them. He held both Elucidators high over his head, out of their reach. Katherine and Jonah scrambled to their feet, but Jordan anticipated that, too. He took off running toward the door.

"Jordan, you don't know what's out there!" Katherine called after him.

"Stop!" Jonah hissed.

Jordan reached the door and wrapped his hand around the knob.

I'll show them. I'm not as careless as they think, he told himself. He pulled the door open only a crack, so he could peek out, just in case.

Outside the lab he saw an empty hallway. Maybe it was wildly futuristic; maybe the walls and floors and ceiling were made of some bizarre substance that didn't even exist in the twenty-first century. Jordan didn't pay attention to any of that. All he cared about was that the hall was empty. He gave himself an extra second of glancing around to see if there were security cameras anywhere in sight. His brain threw an irritating thought at him: *Maybe in the future, security cameras are just woven into the wallpaper or otherwise completely undetectable.* . . . But if there were security cameras, wouldn't the three people who'd come into the lab already have shut them off? Jonah and Katherine had almost caught up with Jordan. He didn't have time to worry about every little possibility.

Out of the corner of his eye, Jordan could see Jonah and Katherine reaching for him. Just as he felt them grab for his shirt, he yanked the door open and stepped out into the hall.

"Elucidator, take the three of us ahead to five o'clock today!" Jordan muttered.

The next thing Jordan knew, a very large man smashed into him.

"Where did you come from?" a deep voice asked.

TWELVE

Jordan slammed to the floor, which may have been cushioned more than a typical twenty-first-century floor, but he didn't care about that either. His brain had just figured something out, way too late: *Just because the hallway was empty and clear at the time you were leaving, that doesn't mean it would be empty and clear in the time you traveled to. In fact, you knew three people were planning to be in this area at five o'clock. Stupid, stupid, stupid!*

Dimly, he realized that Jonah and Katherine had also toppled to the floor behind him. The fact that they had been reaching out of the protected room to grab him was evidently enough to make them travel through time too. And so all three of them fell like dominos when they ran into the large man.

"Who are you?" the man demanded, still in that amazingly deep voice.

Dub. He's the man you were thinking of as Deep Voice, when you were eavesdropping from your safe, secure hiding place, Jordan realized. *Of course Deep Voice or one of the other two would be walking into the lab for their meeting now.*

Why did his brain have to get so smart now, when it was too late?

He decided to let Jonah or Katherine deal with Deep Voice's questions.

But the man didn't wait for any answers. He quickly glanced around, beads swinging out from his head—*beads all over a man's hair? Is that some typical fashion in the future?* Jordan wondered. Then the man kicked the door behind them completely open and shoved all three kids back into the lab.

Jordan, Jonah, and Katherine somersaulted over one another. It was like some pileup on a soccer or football field, where Jordan lost track of whose elbow was in his ear and whose knee was in his stomach.

Jordan had never felt so guilty about causing a pileup in soccer or football.

"Sorry," he muttered. "Sorry. I should have thought . . ."

"Shh," Katherine hissed at him, as if she still hoped she could hide, even as Deep Voice stared down at them.

No, not just Deep Voice. Two other people were staring down at them, too: A woman in a bright purple robe and a man with what seemed to be tattoos of eagles and trees across his face.

Maybe Jordan shouldn't have gotten so distracted looking at clothes and tattoos and beads. In the next instant, Deep Voice snatched the two Elucidators from Jordan's hand. And the woman went into a defensive stance and pointed something that looked like a flash drive at all three of the kids.

"Don't move!" she commanded, just as if she were pointing a gun at them.

Oh, um, maybe she is? Jordan realized. *Maybe that's what guns look like in the future?*

"Spies," Deep Voice growled.

"The question is, who are they spies for?" the woman asked, still in her *Don't move or I'll shoot you* stance.

"We'll interrogate them separately," the tattooed man announced. "That should help."

Jordan thought that would mean he'd have a few moments to whisper to Katherine and Jonah while they were being taken away. But the tattooed man pointed at three corners of the room, one after the other. Shimmering walls appeared instantly in each of those corners, creating small private cubicles.

"I'll take the girl," the woman announced, pulling Katherine up and away from Jordan and Jonah.

"You want old-timey-clothes boy number one or old-timey-clothes boy number two?" Deep Voice asked Tattoo Face.

Jordan wanted to protest, *I'm not wearing old-timey clothes!* But if this was the future, he guessed maybe his clothes would look old-fashioned. Did his T-shirt and sweatpants look as strange to the two men as their tattoos and beads looked to him?

"Don't—" Jonah started to whisper in Jordan's ear, but Deep Voice and Tattoo Face were already yanking them apart.

"Except for their clothes, it looks like they're pretty much the same person," Tattoo Face muttered. "So it's probably not going to matter."

Deep Voice pulled Jordan to the nearest cubicle. Although the walls looked see-through from the outside, they seemed to turn solid as soon as Deep Voice yanked Jordan inside.

"Let me go!" Jordan cried, jerking his arm away from the man. Evidently Jordan caught him off guard—Jordan slipped through his fingers. Immediately Jordan sprang up and hurled himself back toward the opening they'd just walked through.

It still *looked* like open space, but Jordan seemed to slam into a solid wall. He bounced back and landed on the floor once more.

"Lucky me, I got the spaz kid," Deep Voice muttered. He settled into a chair at a table Jordan hadn't noticed before. "Want to try that again, so I can laugh?"

Jordan ignored him, and put his hand out to touch the invisible wall.

Nothing, nothing, nothing . . . Jordan had his whole arm extended out of the cubicle, and hadn't touched a wall yet. He rose up, intending to ease the rest of his body out too.

Maybe you just have to be slow passing through the doorway . . . , he thought.

His shoulder hit solid wall again, bouncing him back into a heap on the floor.

Deep Voice chuckled. "It's so much fun watching time primitives encounter actual technology," he murmured.

"I'm not from a primitive time!" Jordan protested. "We have computers! We have, uh, walls that look like mirrors from one side but are see-through from the other! That's not so different from this! And we, um—"

Belatedly, Jordan realized that he might as well be telling Deep Voice what time period he was from. And Jonah's *Don't* had probably been the start of *Don't tell them anything*.

"Oh, sorry," Deep Voice said, not sounding the least bit sorry. "I didn't mean to insult your highly advanced time period."

Make him start telling you about his time period, Jordan told himself. *Trick him into revealing stuff the way he tricked you.*

What Jordan really wanted was to know was where his parents were and how he could get them back. But he didn't trust himself to ask anything about them.

"Did you find out where Gary and Hodge are, and why they're not answering you?" he asked instead.

Deep Voice narrowed his eyes.

"How did you know . . . ?" he began. His eyes were just slits now. It was amazing how terrifying this made him look. He was a mountain of a man, even with beads in his hair. "Did you overhear at lunchtime? After Doreen scanned the room and was certain it was empty?"

"Maybe there's stuff you and Doreen and that other dude don't know," Jordan taunted. "Maybe *your* technology isn't all that great, either, if your scanners can miss three whole people."

Deep Voice glowered at Jordan.

"Sit," he said, pointing at the chair opposite him at the table.

Jordan considered refusing, but didn't see how that would help.

"I'm not telling you anything," he said, even as he eased into the chair. "Not unless we trade information. You get one question, I get one question."

That was how real spies would do it, wasn't it?

Deep Voice didn't look impressed. He stared down at something in his hands—maybe an Elucidator of his own, maybe one of the two that he'd grabbed away from Jordan.

"I've already done the DNA scan," he said. "In a moment, I'll have more information about you at my fingertips than you could ever tell me. And I'll know *my* information is accurate."

A DNA scan couldn't really tell all that much, could it?

Jordan stayed silent. An instant later Deep Voice jumped, and glanced up at Jordan with an amazed expression on his face.

"*You're* Jonah Skidmore?" he asked.

"Why do people always guess his name first?" Jordan complained. "Have you never heard of identical twins? Same genes and all? I'm not Jonah, I'm—"

At the last moment, he realized maybe he shouldn't say his name. Maybe he shouldn't have even said that about being identical twins.

The amazement left Deep Voice's face.

"Oh, right," he murmured. "Of course. It's the *other* boy who's Jonah Skidmore."

Ouch, Jordan thought.

He guessed Deep Voice had done the futuristic

equivalent of googling someone with the same name as a famous person, and all the stuff about the famous person came up first.

In this case, Jonah was the famous person. Jordan wasn't.

"I see there was a twin left to die in the nineteen thirties," Deep Voice said. "It was Claude and Clyde Beckman originally—looks like you're Clyde. Gary and Hodge must not have thought you were worth rescuing."

Not worth rescuing? That really hurt.

Jordan opened his mouth to protest, *Don't you see anything about me in the twenty-first century as Jordan Skidmore? Your fancy DNA scan isn't very good after all, is it?*

But probably that was what Deep Voice wanted him to do. Probably Deep Voice was trying to goad him into getting upset and accidentally revealing something Deep Voice wouldn't have known otherwise.

Jordan felt proud of himself for figuring out that psychological game.

But is there any chance this guy really does think I was left behind in the nineteen thirties? Jordan wondered. *What if he doesn't know about me being kidnapped and ending up with Mom and Dad?*

Could that also mean Deep Voice knew nothing about Jordan having his own dimension until Jonah made everything smash together?

And that means . . . .

Jordan barely understood the different dimensions himself. But if Deep Voice didn't know about them either, did that maybe mean that this was some future branch of time where the dimensions *hadn't* blended? Or hadn't blended yet?

Since everything's in such a mess back in the twenty-first century, is it possible that the changes—and news of the changes—haven't reached this future yet? Jordan wondered.

Jordan felt absolutely brilliant figuring that out. But he wasn't sure what he could do with the information, or if it was even right.

What if it just means everything was ruined so badly with Mom and Dad being the wrong age that it's too late to stop all of time from ending?

Okay, that wasn't the right way to go for his next thought.

"The question is, how did you get *here?*" Deep Voice asked.

Now the man was looking down at the cell phone–like device and the plastic card that he'd grabbed from Jordan.

What if they worked well enough to tell Deep Voice everything?

"I'll tell you what happened," Jordan said, trying to keep the panic out of his voice. "The time agency sent me here. They gave me those Elucidators. They know where I am. You've got to let me go, or the time agency will come and arrest you!"

"It's interesting that you would say that," Deep Voice muttered. Strangely, he laid both the cell phone and the plastic card out on the table, where Jordan could easily reach them. The only thing that stopped Jordan from grabbing them was Deep Voice's next words: "Because neither of these objects is a working Elucidator."

THIRTEEN

"What?" Jordan asked. "They're not? But—but—"

Had JB lied to him? Had Jonah? Had Second?

It wasn't as if Jordan had understood much about Elucidators before. But this was even more confusing.

"But those Elucidators made us travel through time," Jordan protested. "They did! We were at home, my whole family was—and some other people too—and then all that disappeared and we were in the dark and spinning and then we were here. And then we were in a time hollow and—"

Too late, Jordan realized that he probably shouldn't be telling Deep Voice so much. But he wanted Deep Voice to admit, *Oh, sorry. My mistake. You're right. These are Elucidators.*

"Huh," Deep Voice grunted. "If what you've told me were actually true, that would be very interesting."

"Why?" Jordan asked. His head was spinning again.

Am I getting even sicker? he wondered, even though all his travels through time had mostly distracted him from remembering he'd been sick back home. *Did I bring my germs to the future with me?*

What did it matter? His problems now were so much bigger than a minor twenty-first-century cold.

"You *claim* the time agency sent you here," Deep Voice said. "And yet the time agency recently issued an edict prohibiting all travel bringing time natives from the past to the present. My present, I mean—your future. Why would the time agency break its own rules for a kid like you? One who wasn't even worth removing from the nineteen thirties, when it was easy?"

Deep Voice sounded triumphant, like he thought he'd caught Jordan in some huge lie, and now he expected Jordan to spill everything.

Dude, I've got nothing to spill, because I don't understand any of this! Jordan wanted to protest.

He started grasping for something—anything—that he might be able to figure out.

"So . . . it's illegal now to bring people from the past to the future?" Jordan asked. "Doesn't that make things hard for Gary and Hodge? Isn't that what they do all the time, kidnapping babies?"

"They rescue endangered children from the past," Deep Voice said, so smoothly it seemed as if that might be an official slogan. "We here at Interchronological Rescue perform a strictly humanitarian function. So of course we have protested the time agency's edict. And we've sued for damages."

"And Gary and Hodge disappeared," Jordan said.

Were all those things connected?

Jordan remembered that Jonah claimed he knew why Gary and Hodge had disappeared: because Charles Lindbergh had turned them back into babies.

Did Charles Lindbergh work for the time agency too? Why hadn't Jordan asked Jonah that question?

Was the time agency going to let Gary and Hodge grow up all over again, and hope that this time they didn't become kidnappers capable of ending all of time?

And what did any of that have to do with Mom and Dad looking like teenagers again? *Were* they still teenagers, wherever Second had taken them? Were they still in this same time period as Jordan?

Maybe Jordan shouldn't have been so hard on Jonah and Katherine for wanting to sit around waiting and thinking and talking endlessly before actually doing anything. Jordan could really use some more information right about now.

"What are you and Doreen and that other guy going

to do about Gary and Hodge disappearing?" Jordan asked Deep Voice. "What are you going to do to stop their plan from ending all of time forever? What are you going to do to me and Katherine and Jonah?"

Deep Voice swept his hands across the table, knocking the plastic card and the cell phone to the side. He didn't bother putting them back in place. He acted like they were as worthless as an empty gum wrapper or a used Kleenex— or as worthless as he'd accused Jordan himself of being. Something you forgot about once you were done with it.

"This interrogation is over," Deep Voice rumbled.

He stood up and walked out the doorway of the cubicle as though it were the easiest thing in the world.

But of course when Jordan tried to sneak behind him, Jordan hit a solid wall and smashed to the floor once more.

"Wait!" Jordan cried. "Come back! You can't just leave me in this . . . this jail cell!"

Deep Voice kept walking away. An instant later the see-through area of the cubicle clouded up, completely blocking Jordan's view of anything outside the cubicle.

He *was* in a jail cell. No, worse than that—he was in a jail cell with no door. There was nothing he could do to escape.

And if Deep Voice thought he was worthless, would anyone ever bother coming back for him?

FOURTEEN

Jordan panicked.

He pounded his fists against the walls and screamed, "Let me out! Let me out!"

He screamed himself hoarse before it occurred to him that this was a cubicle made for interrogations, and so it was probably soundproof.

Probably nobody could hear anything he said, no matter how much he screamed.

He slammed his shoulders against first one wall, then another, hoping to find some weak spot, some crack in the defenses.

That just made his shoulders ache.

He snatched up the cell phone and the plastic card from the table. Even though Deep Voice had said they weren't Elucidators—and Jonah had said they were suspicious—Jordan shouted commands at them anyway.

"Talk to me! Tell me what to do!"

Nothing happened.

"You answered questions before! Answer questions now!"

Still nothing.

"Where are all the glowing words?" he asked. He put the plastic card down, and yelled into the cell. "Even if you're just, like, a smartphone from the twenty-first century, can't you answer anything?"

If he was holding a smartphone from the twenty-first century, it was one with a dead battery.

He slumped against the wall. Nobody could hear him. Nobody could see him. So he let himself do what he really wanted to do.

"Mommy? Daddy?" he moaned. "Why can't you come and find me? I'm sorry! Come and fix everything I messed up! And everything everybody else messed up, too . . ."

Nobody came. It was entirely possible that he would be stuck here until the end of time—especially since Gary and Hodge's coworkers seemed to think that could happen soon. Which was worse, being stuck in a doorless cubicle when time ended quickly, or having to spend weeks and months and years in a doorless cubicle, and then just dying of old age?

I wouldn't die of old age here, Jordan realized, looking around at the tiny, blank space around him. *I'd starve, or die of thirst, or . . . or maybe there isn't even enough air in here . . .*

He had to gasp for breath, but maybe that was just because he was thinking about suffocating. He did know there wasn't any food around, and this was clearly not a time hollow, because he was getting really hungry. Hungry and thirsty, and he kind of needed to go to the bathroom, too. . . .

Katherine would make fun of me thinking about bathrooms at a time like this, Jordan thought despairingly.

Was Katherine maybe stuck in a doorless cubicle of her own, thinking she was going to die? Was she going to die being furious with him, because it was his fault both of them were stuck?

She could be so annoying sometimes. But she was still his sister, and he really didn't want her to die hating him. He didn't want her to die at all.

And Mom, and Dad . . . It's pretty much my fault that they're stuck wherever they are too.

"I was trying to help," he said aloud. "Really I was."

But had he been? Or had he been trying to show up Jonah and Katherine?

Jordan didn't like the thoughts in his head. It was no fun sitting around thinking when every thought led back to something he'd done wrong.

Just to distract himself, he began running his hands slowly along the walls, trying to figure out how they worked. Would he be able to feel any difference between the part of the wall that had seemed solid all along, and the section that Deep Voice had walked through?

All the walls felt exactly the same.

Jordan switched to feeling along the floor. Then he climbed onto the table and felt along the ceiling, looking for an exit there.

Nothing.

He went back to the walls again.

Deep Voice got through, he told himself stubbornly.

Maybe the walls recognized Deep Voice's molecular structure, and they didn't recognize Jordan's. Maybe even walls were that individualized in the future.

Why make things so complicated? Jordan wondered.

He sounded like his grandparents, who complained about their cell phones being confusing.

He sat down at the table. He hadn't run his hand over every inch of the table and chairs yet, so he did that, too.

Nothing, nothing, nothing . . .

He had his hand under the chair Deep Voice had sat in, when he felt a little ridge. It was probably just a rough spot in the wood—or plastic, or whatever the chair was made of. But, just in case, he flipped the chair over.

Words glowed up at him from the underside of the chair: TO EXIT, PRESS HERE.

Jordan pressed.

Instantly three of the cubicle walls vanished, and he was staring out at the lab, which was much darker than it had been before. He couldn't even make out the two cubicles on the other side of the room where Jonah and Katherine had been taken.

Maybe I figured out how to get out before they did, he thought. *And I can rescue them, and that will make up for getting them stuck in the cubicles in the first place.*

Or maybe they'd figured out how to escape hours ago, and hadn't bothered coming to rescue him.

Jonah probably wouldn't care, but Katherine would have rescued me, if she could. Wouldn't she?

Jordan took a step forward, stepping into a spot where there'd been a wall only moments before. So now he *was* out. This wasn't just another illusion.

Jordan's step forward also enabled him to see a figure sitting in the darkness, back by the desk where Jordan, Katherine, and Jonah had hidden earlier in the day. Whoever it was wasn't enormous enough to be Deep Voice. Jordan didn't think it was Doreen or Tattoo Face, either.

"Katherine?" Jordan whispered hopefully. "Mom? Dad?"

"Guess again," a voice called back.

It was Second.

FIFTEEN

"You—You—" Jordan sputtered. "You've just been playing tricks on us, haven't you?"

"Maybe," Second admitted.

Jordan rushed toward him, his hands out. He hadn't quite decided yet if he was going to grab Second by the shoulders and shake him, or if he was going to go straight into punching mode.

It didn't matter. Jordan felt himself completely immobilized in running pose, his feet inches off the floor, his outstretched hands a full yard away from Second's shoulders and face.

"Now, now," Second scolded him. "That hot temper of yours isn't going to help."

"You're just manipulating me!" Jordan accused. "You've been manipulating all of us all along, haven't you?" His mind started putting things together. "Were you manipulating the Elucidators, too? And Deep Voice didn't get out of that cubicle by pressing a button on his chair, did he?"

"Deep Voice?" Second asked blankly. Then he chuckled. "Oh, you mean Interchronological Rescue employee Markiel Katun? 'Deep Voice' really isn't a bad name for him. Though you also could have gone with 'Bigfoot' or 'Mount Human' or—"

"Stop joking around!" Jordan demanded. "Tell me the truth! Was all this some big setup? Do those people who captured us even work with Gary and Hodge, or was that a lie too?"

"Now you're thinking," Second congratulated him.

Jordan felt himself land on his feet again. He moved his arms forward and back, experimentally. He wasn't frozen anymore. But he figured it could happen again if he took another step toward Second.

He stayed where he was.

"Ah, and now you're showing some self-restraint. Good for you!" Second continued.

Jordan still felt like punching him. He went back to asking questions instead.

"Well? What's really going on? What did you do with Mom and Dad? What are you trying to manipulate Jonah and Katherine and me into doing? Why are you being so mean?"

Second held up his hand.

"I assure you, there is a point to everything I'm doing," he said. "I worry about you, little Jordan."

Jordan thought about telling him that absolutely no thirteen-year-old in the universe liked being called "little." But he held himself back.

"You see," Second went on, "you're so *callow*. Oh dear, have I maybe used a word that you don't even know?"

Of course Jordan was not going to admit that he'd never heard of the word "callow."

"That means inexperienced," Second said. "Immature. Naturally, you are just thirteen, but you've also led such a sheltered life. Those parents of yours—"

"Don't you say anything bad about my parents!" Jordan muttered.

"Ah, yes, loyalty—what a good trait!" Second cooed. "I'm just saying that they've made the choice that many of their time and place do: In their attempts to raise you wisely and well, they've perhaps kept you too ignorant of what we might call the seamier side of human existence."

Jordan had no desire to discuss how his parents had raised him.

"That has nothing to do with time travel or your lies or anything that matters right now!" he complained.

If he slid forward so gradually that Second didn't notice, could he perhaps grab a real, working Elucidator from Second and make Second freeze and then force the man to tell Jordan where his parents were and how Jordan could rescue them?

No—that would require Jordan actually being able to recognize a real, working Elucidator.

"Tell me the truth!" Jordan demanded.

Second sighed. "This is not all an elaborate setup," he said. "Just . . . partially. I did place that button in your cubicle. For your benefit, I might add. But Markiel Katun, Doreen Smith, and Liam Gonzalez really do work for Interchronological Rescue, the, shall we say, erstwhile employer of your unreasonably detested Gary and Hodge. I mean, contemptible as they are, those two really did save you and your twin from starving to death during the depths of the Great Depression—"

"Stop trying to change the subject!" Jordan said. "I don't care about ancient history—just tell me about what affects now."

"Ah, but is any history really all that ancient?" Second asked. "Doesn't every moment from the past affect the present?"

This man was more annoying than any history teacher Jordan had ever had.

"I just want my parents back," Jordan said. "I just want my family back, and my regular life. . . . And okay, if there's some danger that all of time is going to end, I'd like to help stop it, if I can. . . ."

"Naiveté," Second said. "Such a combination of blessing and curse."

Did this man do anything but speak in riddles? And mess with people's minds?

Second smiled, almost as if he knew what Jordan was thinking.

"Lucky for you," Second said, "I'm going to let you have one other family member help you achieve the tasks ahead of you. Which would you choose?"

"Dad," Jordan said instantly. Then he reconsidered. "Though, I guess if it's their kid versions, maybe it should be Mom. Or really, even Katherine would be all right."

He wasn't going to admit that Katherine might be more useful than either of his parents right now.

"Ennnhhh," Second said, making a sound like a buzzer signaling a mistake. "You're missing the obvious choice. Look over there."

Second pointed across the room, toward the corner cubicle farthest from Jordan. The walls of the cubicle began to glow slightly. Then they became see-through. Then, rapidly, they went dark and disappeared, but not before Jordan had seen who was sitting calmly inside that cubicle. It was the person Second had chosen to work with Jordan.

Jonah.

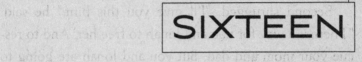

SIXTEEN

"He's not part of my family!" Jordan protested.

"Think again," Second said, narrowing his eyes disapprovingly. "And be careful. You wouldn't want to hurt his feelings."

Jordan squinted, catching just enough movement from the other side of the room to figure out that Jonah was edging along the main wall of the lab, inching toward the only cubicle left—the one that probably still held Katherine inside.

"Let Katherine help too," Jordan argued. "It's not fair to leave her stuck in that awful cubicle while Jonah and I are out free."

"Ah, but who is that situation unfair to?" Second asked. "Katherine, or you and Jonah? Who would be advantaged and who would be disadvantaged?"

Was talking to Second always this infuriating?

"You know what I mean," Jordan mumbled. Then he felt his stomach twist, as if it had caught on faster than his brain had. "Er . . . do you mean that Katherine's safer in that cubicle than she would be with Jonah and me? Or than Jonah and I are going to be?"

Second shrugged. "I'll give you this hint," he said. "There *is* a way for you and Jonah to free her. And to rescue your mom and dad. But you and Jonah are going to have to figure it out."

He took a step back and raised his arm melodramatically, and the gesture seemed familiar.

Because—wasn't that what Second did right before he disappeared from the time hollow? Jordan wondered.

This time Second didn't disappear immediately.

"Oh, wait," he said. "Just for fun, let's make this a little more challenging. Look."

He pointed behind Jordan.

Jordan wasn't going to fall for that trick.

"Oh, no, you don't," he said, starting to step forward, toward Second.

But Second was already gone. Jordan swiped his hands uselessly through the air anyway, touching nothing. But then, out of the corner of his eye, he saw something glowing behind him. He whirled around, and the glow grew.

A long line of flames stretched across the floor, crackling up toward the ceiling and cutting Jordan off completely from Katherine's cubicle, from Jonah—and from the door.

SEVENTEEN

For a moment, Jordan could do nothing but stare. How could those flames have appeared out of nowhere, so quickly? How had there been time for someone to dump a line of gasoline across the floor and set it on fire? And then for that fire to reach all the way to the ceiling . . .

Jordan realized Jonah was screaming at him. "Jordan! Get the Elucidators!"

Jordan whipped his head back and forth, looking toward the table where Deep Voice had left the plastic card and the cell phone. That table was on Jordan's side of the flames.

It figured—Jonah got the door on his side, and Jordan got the worthless junk.

"Those don't work!" Jordan yelled back at Jonah.

"I know!" Jonah yelled back. "But sometimes they work—please, we have to try—"

Jordan ran for the table. As soon as he had his hands around the phone and the plastic card, he heard Jonah yell over the crackling flames, "Now say, 'Get all three of us out of here! Take us someplace safe!'"

"Why don't I just say, 'Put out the fire'?" Jordan screamed back. "Put out the fire!"

Instantly a line of sprinklers opened in the ceiling, right above the flames. Water poured down onto the flames, and in seconds nothing remained of them but a little trail of leftover smoke.

"Okay, that worked too," Jonah admitted, grinning.

It was the first time Jonah had actually worn a pleasant expression looking toward Jordan.

"How did you know the Elucidators would still work?" Jordan asked. "The guy who interrogated me said they were just fakes or totally broken, or something like that."

"I had this theory, and then I just came out and asked the guy who interrogated me, and he said . . ." Jonah's voice trailed off. His gaze shifted away from Jordan, toward something just past Jordan's right shoulder. Jonah's eyes got big.

"Jordan," he whispered. "Step closer to me. Stay in the shadows. No—tell the Elucidators to make us invisible. . . ."

"That doesn't work in here, remember?" Jordan started to protest. But the worry in Jonah's expression made him decide to turn around instead, even as he took the first step toward Jonah.

Everything had changed behind him. Somehow the futuristic laboratory had changed into a medieval-looking space—were they in a castle now? A cathedral? A dungeon? Stone walls soared high into the shadows above Jordan's head. And footsteps echoed ominously against the stone floor. Jordan could see a line of figures in dark robes marching toward him. Were there fifty of them? A hundred? A thousand?

"Jordan! Hide!" Jonah whispered. "Maybe they haven't seen us yet!"

"Where?" Jordan asked, glancing around frantically at solid stone walls and stone floors with no breaks or crevices or cubbyholes. "There's nowhere to hide!"

It was too late anyhow. The man in the front of all those robed men was practically toe to toe with Jordan now. Jordan could see the man's eyes narrow with disgust, maybe even hatred.

"Halt!" the man called, and the word echoed against the vaulted ceiling, high overhead.

The long line of men behind him ceased their marching. Somehow the sudden silence was even more terrifying than the echoing footsteps had been. How could so many men stay so still?

The man in the lead glared at Jordan.

"Why hast thou intruded upon this sacred moment, the king's coronation?" the man snarled. He looked Jordan up and down. "How dare you! And attired in such ridiculous garb . . . Such disrespect! Quick! Answer me and answer me well, lest I summon the executioner!"

Jordan gulped. "You mean . . . you'll kill me if I don't give the right answer?" he asked, his voice trembling.

The man's glare intensified. Jordan could feel the fifty men behind him glaring as well. Or maybe it was a hundred glares, or a thousand. All aimed at him.

"Yes," the man hissed. "Answer well or die!"

EIGHTEEN

I'm dead, Jordan thought. His brain seemed incapable of coming up with anything else except *um . . . er . . . uh . . .*

And then Jonah stepped up beside him and wrapped his arm protectively around Jordan.

"Good man of God, I pray thee, have pity," Jonah told the glaring man, and the entire line of glaring men behind him. "We are simple folk, come from another land to pay homage to your new king. We meant no disrespect, only, uh, honor. Our strange garb represents the finest raiment of our land, worn only for the most honorable occasion. And, uh, this one has been struck dumb—or into foolishness, anyway—by his awe for your, uh, awesome kingdom. . . ."

The glaring man looked even angrier than before.

"Do I see double?" he asked. "What devilish trick is this?"

Oh, man, Jordan thought. *That's so not fair! Now he wants to kill us just because we're identical twins?*

Jonah didn't even flinch.

"Nay, nay, honorable sir," he said, his voice as smooth as glass. "'Tis God's blessing, not the work of the devil. That is how our parents always accounted it. They rejoiced that God had given them two strong twin sons to work their land. . . . They would mourn so, to lose either of us. I pray thee, do not deprive such fine, God-fearing folk of either of their beloved sons. Especially when we are here to honor your king, who of course would not want war with our land. . . ."

War? Was Jonah maybe laying it on a little too thick?

The glaring man still looked suspicious.

"Tell me, then, young knave," he said. "Which king do you revere above all others in this land?"

Oh, crap, Jordan thought. *That's not a fair question. How are we even supposed to know what land we're in?*

He bent his knees, because clearly all they could do was run. And clearly that was hopeless when they were so outnumbered.

But Jonah kept his arm tight around Jordan and answered steadily, "Why, Richard the Third, of course, good sir."

In the next instant the glaring man and all the other glaring men behind him simply vanished.

Jordan felt his knees go weak. He felt insanely grateful that Jonah didn't drop his arm immediately. It took a moment before Jordan felt safe pulling away on his own, before he felt certain that he could stand on his own two legs.

"What was *that* about?" Jordan demanded. He started laughing, making a burbling sound that might have been tinged with hysteria. "That was *crazy!* How did you know what to say? 'Good man of God, I pray thee, have pity'— really? *Really?* And Richard the Third? Who even knew there was a king called Richard the Third? Like, ever?"

"Jordan," Jonah said quietly. "Shh. I think this is a test. And I don't think it's over. Keep a hold on that plastic card—the fake Elucidator—even if it changes into something else in your hand. And stay with me. Do what I say."

A moment later, someone swung a flaming torch at Jordan's head.

NINETEEN

"What the—" Jordan screamed, throwing himself to the floor.

The torch hissed past the crown of his head, close enough to singe his hair.

Jordan dared to turn his head, and instantly wished he hadn't. A row of torches was advancing toward them.

Jonah grabbed Jordan's hand, the one that held the plastic-card Elucidator.

"Elucidator, make us invisible," Jonah cried in an urgent whisper. "Jordan, run for the tapestry!"

Tapestry? Jordan thought numbly.

Jonah pulled him toward some huge, musty wall hanging. In the dim light Jordan caught a glimpse of the needle-point design on the tapestry: knights with lances impaling a wild boar.

But as soon as Jordan crouched behind the tapestry, it disappeared.

Fortunately, so did the torches.

"Whew. That was close," Jordan mumbled, closing his eyes in relief.

When he opened them a second later, he thought the tapestry had come to life: He could see knights all around him, their armor gleaming in sudden, unexpected sunlight. But their lances were aimed at people, not animals. And there were battle-axes slashing against the armor, and cannonballs flying overhead. . . .

"Run!" Jonah screamed in Jordan's ear, his voice blending into the screams of horror and fear and death echoing all around them. "We've got to get off the battlefield!"

Jonah tugged on Jordan's arm, yanking him past foot soldiers and knights on horseback and a long row of wheeled cannons being shoved forward. They reached a clump of trees, and Jonah pulled Jordan behind the thickest trunk.

"Is it . . . over now?" Jordan mumbled.

This time he didn't even dare to blink. That was a good thing, because an arrow came whizzing toward him. It would have stabbed him right in the heart if he hadn't dived to the ground, knocking Jonah with him.

"Is this . . . still the battlefield?" Jordan moaned.

"No—they're shooting at deer, not us," Jonah whispered back. "Just stay down, and we'll be fine."

Jonah pointed, and Jordan gaped: All the medieval knights had vanished. Now he and Jonah were in thick woods, and two boys in loincloths were shooting arrow after arrow toward a deer that crashed past Jordan and Jonah.

"Are those...Indians?" Jordan asked. "Native Americans?"

But they'd already vanished, and so had the woods. Now he and Jonah seemed to be in a boat—an old, decrepit, icy boat heaving up and down on roiling waves.

"Going to be . . . sick," Jordan moaned.

He turned his head, trying to find something to focus on, and he saw what the boat was lurching toward: a towering cliff of ice, so enormous it was sure to smash the boat into slivers.

"Row!" Jonah screamed in Jordan's ear. "I don't care how sick you are—row hard!"

Somehow Jordan found an oar in his hands. He shoved both Elucidators into his pocket and clutched the oar with both hands. Then he slapped the oar's blade into the water, into the waves that rose and fell, crashing into the boat.

"Row harder!" Jonah demanded, and Jordan threw all his muscle into it.

The ice—an iceberg? A glacier? A continent?—slid

past them, so close that Jordan's oar splintered off shards that sparkled even in the gloom.

And then the ice and the boat were gone. Jordan and Jonah were lying on solid ground again, on dead-looking tufts of grass.

"Bear!" Jonah screamed. "Bear!"

Jordan had only ever seen bears in the zoo, usually when they were sleeping.

The monstrous creature galloping toward them did not even seem to be part of the same species. It was the size of a house; its teeth looked as long as knives. Its giant face was constricted with rage.

"Elucidator!" Jonah screamed. "Give us a . . ."

Why was he hesitating?

"Gun!" Jordan filled in. "Give us a gun!"

Something slammed into Jordan's right hand. He raised his arm and looked. Was it a rifle he was holding?

The only time Jordan had ever shot a gun was at camp, and that was only a BB gun. But he guessed this one would sort of work the same way. The bear was getting closer and closer. Jordan lifted the gun higher and aimed and squeezed the trigger. The recoil was so strong that it knocked Jordan down, but he could still see the bullet soaring off into the sky—seemingly miles away from the bear.

"I think this is the sixteen hundreds!" Jonah screamed. "Guns weren't very accurate then! We need something else . . . a spear! Elucidator, give us a spear!"

A long, thin spear appeared in Jonah's hand. The bear was so close now it practically could have slobbered on the spear's tip. Jonah reared back and drove the tip of the spear deep into the bear's chest.

And then the bear was gone. So were the gun and the spear.

"How was I supposed to know it was the sixteen hundreds?" Jordan moaned.

But they were already someplace else, maybe sometime else. Indoors this time, in a room that didn't seem too terribly old-fashioned. Wallpapered walls, a table covered with a lace cloth—was this the eighteen hundreds? The nineteen hundreds?

A man walked toward them, not glaring or screaming but just mumbling, "Where did you come from? What are you doing here?"

He had wiry hair and a thick moustache, and he looked like a strangely young version of . . .

Albert Einstein? Jordan wondered. *Could that be Albert Einstein?*

Jonah picked up a piece of paper from the table in front of him.

"Weren't you thinking about trains?" Jonah asked the

man. "Trains and light, and how beams of light would look different on a train going the speed of light?"

"Ah, yes," the man said vaguely, a distant look slipping into his eye. "Such fascinating subjects to contemplate . . ."

And then he vanished too.

"We were supposed to be afraid of Albert Einstein?" Jordan marveled. "*He* was supposed to be a danger to us like bears or battles or, or—"

"It's the other way around with him," Jordan said. "*We* were the danger there. If we'd distracted Einstein, we could have ruined time."

"Isn't that better than *our* lives being in danger?" Jordan asked, but probably Jonah didn't hear him, because the scene around them was changing.

The sunny, pleasant room disappeared, replaced by a dim, dingy space lit by a single lightbulb. In the center of the room, a group of people—maybe a family?—clung to one another in what had to be absolute terror. But Jordan and Jonah apparently weren't the danger here. The terrified family seemed to be looking past them, toward an open doorway.

Jordan whipped his head around. A line of men in vaguely Russian-looking clothes were lined up in the doorway, all of them holding guns or bayonets. And the guns were aimed at the family, at women and children and even a dog.

"Freeze time!" Jonah yelled. "Stop the assassination!"

And then the family and the men and guns and bayonets vanished too. In their place, the scene around Jordan and Jonah became the cockpit of an airplane—maybe even a jet. Both boys landed half in, half out of the copilot seat. There wasn't enough room for both of them, and Jordan's elbow knocked against a lever on the control panel.

Could that make the plane crash? Jordan wondered. *Oh, no—what if that's what we're here for, to stop a plane crash?*

He jerked his head toward the pilot's seat, expecting to see a terrorist or a hijacker—someone Jordan and Jonah might have to overpower. A tall man sat there, wearing, oddly, an old-fashioned brown suit and hat. His gaze practically drilled holes in the window in front of him.

"I'll do anything to get my son back," the man said, jutting his jaw out.

"Crashing the plane isn't the answer," Jordan said weakly. Because didn't this have to be a hijacker? Didn't the man's lack of a pilot's uniform prove it?

It was all he could do not to add, *I don't know how to fly a plane! I don't think Jonah does either! Please give it back to someone who does! Please don't kill us!*

Jonah drove his elbow deep into Jordan's side, a signal that had to mean, *Shut up! Let me handle this!*

"Gary and Hodge lied to you. I'm not your son, and

neither is Jordan," Jonah told the man. "Here's the evidence. You can test it yourself."

He pulled a hair from his own head, a hair from Jordan's, and one from the man's jacket. Then he held all three hairs out to the man.

When the man lifted his hand to reach for the hairs, the whole scene began to fade away. The man and the cockpit disappeared.

"*Hair* was the answer there?" Jordan cried. "How were we supposed to know that?"

"That was Charles Lindbergh," Jonah said. "He just needed proof. I was scared to death we'd need to give him an Elucidator, too, and I couldn't decide which one to hand him, which one to keep . . . ."

Jordan could barely listen. He had to stay braced for the next emergency, the next moment that would put him and Jonah on the verge of yet another disaster. He was so much on edge, so ready to make the next hair-trigger response, that it took him a moment to realize that the scene around him was the futuristic lab once again.

The flames! he thought, looking down at the floor. But all evidence of them was gone. Even the smell of smoke had vanished, as if there'd never been a fire.

Jordan looked back up, his eyes searching the dim

room for the next threat to his life. He could see clear to the opposite corner now.

No danger, no danger, please, no more danger . . .

Something moved in the corner where Katherine's cubicle had been. But—Jordan squinted—the cubicle was gone now.

Katherine came stepping out of the shadows.

"Did I miss anything?" she asked.

TWENTY

Jordan cracked up.

"Did you miss anything?" he repeated. "Are you kidding? Jonah and me, we're lucky to be alive! We just survived bears and battlefields and guns and bows and arrows and fire and—"

Katherine looked toward Jonah with an expression that seemed to ask, *Has Jordan completely lost his mind?*

Jordan realized his laughter sounded a little maniacal.

"It's true!" he said. "It was all real! It—"

"—was definitely not real," Jonah finished for him.

Now Jordan and Katherine both squinted at Jonah. Jonah leaned gingerly against the desk behind him.

"I think Second just sent us through either the training program or the final test—or something like that—for people trying out to be kidnappers like Gary and

Hodge, working for Interchronological Rescue," Jonah said. "I think that's what the plastic-card Elucidator is for, testing like that. It was like some virtual-reality thing, giving us different scenarios and different time-travel problems."

"No—I *felt* that bear's breath on my face! I felt his slobber! That wasn't just some *training* exercise," Jordan protested. "You know, with virtual-reality stuff—you can always tell it's not real!"

"A *bear*?" Katherine repeated. "And fire? And a battle-field . . ."

She looked questioningly at Jonah.

"Oh, yeah, and it was like we were in Albert Einstein's living room, talking to him too," Jordan remembered. "Like we were supposed to be scared of *him*. And on a plane with Charles Lindbergh . . ."

Katherine raised an eyebrow.

"So it was stuff Jonah and I already lived through, rescuing our friends," Katherine said. She seemed to turn a little pale. "Please tell me you didn't have to kill a bear with a tiny knife again."

"No, Jordan asked the Elucidator for a gun, and that gave me the idea to ask for something that would work even better," Jonah said.

Jordan could have been annoyed that Jonah thought

his ideas were so much better than Jordan's. But his mind was still stuck on Katherine's words.

"You . . . you rescued other people in the midst of fires and bear attacks and battles and all that other stuff?" Jordan asked. "You didn't just . . . barely manage to keep yourself alive?"

Jonah and Katherine exchanged a look.

"Yeah," Katherine said softly. "We did."

Jordan waited for her to start gloating. The Katherine he'd known his whole life would normally have added something like, *See, Jordan, that's why I'm so much better than you, so superior. You go through all those dangers, and you just barely come out of it alive. Jonah and me, we were like superheroes doing all that. We saved ourselves and lots of other people too.*

Somehow having her not gloat actually made him wonder, *Are she and Jonah truly better than me? Going through the fire, the battle, the bear attack, and everything else, pretty much all I could think about was how I could keep from dying.*

"How many people?" Jordan asked. "How many of your friends did you rescue?"

"Katherine saved Chip and Alex in the fourteen hundreds," Jonah said.

"Jonah saved Andrea, Brendan, and Antonio in the sixteen hundreds," Katherine said. "And, oh yeah, he also saved JB and Dalton and Andrea's grandfather and an entire Native American village."

Jonah winced, like this brought back bad memories.

"But Katherine, you're the one who went back to save the Romanovs and Leonid. And Chip, *again*," Jonah said.

Was that why that Chip guy seemed so thrilled to see Katherine? Jordan wondered. *Because she keeps saving his life?*

Katherine gave a rueful frown.

"Actually, if you count all the stuff that happened with the plane, Jonah deserves every bit of the credit," she said. "Just about everyone I saved would have died anyway if it hadn't been for Jonah. Because he saved all the other thirty-five kids from his plane. And me. And you, Jordan. He saved you."

Was that true?

"Second said Gary and Hodge saved my life by kidnapping me," Jordan said.

"That was just the first time your life was in danger," Katherine said. "Jonah saved you the second time."

"Jordan wouldn't necessarily have died that time," Jonah protested. "He just . . . probably would have been adopted by somebody else."

"And see, that would have been a fate *worse* than death," Katherine teased. "Jordan, it would have killed you not to have me for a sister!"

Jordan wanted to zap her with a witty comeback that made it clear his life would have been better without her.

But he'd just lost her and regained her. He'd had that moment with the line of flames between them when he'd felt certain he'd never see her again.

"Right," he mumbled. And the way he said it, it really could have been taken two different ways: sarcastically— or as if he really couldn't imagine his life without her.

Jordan didn't want to watch Katherine's face to see how she interpreted his comment. He turned to Jonah.

"So was *everything* we went through something that already happened to you before?" Jordan asked.

Jonah nodded.

"So why train or test you for something you've already lived through?" Jordan asked.

"I'm not sure," Jonah said slowly. "Either Second's trying to catch you up with Katherine and me, or . . . or it's based on my fears. Maybe the training program read my mind and gave me the scenarios I would be most afraid of."

"You're still afraid of stuff you already survived?" Jordan asked. "Why? You survived! It's over!"

"Nothing's over," Jonah muttered.

Jordan held back a shiver. After what they'd been through—all three of them—he didn't want the others seeing that two words uttered in a spooky voice could frighten him.

"You're talking about Second, aren't you?" Katherine

asked. She turned to Jordan to explain. "Second got everything he wanted from us the last time we had to deal with him, back in the sixteen hundreds. He outsmarted us, every time."

"We've got to outsmart him this time," Jonah murmured. He gritted his teeth. "We have to."

He looked around the room that only moments before had seemed like a medieval castle, a battlefield, an icy sea, and Albert Einstein's living room. Jordan followed the other boy's gaze. The room just looked like an empty, quiet lab once again. It didn't even seem so wildly futuristic anymore—Jordan was starting to get used to the suspended images that seemed to glow from TV screens that weren't even there. But Jonah was pivoting his head frantically, as if he saw potential danger at every turn.

"I know what we have to do next," he said.

Before Jordan and Katherine could respond, Jonah took off running. In three strides he was beside the door.

And then he yanked open the door and ran out into the hall.

TWENTY-ONE

"Are you nuts?" Katherine cried, scrambling after Jonah.

"You yelled at me when I did that, and now you're . . ." Jordan realized no one was listening. "Wait for me!"

He ran after Jonah and Katherine. Both of them were halfway down the hall before Jordan caught up.

"At least give us some warning before you make sudden moves like that," Jordan panted.

Jonah glanced quickly toward Jordan, then snapped his head back toward the front. Jordan realized the other boy was studying everything around them.

"I can't warn you, because that warns Second, too," Jonah said. "He spent his whole life making predictions about what people would do—so we have to be unpredictable."

"This is unpredictable all right," Katherine muttered. "Are you *trying* to get caught?"

"It wouldn't be the worst thing in the world," Jonah said calmly.

They reached an intersection with another hallway, and Jonah plowed right on through as if it didn't matter if anyone saw them.

"You're nuts," Katherine said, running a little to catch up. "Could we at least tiptoe? And whisper?"

"We have to show confidence," Jonah said. "Fake it, anyway. That's the only way this is going to work."

"*What* is going to work?" Katherine wailed.

Jordan felt a rush of air behind him. He turned around, and saw nothing out of the ordinary. But something made him reach his hand out.

His fingers hit a solid wall, even though his eyes told him he was waving his hand through empty air.

"Oh, no," he moaned. "Not again. Katherine, Jonah, look. Er—feel this, I mean."

But when he turned back toward the other two, he saw that they seemed to have encountered an invisible wall ahead of them as well. Jonah bounced back from what looked like empty air; then he and Katherine put their hands out flat in the space right ahead of them.

Either both of them were very talented mimes, or Jordan, Katherine, and Jonah were all trapped inside the same kind of sometimes-invisible walls that had held

Jordan prisoner back in the interrogation cubicle.

Jordan stretched his hand toward Katherine, and was relieved when he brushed the tip of her ponytail. At least each of them wasn't trapped in an individual cubicle again.

"Intruders have been isolated," a robotic-sounding voice intoned above them. "Intruders, do not try to escape. It is impossible. Our security forces will be by to collect you within the next twenty-four hours."

A sudden wind that felt as strong as a tornado seemed to hit Jordan out of nowhere, tugging his clothes upward and making his hair stand on end. He had to grab the bottom of his shirt to keep it from flying up against his face. So he almost missed seeing the plastic card and fake cell phone zip past his head.

"The Elucidators!" he screamed.

He swiped his hands uselessly through the air, trying to catch the two Elucidators that had flown out of his pocket. He missed. He bent his knees and jumped and tried again, but it was too late. The Elucidators slammed against the ceiling. No—they were being sucked up through the ceiling, along with the ponytail rubber band that had been holding back Katherine's hair.

All three items vanished completely. The wind stopped.

"We have retrieved all items that might provide you any assistance during the next twenty-four hours." The robotic voice spoke again. "They will not be returned to you. Ever."

Geez, what could we have figured out to do with that rubber band? Jordan wondered. *And how could those three things, which are solid, pass completely through a solid ceiling?*

"You just made us lose the Elucidators!" Jordan accused Jonah.

"They didn't work right, anyway," Jonah said defensively. "And . . . I bet Second could track everything we did with them. So it doesn't matter."

But his voice trembled, making him sound like he wasn't sure.

Katherine smoothed down her freed, tangled hair, and hit the palm of her hand against one of the invisible walls.

"Didn't you think about something like this happening?" she demanded, glaring at Jonah. "Is this what you *wanted?*"

Jonah rolled his bottom lip up over his top lip, a motion that Jordan recognized.

Isn't that what I do when I want people to think I know what I'm doing but I really don't? Jordan thought.

But Jonah cocked his head and started talking back to the ceiling. "We are in possession of information that could be crucial to the future well-being of Interchronological Rescue," he said, and he had control of his voice again.

Anyone who didn't know him would probably think he was completely at ease. "We were on our way to see Curtis Rathbone, your CEO. It would be in your company's best interest to take us there immediately."

Jonah's supposedly thirteen, just like me, Jordan thought. *How can he talk like that?*

It was almost as strange and impressive as when he'd talked in a medieval way with the virtual-reality monks.

Then Jonah's words sank in, and Jordan realized what Jonah was asking.

Was Katherine right? Jordan wondered. *Has Jonah totally lost it?*

Katherine still looked like she thought Jonah was nuts. Her eyes were practically popping out of her head.

"You *want* them to take us to Curtis Rathbone?" she asked incredulously. "What exactly are you planning to tell him? Which piece of information do you think—"

"Shh," Jonah said. "I'm sure they can hear everything we say. Don't give anything away yet."

Katherine shot Jonah the same kind of look she usually gave Jordan, the mix of *You're an idiot* and *I can't believe I'm stuck with a brother like you* and *It's a good thing you're adopted because I really would not want to share any of the same genes as you.* Except maybe there was a little bit more to this look; maybe she was also thinking, *I really hope you know what you're doing,* and *Even if you're a total fool, I've got your back.*

Was it possible those extra messages had always been in the looks Katherine shot Jordan, too, and Jordan just hadn't noticed?

"Your appeal has been duly noted, and it has been decided that you will be allowed to proceed," the voice from the ceiling intoned, just as robotically as before.

Arrows lit up on the floor, evidently pointing toward Curtis Rathbone's office.

Jordan waited until Jonah and Katherine took their first steps forward, through the space where the invisible wall had been moments before. He didn't know about the other two, but he had had enough of bouncing off walls he couldn't see.

"Do you think Interchronological Rescue only has, like, nine or ten actual human beings working here, and everything else is automated?" Katherine muttered, glancing around.

Jordan guessed that she was as creeped out as he was that invisible walls could evidently just materialize out of thin air, anywhere and anytime. So could tornado-strength winds that could suck solid objects through the solid ceiling.

"I think they want us feeling primitive and ignorant," Jonah muttered back. "We can still outsmart them. We know stuff they don't know."

I don't, Jordan wanted to say. But Deep Voice, Tattoo Face, and Doreen had acted like Curtis Rathbone didn't know Gary and Hodge were missing. Maybe the CEO also didn't know about Second or Jordan's parents or Charles Lindbergh or the different dimensions or . . .

What good does knowing about all that stuff do when I don't understand any of it? Jordan wondered.

"Come on, Jordan," Katherine said, turning back to face him for a moment.

Jordan realized he'd let the other two get way ahead of him. It was amazing how good he felt that Katherine had noticed and didn't want to leave him behind.

He scrambled to catch up.

"What—" he began.

This time both Katherine and Jonah turned to him with fingers over their lips and hissed, "Shh!"

The three of them continued on in silence, following lit-up red arrows that vanished the instant the kids passed by.

What if it's all just a trap? Jonah wondered. *What if it's another elaborate virtual-reality setup by Second?*

Why would anybody bother to lead them into a trap when they'd already been imprisoned and released twice?

Maybe that's not the best thing to think about, since it doesn't do any good anyway, Jordan thought.

To distract himself, he tried to study the hallways they passed through. They had to be full of all sorts of sensors and speakers and robotic capabilities. But the hallways didn't *look* that odd. Jordan had seen the office buildings where his parents worked; these hallways were just as nondescript, with taupe flooring and beige walls.

So maybe we're not that crazy far into the future, Jordan thought. *Maybe it's not much past the twenty-first century.*

Or maybe these hallways were so advanced he didn't even know what he was seeing.

Then he started noticing the artwork on the walls. First there'd be a photograph that looked like it came straight from some history book: a child crying in the ruins of a bombed-out city, parents clutching bundled-up babies and running from scenes labeled THE GREAT FIRE OF LONDON, 1666 or INDIAN OCEAN TSUNAMI, 2004, or simply HIROSHIMA, 1945. Then, right after the historical artwork, there'd be a photo of some happy kid grinning ear to ear in the midst of playing what must be futuristic versions of soccer or Monopoly or video games.

Oh, Jordan realized. *It's always the same kid in each pair of pictures. First in miserable history, then in the happy future. Before and after.*

"Are there pictures like these somewhere of you and me?" Jordan asked Jonah.

Jonah squinted like he hadn't been paying attention, and Jordan pointed at the nearest set of pictures: a toddler crying in what seemed to be a deserted Asian palace, then the same child joyously hugging a man with the same kind of beaded hair as Deep Voice.

Jonah snorted.

"Interchronological Rescue wouldn't hold up either you or me as a success story," he said bitterly.

"This is all just . . . propaganda," Katherine muttered, sweeping her arms toward the artwork. "Like we studied in language arts. They're trying to make people think that Interchronological Rescue is like a charity or something, when really they're kidnappers and baby sellers and . . ."

"Katherine, they can hear you, remember?" Jordan interrupted.

"I don't care," Katherine said. "I'm not going to lie about this. Gary and Hodge wanted to steal Jonah away from our family, and they sent Charles Lindbergh to steal me away, and . . . the whole company needs to know we won't let anything like that happen ever again!"

Jordan expected Jonah to shush Katherine once again, but Jonah didn't seem to be listening. He'd stopped in front of a huge wooden door framed by actual pillars.

Okay, that is kind of different from Mom's and Dad's offices, Jordan thought.

But then, neither of his parents was a CEO.

It took Jordan a moment to realize that the entire floor was lit up with arrows now—all pointing toward the elaborate door.

"Katherine," Jonah said, under his breath. "I know it's hard for you to be quiet, but could you let me do the talking in there?"

Katherine fixed him with a steady gaze.

"Do you have a really good plan?" she asked. "Have you thought it through?"

"I think so," Jonah said. "It's the best I could come up with."

"Okay, then," Katherine agreed.

Jordan gaped. Was this the real Katherine standing in front of him? He'd never once seen his sister agree to let someone else do all the talking.

Then Katherine slugged Jordan in the arm, which made her seem more normal.

"Don't you ruin things either," she hissed.

"But, I—" Jordan began.

Jonah was already reaching for the doorknob, and Jordan shut up.

As soon as Jonah's finger's brushed the huge brass knob, the door completely vanished. It didn't creak open, it didn't slide to the side—it just disappeared.

"I could live in this time period a million years and I would never get used to that," Jordan muttered.

"Shh," Katherine whispered.

Jonah was already stepping across the threshold. He seemed to be very deliberately easing his feet forward on the lustrous carpet, almost as if he expected a trapdoor to open beneath him.

Jordan had to resist the urge to huddle close to Katherine. Or to cower down behind Jonah and hope nobody saw him.

A man was waiting for them behind a desk that seemed as enormous as a yacht. The man—Curtis Rathbone?—was wearing an ivory robe rather than a business suit, but Jordan thought it was probably a really, really expensive ivory robe, intended to let everyone around him know, *I'm powerful. Don't mess with me.* Probably the president of the United States had one just like it—if there was still a president of the United States.

Mr. Rathbone raised one eyebrow, as if to say, *Don't waste my time. I know who you are. Get to the point.*

Jonah stopped so abruptly that Jordan and Katherine almost ran into him.

Is Jonah secretly carrying some weapon I don't know about? Jordan wondered. *Something the wind didn't pull away? Is he going to threaten this guy? Does he think he has time to do anything before invisible walls fall around us and trap us once more?*

Jonah cleared his throat.

"Your employees are afraid to tell you that your top performers, Gary and Hodge, have vanished," Jonah said. His voice trembled only a little. "But I know where they are. I'll make you a deal. You give us a working Elucidator, and we'll help you out. We'll rescue Gary and Hodge."

TWENTY-TWO

Jonah's switching sides? Jordan thought. He was so stunned his brain could barely keep up. *Jonah hates Gary and Hodge, but now he wants to rescue them? He wants to work for their company and fight the time agency?*

It took him a ridiculous amount of time to figure out, *Oh. No. Jonah's lying. He's just trying to trick this guy into giving us a good Elucidator. One that has no connection to Second.*

Would it work?

Jordan glanced back at Mr. Rathbone. The man's expression hadn't changed. Did *he* know Jonah was lying?

"Jonah Skidmore," Mr. Rathbone said in a booming voice. "I finally get to meet the famous Jonah Skidmore. And this is your sister, Katherine?"

So he's just going to ignore Jonah's offer? Jordan wondered.

Jordan was really bad at figuring out people's motives

when they didn't just come out and say what they wanted, or what they planned to do. That was probably part of the reason he never had any hope of being one of the cool kids at school, but would be doing well to just stay a not-so-cool kid, not a total loser. But he could tell that Mr. Rathbone was one of those people that Jordan's dad always called "a real operator."

He's playing some kind of game, Jordan thought. *We're going to have to be really careful, or he'll outsmart us.*

But Jordan's next thought was, *Hey, why does he recognize Jonah and Katherine, but he's acting like I don't even exist?*

Jordan forgot that he'd been trying to hide behind Jonah. He inched to the right a little, so Mr. Rathbone had to see him.

Mr. Rathbone tilted his head slightly and squinted at Jordan curiously. But Jordan couldn't tell if he was actually surprised, or if he was just pretending.

"Why, Jonah," Mr. Rathbone said, peering back at Jonah. "I see that you went back to the nineteen thirties and rescued your doomed twin. Should I applaud your humanitarian instincts, so similar to the ones that inspired me to found Interchronological Rescue? Or should I remind you that the time agency thoroughly discourages such blatant meddling, unless it can be absolutely proved that the removal of the child will have no effect on time?

Did *you* do all the necessary impact studies? Did *you* fill out all the necessary paperwork, and file it the necessary six months in advance of any rescue trip, so the agency had ample time to review all the plans and mount any possible objections? Did you—"

"The time agency knows about Jordan," Jonah interrupted.

It was on the tip of Jordan's tongue to say, *No, wait. I thought Gary and Hodge were the ones who rescued me from the 1930s. Jonah was just the one who took me to my parents in that whole mix-up with the different dimensions. Doesn't Mr. Rathbone know about Gary and Hodge rescuing me? Or is he just trying to psych me out, like Deep Voice did?*

"Jonah didn't do anything wrong," Jordan began. "He—"

Before he could say anything else, Katherine dug her elbow into Jordan's side, and Jordan remembered that he and Katherine were supposed to let Jonah do all the talking.

This wasn't the right place for Jordan to ask all his questions about the different dimensions.

Mr. Rathbone tilted his head a bit more.

He saw Katherine trying to shut me up, Jordan realized. *Oh, no—what if he decides to interrogate all three of us in separate cubicles?*

Jordan resisted the urge to inch back to the left, to hide behind Jonah again.

But Mr. Rathbone didn't even seem to be looking at them now. His eyes were focused on what seemed to be empty air right above his desk, where a computer screen might sit in a twenty-first-century office.

Could he have a computer screen that he can see from that side, but we can't see at all? Jordan wondered. He thought he'd seen something like that in a science-fiction movie. It seemed possible.

"Interesting," Mr. Rathbone murmured. "Fascinating . . ."

He's trying to get us to ask, "What's interesting? What's fascinating?" Jordan thought. *Isn't he?*

Jordan sneaked a glance at Katherine. She had her lips pressed firmly together. If Katherine could stay silent, so could Jordan.

After a moment Mr. Rathbone looked back at the three kids.

"I'll confess, the nineteen thirties exhaust even my capacity for compassion," he said. "So much human misery compressed into one short decade. Worldwide economic collapse, the Japanese invasion of China, the rise of the Nazis in Germany, the Spanish Civil War, the Italian invasion of Ethiopia, the start of world war . . . and, oh, lest we forget, that poor little Lindbergh baby . . ."

"I know I was never the Lindbergh baby," Jonah said in a tight voice. "I know Gary and Hodge were planning to use me as a fake."

Mr. Rathbone lifted an eyebrow again.

"I never endorsed such a deception," he said. He pushed back from his desk. "In truth, Gary and Hodge exhaust me as well. They exhaust my patience, and there is always the danger that their . . . tactics . . . could exhaust the goodwill the public has toward Interchronological Rescue. The time agency has become pricklier than ever—perhaps it would be best for Interchronological Rescue if Gary and Hodge were never found. We could arrange such a lovely ceremony honoring their memories. Now, that would be *good* PR. We could invite all the children who are here only because of Gary and Hodge's skill at time extraction. . . . Happy children always stifle any possible criticisms. . . . It's so petty to ask nitpicky questions in the face of a smiling toddler. . . ."

Jordan turned to stare at Jonah. If Mr. Rathbone didn't even want Gary and Hodge back, then Jonah's plan had completely bombed. Jonah, Katherine, and Jordan had given themselves up to an enemy—and they weren't going to get anything in exchange.

Jonah's face might as well have turned to stone.

"But we—we—" Jordan began, because didn't

somebody have to come up with a backup plan? He didn't know what it should be, but wasn't there something they could still offer?

Katherine slapped her hand over Jordan's mouth so fast he didn't even see her move.

"Shut. Up," she hissed through gritted teeth.

Mr. Rathbone started laughing.

"Ah, I can see who *didn't* want another brother," he said. "Don't worry, Katherine. I'm sure he'll grow on you. Or perhaps he'll just grow up eventually, and you can be done with him. Though of course Interchronological Rescue doesn't ever mention that ultimate way out of having inconvenient children in any of our advertising. . . ."

"Katherine has always had me as her brother!" Jordan tried to say, just to show this horrible man that he didn't know everything. But Katherine's hand was pressed so tightly against Jordan's mouth that it just sounded like he was grunting.

"Aren't you worried that Gary and Hodge could make more trouble for Interchronological Rescue?" Jonah asked. "Wouldn't you want them brought back to you, just so you know where they are and what they're doing?"

Mr. Rathbone kept his poker-face calm expression.

"Oh, I've always got deniability," he said. "There are resignation letters I could always release to the public—or perhaps I'd want to reveal that they'd been secretly fired years ago? I'd have to decide based on the situation. . . ."

Was Mr. Rathbone talking about going back in time and forcing Gary and Hodge to sign those resignation letters? Or did he already have them on file, just in case? Or was he talking about faking them?

Jordan wished he knew more about business, as well as time travel.

Katherine had let her hand slip from Jordan's face just enough that Jordan saw his opening.

"I bet . . . I bet there's *something* we could do for you," he offered. Because otherwise, weren't they only a second or two away from more of those invisible walls slamming down around them?

Mr. Rathbone smiled in a way that made Jordan dislike him even more.

"As a matter of fact, there is," he said. "It's something the three of you would be uniquely qualified to do."

"There is?" Katherine repeated, sounding numb. "We are?"

Mr. Rathbone nodded, his eyes glinting.

"Absolutely," he said. "I want you to go back and finish the job that Gary and Hodge botched the worst. The one that sent them down the path to total failure and oblivion."

TWENTY-THREE

For a moment it felt like all three of the kids had been struck dumb. Then Jonah mumbled, "You really know how to sell a job."

"Just letting you know what you're getting into," Mr. Rathbone said, his voice steady, almost light.

"Can you tell us what the job is?" Katherine asked in a small voice. When even cheerleader-boisterous Katherine was cowed, Jordan knew things were bad.

Mr. Rathbone was back to looking at the empty air above his desk.

"Let's just say that the time agency was always wrong about the reason Gary and Hodge's plane time-crashed where and when it did," he said, his eyes focused away from any of the kids.

"You mean the plane I was on?" Jonah asked. "The time

agency never thought there was a reason for when and where it landed. They always said it was random."

Mr. Rathbone snorted. "You'd think, as much tax money as they eat up, the agency would hire a better class of investigators," he said, shaking his head.

"So . . . the crash wasn't random?" Katherine asked.

Mr. Rathbone palmed something in midair. Jordan had the feeling he'd just seen the futuristic version of a flash drive being ejected from a computer. Or maybe a new object being pulled out of a 3-D printer.

"All the details are contained in this Elucidator," he said, holding out his hand. "But I can tell you—Gary and Hodge were *supposed* to rescue an important child that day. One who, alas, will stay endangered. Unless you help."

Jonah took the Elucidator from Mr. Rathbone. It looked like nothing more than a watch battery.

"It's so small," Katherine objected. "What if we lose it?"

"It will adhere to Jonah's skin during your trip," Mr. Rathbone said. "And remember, it will look like some common item from the past when you get where you're going. You'll be fine."

There was something suspicious about his smile, and Jordan shifted uncomfortably from one foot to another. He wanted to whisper to Katherine, *What if we're making a huge mistake?* But of course he couldn't do anything like that without Mr. Rathbone noticing.

"Who is this child?" Jonah asked, focusing on a detail that Jordan had already forgotten. "Why's he so important? Why's he in danger? What—"

Mr. Rathbone held up his hand.

"Now, now," he said. "Can't you see I'm a busy man? Get your explanations from the Elucidator. Bon voyage!"

He pressed something on his desk—maybe the invisible futuristic version of a computer mouse. And then Mr. Rathbone and his office disappeared.

"But—wait!" Katherine cried. "We—"

"Too late," Jonah and Jordan said, practically speaking together.

They were already floating through time again, zipping off toward some unknown child in some unknown danger.

Even in the near darkness, Jordan saw Jonah clench his fingers against the palm of his hand, clutching the Elucidator as tightly as he could. Jordan didn't even want to think about the danger Mr. Rathbone was sending them into, or the kid they were supposed to rescue.

Maybe he didn't have to.

"We have an Elucidator that works now!" Jordan crowed. "We can go anywhere we want! We can rescue Mom and Dad from Second! We can make them the right age! We can go home!"

Jonah and Katherine just looked at Jordan. What was wrong with them, that they weren't excited too?

"No way he would have given us anything but a parental-controls Elucidator, right?" Katherine muttered to Jonah.

"Huh?" Jordan said. "What do you mean, 'parental-controls Elucidator'?"

As they flipped and floated through time, Jonah began cautiously poking at the object in his hand.

"It says 'destination locked,'" Jonah said. "So, yeah, I'd say this is like 1918 all over again."

"What? We're going to 1918?" Jordan asked. His voice squeaked. He had some vague sense that there might have been a war going on then. Not the Civil War—wasn't that in the eighteen hundreds? But maybe World War I. Or something like that.

"No, we're not going to 1918," Katherine said. "I don't think. It's just, the Elucidator Mr. Rathbone gave us is probably the same kind we had back then. It was like one of those cell phones people buy for little kids, where they can't call anyone but their parents."

"We can call Mom and Dad?" Jordan asked.

He was already starting to lean toward Jonah's hand when Katherine gave him a shove.

"I didn't say it *was* one of those parental-control cell phones," she said. "I just said it was like that. It'll probably only do a couple things—things Mr. Rathbone wants."

"Oh," Jordan said.

So the Elucidator in Jonah's hand wasn't that much different from the two broken or fake ones Jordan had lost moments earlier.

Jonah hates Second that much, that he thinks this is a better arrangement? Jordan wondered.

"But we'll hide somewhere when we land," Jonah said. "We'll figure out where we are and what's going on, and, I don't know, maybe we can alert the time agency somehow. Maybe we can—"

He broke off then, because they hit the part of the trip where everything intensified and Jordan felt like his body was being ripped apart.

When that ended, and Jordan began struggling back to awareness, he found himself lying flat on his back on what seemed to be frozen ground. Tufts of grass tickled the back of his neck, but they seemed brittle with cold.

"Wish . . . someone had told me . . . to wear a sweatshirt this morning," Jordan said, rubbing his arms where his T-shirt sleeves ended.

Katherine had on a pink-and-purple-striped sweater, and Jonah at least had a long-sleeved shirt under his old-fashioned sweater vest. But they were shivering too.

"Jonah, we are not going to able to sit out here thinking and thinking and thinking and figuring out how to outsmart the Elucidator," Katherine said, sitting up. "We're going to have to find somewhere indoors to—ah!"

Something loomed just above her head. Reflexively, Jordan reached out to grab her arm and pull her down again—to safety. But Katherine was a step ahead of him; she had already thrown herself flat against the ground. A deafening sound roared overhead, so bone-jarringly close that Jordan squeezed his eyes shut in fear.

"What . . . was . . . that?" Katherine screamed as soon as the roar diminished ever so slightly.

Jordan could barely get his eyes to focus. But he could see that Jonah had rolled over onto his stomach and was staring off after the source of the noise.

"Airplane," Jonah moaned. "Oh, no, not again. Do *all* Elucidators hate me? At least we're not right on the runway this time."

"We're at an airport?" Katherine asked, daring to lift her head again. "Oh, no. What year is it? What day? If today's the day, how much time do we have left?"

"What are you talking about?" Jordan demanded.

"If Mr. Rathbone sent us back to the day Gary and Hodge crash-landed the plane, we can't be here when the plane arrives," Katherine said. "Having Jonah duplicated in time—or, I guess, you either, Jordan—that would ruin everything." She reached toward Jonah's hand, as if she planned to grab the round, silvery Elucidator. More of it showed now—maybe it had grown, to look like a battery from an older watch. "Just to be safe, you two should go somewhere else. But I could stay."

"No, Katherine, because after the babies come off that plane, no time traveler can get in or out for thirteen years, remember?" Jonah said, pulling his hand and the Elucidator to the side. "And you're going to be born next December, so *you* would be duplicated in time then too. . . . And, oh yeah, you were here with me anyway, in one of the dimensions, as a baby. . . ."

Jordan let their words flow over him. He didn't really understand the worries about people being duplicated in time or anything about Gary and Hodge's airplane—was it supposed to be the one he arrived on, or the one Jonah arrived on? How weird would that be, to see himself or Jonah as a baby? But he could tell that Jonah and Katherine were really, really freaked out.

Both of them were staring down at the Elucidator now.

"This *is* the day the plane crash-landed," Jonah moaned. "But I can't get the Elucidator to tell us how much time we have left. . . ."

"What if Mr. Rathbone was *trying* to get time to split again?" Katherine asked. "What if he's just tricking us?"

Jordan had had enough of their agonizing.

"How about we just grab whatever kid we're supposed to grab and get out of here?" he asked.

"Do you *see* any kid anywhere around here?" Jonah demanded. "Any kid who looks endangered and in need of saving?"

Jordan started to say no. His eyes still weren't working great. It was like coming out of the eye doctor's after his pupils had been dilated. Even the weak wintry sunshine that seemed to be coming from far, far overhead—and perhaps through several clouds—felt too bright to him. But then he saw a hint of movement off to the right.

"Is *that* a kid?" he asked, pointing. "Or maybe a group of kids?"

A dark shape was moving off in the distance, in a sort of gully or ditch or ravine—an area where the ground sloped downward, anyway. Jordan squinted and managed to make out a fence and a forbidding-looking sign. It was too far away to read, but Jordan had the feeling it said something like KEEP OUT or DANGER! DO NOT PASS!

A dark figure broke off from the other shadowy shapes and began scaling the fence.

"That looks dangerous," Katherine murmured. She was staring off in the same direction as Jordan, and squinting every bit as hard.

Jonah pressed his fists against his face.

"I thought we'd bought ourselves some time," he said. "I thought we'd have time to figure things out. . . ."

"Elucidator, can you take us to a time hollow nearby?" Katherine asked.

A glowing red NO appeared by Jonah's hand. This Elucidator really was as frustrating as the other two.

"We have to do something," Jordan moaned, his voice squeaking with panic. "What if that kid dies right in front of us?"

The dark figure was at the top of the fence now, high above the ground. He—or possibly she—was at a point where the chain-link and metal bars were replaced by rows of barbed wire jutting out at an angle. The climber slowed down and reached carefully, clearly trying to avoid the barbs. Jordan found himself holding his breath as the dark figure flipped one leg over the top line of barbed wire. The climber held on with just one hand. The flimsy wire whipped back and forth, tugged downward by the weight of the climber.

And then the wire snapped, and the climber plummeted out of sight.

TWENTY-FOUR

A chorus of voices rose from the dark figures near the fence. Jordan was too shocked and too far away to tell if the name they were screaming was "Kevin!" or "Kyle!" or "Keith!" It was something that started with a *K* sound. But what happened next was that the figures started screaming, "We've got to get out of here!" And "What if they find out we were with him?"

The figures scattered.

"They're just running away?" Katherine asked, sounding as stunned as Jordan felt. "They're not going to try to help him?"

"We should go get help at the airport," Jordan said, trying to pull himself up into a standing position. He wanted to run for the airport—that would be the right thing to do. But he wasn't sure his legs worked yet.

Jonah glanced up at the sky as if trying to gauge how much time they had left.

"Let's go see if he's still alive," Jonah said grimly. "He may not be able to wait for help from the airport."

Jonah started running toward the fence. He sounded so sure of himself that Jordan found himself stumbling after him. Even Katherine ran along.

They reached the fence, and Jordan saw that the gully on the other side was so deep and filled with trees that he couldn't see to the bottom of it. He saw no sign of a body down below. But now he thought of the climber as a body, not a person. Nobody could survive a fall like that.

Katherine reached up and put her hands on the chain-link fence, as if she were about to climb.

"Katherine, that's not safe!" Jordan cried. "You can't do anything to help! It's too late!"

"I don't have a problem with heights like you and Jonah do," Katherine said.

Jordan glanced at the other boy. Could he possibly hate heights as much as Jordan did?

"Elucidator, can you just carry us down the hill to stand beside the kid who fell?" Jonah asked.

YES glowed above Jonah's hand. I WILL.

In the next instant, the three of them were standing on a flat rock outcropping above what seemed to be a raging river far below. A boy in ragged jeans and a dark sweatshirt lay on the rock beside them, his face hidden in dead leaves.

Jonah bent down beside the boy and gently touched his shoulder.

"Hello?" Jonah said. "Are you awake? Does anything hurt?"

Jordan guessed that Jonah had gone through first-aid training in Boy Scouts too.

"He's bleeding," Katherine said, pointing.

Now Jordan saw that the boy's right leg was twisted, and the jeans below his right knee were dark.

"Does he need a tourniquet?" Jordan asked, crouching down beside Jonah. "A splint?"

Most of what Jordan had learned in first aid seemed to be spinning uselessly in his brain. How were they supposed to know if the bleeding required a tourniquet, or if just applying pressure to the wound would do the trick? Why hadn't his brain held on to such details?

The boy moaned and turned his head, his messy blond hair flopping against the dead leaves.

Katherine gasped. "Is that . . . Doesn't he look like someone?" she asked. "Like . . . maybe the kid version of Second?"

In the next instant the boy reached up, snatched the Elucidator from Jonah's hands—and vanished.

TWENTY-FIVE

For a moment Jordan, Katherine, and Jonah could do nothing but gape at the empty space where the boy had been. The rock was still stained with his blood.

"That—that *was* Second, wasn't it?" Katherine said, sinking down alongside Jordan and Jonah.

"*He* was the kid Gary and Hodge were coming to kidnap?" Jonah asked numbly. "Did Second set this whole thing up so we would rescue him?"

"But then how was he in the future to begin with, if nobody rescued him in original time?" Katherine asked. "And Curtis Rathbone sent us here, not Second—or did Second somehow know that all of this would happen?"

"Could *Second* have an identical twin?" Jonah asked.

All the time-travel questions and speculation made Jordan's head ache. And he didn't like the way Jonah looked accusingly at Jordan when he said the words "identical twin." Jordan's mind jumped ahead to a different question.

"How are we going to get off this rock without killing ourselves?" he asked.

Jonah winced. "And how are we going to get out of this time period without an Elucidator?" he asked. He glanced up at the sky. "I don't know what time it is now, but we have to get out before the plane arrives. No—we have to get out before *I* arrived with you as a baby, Katherine. We got here thirty minutes before the plane. It was already kind of dark then, but . . ."

Jordan craned his neck to peer up toward the sky, too. It seemed much more shadowed and dusky than it had when they were standing up by the fence. He hoped that was mostly because of all the trees now towering above them.

"We should be able to climb down from here," Katherine said. She leaned out and peeked over the side of the rock and seemed to change her mind. "Or up. Remember, distances are kind of messed up when you're suffering from timesickness. Probably this ravine isn't deep at all, if falling into it didn't kill that kid. Didn't kill Second, I mean."

Jordan really didn't want to think about falling right now. Or Second.

Does he even care that we're stuck here now? Jordan

wondered. He didn't understand all the ins and outs of time travel, but he could tell that Jonah and Katherine thought it would be disastrous if any of them were duplicated in time. Did Second want that to happen? Was he trying to ruin everything? How did the kid version of Second (or his twin) know to grab the Elucidator anyway?

"This tree looks pretty sturdy," Katherine said, tugging on a tree that stood beside the rock. She squinted upward. "If we climb to the top, we can probably grab the bottom section of that fence, and then . . ."

Then fall just like that kid did, Jordan thought.

"You don't have to use any tricks like you did to get me to climb the mast of Henry Hudson's ship or that tree when we were hiding from the Serbians," Jonah told Katherine. "I'll climb it on my own . . . in a minute."

Jordan didn't like hearing about adventures Jonah and Katherine had had without him. But something in Jonah's expression looked familiar.

"Hey," Jordan said. "Did *you* almost fall off the climbing wall at Boy Scout camp last year too? Because Dustin and Keenan were playing a trick with the ropes? And that made you scared of heights?"

"It was Dustin and Keenan's fault?" Jonah asked. "I thought I just slipped."

"Could it have been their fault in my dimension and not in yours?" Jordan asked.

"Guys," Katherine said. "Talk about this *while* you're climbing. We don't have much time!"

Automatically, Jordan reached for the bottom branch of the tree. It was pretty stupid to talk about being afraid of heights while climbing a tree you were afraid to climb. But he had other questions for Jonah.

"Do you think a lot of the same things happened to us in our different dimensions?" Jordan asked, pulling himself up. "Did you . . . drink a whole two-liter of Mountain Dew once at a birthday party?"

"I did!" Jonah said, starting to climb the tree himself. "Are you trying out for the seventh-grade basketball team?"

"Yeah," Jordan said. Honesty forced him to add, "But it looks like I'll be sitting on the bench a lot."

"Huh," Jonah said, in a way that made Jordan suspect that Jonah might somehow be first-string in his dimension.

"Who do you like better, the Reds or the Indians?" Jordan asked, reaching for a higher branch. "The Browns or the Bengals?"

"Reds and Bengals," Jonah answered. "Of course."

"That's because *Dad* always liked the Cincinnati teams instead of Cleveland's," Katherine said. "In both of your dimensions. Don't have some big bonding moment over something stupid like that."

Did Katherine actually think Jordan and Jonah were bonding?

Something shut down in Jonah's face, but Jordan couldn't tell if it was because they were getting higher and higher in the tree, or because hearing Dad's name reminded him they still hadn't rescued their parents. And how were they supposed to do anything now without an Elucidator?

"If all three of us make it to the top of this tree, what are we going to do then?" Jordan asked.

What if he was risking his life for nothing?

"The last time I was in this time period—I mean here, right before the plane crash—I gave Angela a note at the airport," Jonah said. "And then that led to this other time agent, Hadley Correo, getting an Elucidator to me. Maybe if we work fast, we can kind of do the same thing all over again. Maybe there's still time."

He looked up at the sky again. Jordan did the same thing. It really was starting to get dark.

Jordan reached for a higher branch.

"What if talking to Angela again messes up you getting an Elucidator at all?" Katherine asked. "What if it changes the version of time we needed before to fix everything?"

"If none of us can think of a better plan, we're going to have to take that chance," Jonah said quietly. "Maybe it can work out somehow with the three different dimensions. Because they were separate for thirteen years after the plane crash."

"Except weren't you already in all three of the dimensions, at least briefly, right after the plane crash?" Katherine asked him. "Wouldn't having you here when the plane crashes in any dimension ruin everything?"

Jonah didn't answer. Jordan's head throbbed.

I just want to make Mom and Dad the right age again, he thought. *I just want everything to go back to normal.*

"Keep climbing!" Katherine called behind him. "Hurry!"

The tree thinned at the top, and it was scary reaching for smaller and smaller branches.

What if the next one I reach for can't hold me? Jordan thought. *What if I fall and knock Jonah and Katherine to the ground too?*

He drew even with the top of the gully, where the fence was. The branch he was on started to tilt the other way. Before he could think about what he was doing, he flipped over toward the fence. Even as he dropped, he wasn't sure if he was going to land on nice, safe dirt or hard rock far below.

"Open your eyes and get out of the way!" Katherine yelled at him. "Before Jonah and I fall on you!"

Oh, Jordan realized, feeling spiky grass beneath him. *I guess I landed by the fence.*

He rolled over, and Jonah and Katherine landed right beside him.

"Glad that's over," Jonah muttered.

"Yeah, except now don't we have to climb the fence to get back to the airport?" Katherine asked, pointing up again.

Jordan's knees got shaky.

"Can't we wait a *little* before we do that?" he asked. "Or—I know—why don't we walk along the fence and find, like, the road that normal people take to get to the airport—without risking their lives?"

"I don't think there's time," Katherine said, glancing up toward the sky. Jordan realized that the sun had dropped even farther while they were down on the rock and climbing the tree. "I'm not even sure there's time to climb the fence and run across the runways and—"

"We've got to try," Jonah said grimly.

He reached for the fence first, but Jordan and Katherine were almost as fast.

As soon as Jordan touched the fence, he heard a thump behind him.

"No, no, no, no, no," a voice cried from just over Jordan's right shoulder. "Grab on to me! We've only got three minutes to get all of you out of here!"

Jordan whirled around.

A huge man stood behind them, wobbling at the edge of the gully. There was no room for him on that edge, and he looked even more enormous here than he'd looked back in the lab at Interchronological Rescue.

It was Deep Voice.

TWENTY-SIX

Jordan froze. Was he supposed to trust his own fence-climbing and running skills—or the supposed help of his enemy and interrogator? Could Deep Voice possibly be right that they had only three minutes?

Jonah and Katherine seemed equally paralyzed.

"It's true!" Deep Voice roared. And then he lunged for them, his massive arms yanking them away from the fence and into a clump.

"Take us back to headquarters!" Deep Voice screamed. "Now!"

The fence disappeared. The gully disappeared; the lights of the airport off in the distance vanished as well.

They were speeding through time once again.

"What—who—did you just rescue us?" Katherine demanded. "Did Curtis Rathbone send you? We didn't do what he wanted. We—"

"I don't care about Curtis Rathbone," Deep Voice growled. "I'm trying to save time. And my own backside. And the three of you."

"But . . . you *interrogated* us," Jordan complained. "If you were on our side all along, why didn't you say so?"

"I—" Deep Voice began. Then he grimaced and reeled his head backward. "Whoa. Is traveling through time always so awful? I'm not used to this. I'm just a . . . what would people from your time call it? A desk jockey?"

Jordan had never in his life heard the term "desk jockey."

"This is actually kind of the easy part of time travel," Katherine said apologetically. "We're just gliding now. It's fun."

Deep Voice didn't look like he thought it was fun.

"It gets worse?" he asked. It was hard to tell in the dim light, but his face was starting to look almost greenish. "I, um, I think I kind of blacked out for a while on my trip to get you. Didn't wake up until I landed. And then we only had three minutes, so I didn't have time to think. . . ."

"Why didn't you get us when we were down on the rock?" Jonah asked. "Then we wouldn't have had to risk our lives climbing that tree, and you would have had an extra twenty or thirty minutes to get us out."

Deep Voice winced. "We ran the numbers on that," he

said. "The force of me—or even Doreen—landing there would have knocked that rock down into the river below. Someone could have died."

Jordan shivered. Had the rock really been that fragile beneath them? Deep Voice was huge, of course, but Doreen wasn't. When Jordan, Jonah, Katherine, and the mystery kid had all been on the rock together, had they been close to falling into the river?

"You could have landed at the top and lowered a ladder down to us," Jonah suggested.

"Would you have trusted me?" Deep Voice asked.

No, Jordan thought.

"Or . . . you could have just had the Elucidator pull us up to the top of the gully with you," Katherine suggested. It was almost as though she and Jonah were quizzing Deep Voice to test his motives.

"I'm not used to Elucidators," Deep Voice said. "Believe me, I was doing well to get to the past at all. This was all planned on the fly. It's possible I'll be arrested when I get back. But I *had* to do this."

"Why didn't you or someone else from your company just go back and get that kid to begin with?" Jordan asked. "Why did Curtis Rathbone say Katherine and Jonah and I were . . . what did he call it?"

"Uniquely qualified," Katherine muttered.

"Because you two boys are time natives, and Katherine, your natural lifetime is very close by," Deep Voice said. "This isn't my field of specialty, but I believe that made time more . . . receptive . . . to letting the three of you in. And time was very fragile at that point. *I* couldn't have gotten in if you hadn't been there first."

"The time agency and Jonah and everybody—even you—have been telling me that I wasn't in my right time," Jordan said angrily. "They said I was born in the nineteen thirties! Are you telling me now that that was all a lie?"

He was kind of hoping Deep Voice would nod and say something like, *Yeah, about that . . . I was wrong, and so was everybody else.*

But Deep Voice shook his head no.

"You and Jonah *were* born in the nineteen thirties," he said. "And that means you could have still been alive the day of the plane crash if—"

"If we hadn't been kidnapped first," Jonah said.

"*I* was going to say 'if you'd survived childhood in a nineteen thirties orphanage,'" Deep Voice said.

"You really believe all that garbage about how Interchronological Rescue is just a charity that saves kids?" Katherine asked angrily.

Deep Voice looked off into the distance, at the lights growing closer on the horizon. Jordan could tell he was terrified of peering toward those lights—or of seeing any-thing around them as they floated through time.

But maybe right now it was even harder for Deep Voice to look directly at Jordan, Jonah, and Katherine?

"I . . . I used to believe Interchronological Rescue had a noble cause," Deep Voice said. "That was why I applied to work there. But . . . a lot of things have changed recently. I can't just sit at my desk anymore doing my job and ignor-ing everything else. I don't trust Curtis Rathbone any-more."

"But you let us go off and have him send us to the past on a dangerous mission?" Jordan asked. Maybe he'd caught some of Katherine's anger.

"I thought you were all safe in the secret cubicles!" Deep Voice protested. "We thought you were safe until we figured out what to do next!"

"Second let us out," Jonah said. "*Was* that the kid ver-sion of Second who stole our Elucidator? Or was it his identical twin or just someone who looks like him, or—"

"Second?" Deep Voice asked, his tone shooting up an octave. "You mean Second Chance is involved? The for-mer Sam Chase? And . . . you think *he* was the kid down there on that rock? You think this was all a setup? Even Rathbone was set up, even *I* was set up . . ."

He rolled his head around in a way that made Jordan

think of a giant beast—an elephant, maybe—falling down.

"Are we wrong?" Katherine challenged.

"I . . . don't . . . know . . . ," Deep Voice moaned.

If he managed to say anything after that, it got lost in the churning of time travel, as they hit the part of the trip where Jordan felt like his whole body was being torn into tiny shreds.

When Jordan felt like he could see and hear again, Deep Voice was still moaning.

"Not cut out for derring-do . . . scariest moment of my life . . . and now these kids say I was just a pawn for that twisted Sam Chase . . ."

Jordan heard a slapping sound. By squinting, he could just barely make out the sight of someone's hand hitting Deep Voice's face.

"Dude-io Markiel, get ahold of yourself," another man's voice said. It was Tattoo Face. "You rescued all three kids we sent you after. How bad could things have been?"

"You have no idea," Deep Voice moaned again.

Jordan tried to squint past Deep Voice and Tattoo Face—even though Second had told him their real names, the nicknames seemed to fit better. Jordan did remember that the woman who'd been with them was named Doreen Smith. Jordan could just barely make out a blurry shape on the other side of Markiel/Deep Voice. Maybe that was her.

And past her he could see tables, desks, and the glow of what seemed to be a computer monitor. . . .

They were back in the futuristic lab.

Jonah and Katherine were already struggling up into a seated position.

"Please," Katherine was groaning. "Please. If you want to help, find out where Second went. As a kid *and* as an adult. Find out how he's planning to mess up time now. . . ."

There was a rustle off to the right: Doreen moved toward one of the suspended glowing areas that looked like a TV or computer screen.

Deep Voice zoomed from lying on the floor to standing up and rushing to her side. It was like watching a beached whale suddenly jump up and start running.

"Don't!" he cried. "Don't reboot or do anything else to eliminate the information that would have been there before Second changed things—"

"You think he might have released the ripple?" Jonah asked.

Whatever that means, Jordan thought.

He hoped Jonah was just pretending to know what he was talking about, throwing around some time-travel term he barely understood. He hoped Jonah was just a really good actor.

Because otherwise, there was something really scary

that Jonah—and Katherine and Deep Voice and Tattoo Face and Doreen—were all worried about.

Release the ripple, Jordan thought. *Does he mean the ripple of changes from the kid version of Second grabbing the Elucidator out of Jonah's hand? Would there have been some way to hold back those changes?*

He didn't ask, because everyone else clustered around the computerlike screen alongside Doreen. Jordan concentrated on pushing himself off the floor so he could stand beside the others.

"It doesn't do any good to look for traces of Sam Chase, or his alter ego, Second Chance," Tattoo Face objected. "He managed to hide them all—or maybe it was the time agency that did that when Second betrayed everything they stood for?"

"Oh, but I can show you everything about Second's life," Doreen said, sounding less worried than she looked.

"How?" Deep Voice challenged.

"Because," Doreen said, "I just figured out how to get into the secret files Gary and Hodge left behind."

TWENTY-SEVEN

"What if it's a trick?" Jonah asked. "What if Second stealing the Elucidator and traveling through time as a teenager changed things in such a way that *that's* why you are suddenly able to get into Gary and Hodge's secret files? What if Second arranged that to trap you all somehow, and to trap Katherine and Jordan and me?"

"You think he figured all that out as a teenager?" Doreen asked incredulously.

"He's really smart," Katherine offered. "And sneaky."

Doreen touched something on the table in front of her.

"I've always wondered what his story was . . . ," she murmured.

The projection in midair expanded and moved back toward the wall. Suddenly Jordan felt as though he were back on the rock suspended over the gully—or maybe hovering in midair watching the teenage version of Second on the rock suspended over the gully. A small clock in the corner sped through minutes: Second just lay there and lay there and lay there.

"He was *not* there for two hours," Katherine muttered. "This is a different version of time. Or a different dimension."

"Shh," Jonah and Jordan said together.

On the screen a sudden bright light appeared, aimed from above toward the boy on the rock. A dark figure began rappelling down the cliff. The climber landed on the rock and seemed to be checking Second for broken bones and other injuries. And then the climber tied Second to a backboard suspended from a helicopter. The camera seemed to follow Second's precarious progress up from the rock.

When Second reached the top of the gully, Jordan expected to see ambulances and more medical types. Instead a man in a dark suit stepped past the blinding light and bent over Second.

"You!" the man spat. "You were the pilot, weren't you? And like a coward you tried to run away."

"Is that . . . Mr. Reardon?" Katherine asked.

"Who?" Jordan asked.

Katherine glanced cautiously toward the three grown-ups.

"We already know about him," Doreen said, smirking. "He was the FBI agent who was in charge of investigating the plane crash-landing. The agent Jonah and Katherine and your parents went to see to find out about Jonah's background."

"Yeah," Jonah said. "He knew something strange had happened, but he could never figure out what it was. So his goal was just to keep everything secret."

On the screen Mr. Reardon clutched the front of Second's shirt.

"What terrorist group are you working for?" Mr. Reardon demanded. "What are you trying to prove?"

Second only moaned. Mr. Reardon let go. Second's head bounced against the stretcher beneath him.

"Give him medical care, but keep him in a private room," Mr. Reardon said. "Keep a guard outside his door."

The scene shifted into something like time-lapse video, where days and weeks and months were condensed into a few seconds. Second was lying in a hospital bed . . . sitting in a wheelchair . . . struggling on an apparatus that was probably supposed to help him relearn how to walk . . . and then returning to a wheelchair again.

The speeding scenes slowed for the many times Mr. Reardon came into Second's hospital room to interrogate him.

"You say you're an ordinary runaway—why is there

no record of anyone reporting you missing?" Mr. Reardon demanded in his first visit to the hospital.

"I didn't want to be caught. So I hacked into the school and law enforcement and child welfare system computers and eliminated all my records," Second said, staring defiantly up from his hospital bed. "And . . . it's not like my foster parents actually *missed* me. Neither did my caseworker. Or my teachers. No one wanted to try very hard to find me."

"Tell me your foster parents' names," Mr. Reardon demanded. "Tell me what city you lived in, what school you went to. Tell me where to find people who would remember you."

Second turned his face toward the wall and didn't answer.

Beside Jordan, Katherine muttered, "That does sound like something Second would do. He probably was a great hacker even as a kid."

"And he wouldn't give the FBI a straight answer," Jonah agreed, under his breath. "He doesn't give anyone a straight answer."

"But what game is he playing?" Doreen asked. "What does he hope to accomplish? Why doesn't he want to prove he's got nothing to do with the time-crashed plane?"

"Who knows, with Second?" Katherine answered.

On the screen Mr. Reardon shifted tactics.

"Baby smuggling is a serious crime," he said. "There were thirty-six babies on that plane. We could charge you with thirty-six counts of kidnapping."

That, at least, got Second to look back at Mr. Reardon.

"Does FBI mean Federal Bureau of Idiots?" he asked. "If any of you were any good at analyzing footprints, you would know that I fell when I was trying to sneak *into* the airport grounds, not out."

"And why would you do that?" Mr. Reardon asked, hunching forward over a notepad.

"It was a dare, all right?" Second snarled. "I was with my friends and we were talking about what it would be like to stand on a runway when a plane was landing and . . . we decided to try it out."

"That's a crime too," Mr. Reardon said.

Second shrugged. "It ain't thirty-six counts of kidnapping," he said.

"Oh!" Doreen said, sounding surprised. "Gary and Hodge left behind notes on this conversation—Second and his gang had this idea that they could sneak into the airport and pretend to be baggage handlers, and steal all sorts of things from suitcases. And Second didn't want to go back to his foster family because he stole money from them when he ran away."

Tattoo Face leaned over Doreen's shoulder.

"And he thought as long as the FBI wanted information from him, they'd take care of him?" Tattoo Face asked, sounding surprised.

"Looks like he was right," Deep Voice said.

Second, still in a wheelchair, left the hospital for a rehab center. Time flashed by quickly again: Second had books and computers, and he got meals delivered to his room three times a day. Mr. Reardon kept coming to see him, again and again and again.

"Gary and Hodge say Second managed to string along the FBI for thirteen years," Doreen said, as if she was reading from some screen Jordan couldn't see. It kind of made him nervous that he couldn't see it. "He kept Mr. Reardon convinced that he did know something about the plane, but he'd only reveal the information for the right price."

"What happened after thirteen years?" Jordan asked.

"This," Doreen said. Her hands seemed to shake as she waved them through the air, advancing the scene before them.

Jordan saw a nondescript waiting room. The door opened, and four people walked in: Mom and Dad, looking the way they were supposed to, middle-aged and normal; Katherine, carrying the cell phone she was supposed to share with Jordan; and Jordan himself.

What? When did this happen? Jordan wondered.

Was it some event that hadn't happened yet, but was supposed to in his near future, after Mom and Dad were their right ages again, but before he and Katherine grew up much more?

No—somehow he and Katherine both looked ever so slightly babyish on the screen, just a bit younger than they were right now. This was something that had already happened.

"It's the day we went to see Mr. Reardon," Jonah breathed. "Because Dad and Mom actually thought the FBI would tell us the truth about my past. They actually thought the FBI *knew*."

Jordan looked closer. It *was* Jonah, not Jordan, nervously taking a seat in the waiting room. But Jordan had to look for the placement of the chin dimple to be sure.

How am I supposed to keep track of time and different dimensions and tricky Second and everything else when I can't even see the difference between me and Jonah? Jordan wondered.

"And that was the day we saw JB for the first time," Katherine muttered. "Didn't he say it was the first time since the time crash that any time traveler could get in or out? And they could only get in or out at certain spots— points of impact, or something like that?"

"This is just what happened in the antechamber of Mr.

Reardon's office," Doreen said. "Let me see if I can move the focus back to Second. . . ."

The camera angle seemed to move down the hall-way, dipping briefly into an impressive office where Mr. Reardon sat in front of a desktop computer on an impos-ing desk. Then the camera angle moved through the wall into the office next door where Second, still in a wheel-chair, hunched over a laptop.

"Coming through loud and clear," Second said.

"Got it." Mr. Reardon's voice came through the laptop speakers.

"They had things set up so Second could *eavesdrop* on our whole conversation?" Katherine asked, sounding out-raged.

"By now Second is twenty-six," Doreen answered. "He's been working with the FBI since he was thirteen. Mr. Reardon still doesn't trust him—he still thinks Second is keeping secrets—but he's now one of their top computer experts."

"Of course, that's about to end," Tattoo Face muttered.

Before Jordan could ask why, two men suddenly appeared out of nowhere on either side of Second's wheel-chair. One was tall and muscular, the type of guy who probably worked out several hours a day. The other was older and more ordinary-looking. But he carried himself confidently.

"Wh-where did they come from?" Jordan stammered. "Who's that?"

He saw that Katherine and Jonah were staring at the screen with equally stunned expressions. But Katherine took pity on Jordan and glanced his way.

"You don't even recognize them, do you?" she asked. "You don't even know . . . Jordan—that's Gary and Hodge."

TWENTY-EIGHT

"That's what they did the first chance they had to get into our time period after thirteen years?" Jonah exploded. "They went to see Second?"

"I don't think they're just visiting," Doreen muttered.

Second was looking calmly from side to side, sizing up both men.

"You're the ones," he said softly. "You have all the answers Reardon wants."

"Don't think Hodge and I would ever help him!" the muscle-bound man taunted. So that was Gary.

Second leaned back slightly in his wheelchair and slid his laptop lower.

"I wouldn't expect you to," he said. "It wouldn't serve your purposes."

Hodge narrowed his eyes and studied Second's face.

"So, *Kevin*," Hodge said. He raised an eyebrow. "Are you surprised we know the identity you went by before you started working with the FBI?"

Second only shrugged, but Jordan thought, *So it really was "Kevin!" his friends yelled when he fell off that fence!*

Hodge didn't seem to care that Second didn't respond. The two of them just kept staring each other down.

"*You* figured out what the entire FBI couldn't," Hodge said. "You knew that planeload of babies was from another time. How quickly did you put it all together?"

"Are you kidding?" Second asked. "'Tachyon Travel'? You gave yourselves away."

"Huh?" Jordan said.

"Those are the words Angela told the FBI she saw on the side of the airplane," Katherine explained. "Tachyons are these particles that I guess have something to do with time travel. Angela never thought they believed her, but . . . they must have written down what she said. And Second saw it."

"So he knew there was time travel involved," Jonah murmured. "He and Angela both figured it out."

"But the FBI didn't?" Jordan asked, still watching Second.

"Institutions sometimes . . . overlook the obvious," Deep Voice said. He too was staring at the screen. "They get stuck in their ways, caught in their usual pattern of thinking . . . they fail to consider all possible options. The FBI in the late twentieth and early twenty-first centuries would never have considered time travel as a plausible explanation for anything."

"Did you know, in the future there's no need for such a primitive tool as an IQ test?" Hodge was asking Second on the large, glowing screen. "All we have to do is scan a person's brain and we know how smart they are. We don't even have to be in the same time period as the person to do that. And we don't have to worry about them speaking a particular language or having the cultural background to understand the test questions. Our brain scans are an *absolute* measure of intelligence."

"I'm certain I would do well with those scans," Second said with a shrug. "I always do well on IQ tests."

"There is a certain category of children that my colleague and I have done brain scans on, throughout history," Hodge said. "You had the highest score of any of them."

"I'm not a child," Second said.

"You were thirteen years ago," Gary said.

Second blinked. "You could have rescued me," he said. "I was on that ledge, my friends had run away—there was a moment when nobody would have known if I'd simply vanished." He looked down at his legs, immobile in the wheelchair. "I bet you could have even *cured* me. I bet you still could."

"Now, now," Hodge said. "I won't go into the reasons, but it turned out not to be possible to get to you before this very moment. People would notice you missing now. And we only rescue children."

Hodge and Second seemed to be negotiating something. Jordan couldn't understand. Why were they suddenly acting so intense?

Gary stepped closer to Second's wheelchair.

"At the very least, we could show you some of our technology," he said in a bragging tone.

"Just as a professional courtesy," Hodge added. "Because we respect your intellect."

Gary seemed to be holding out an ordinary cell phone for Second to see.

"This totally looks like it belongs in your time period, doesn't it?" Gary asked.

Second grabbed the cell phone from Gary's hands. In the next instant, Second and his wheelchair completely vanished.

So did Gary and Hodge.

TWENTY-NINE

"Those cheaters!" Doreen exclaimed.

"Oh, but they had deniability," Tattoo Face argued. "You saw what happened. They could always claim they were only following customary behavior of the time, one male bragging to another about the superiority of his cell phone. They can claim they had no way of knowing that Second would grab it. Or that he would know how to operate an Elucidator."

"Didn't they see what happened when he was a teenager and he stole the Elucidator from Jonah?" Jordan asked, whipping his head back and forth between Doreen and Tattoo Face and the screen, which now showed only an empty room.

Jordan was confused anyway: How could Second have been twenty-six back in the twenty-first century, if he had stolen the Elucidator from Jonah and left from the ravine as a teenager? How could the FBI have rescued him from the ravine when he'd already escaped on his own?

"Gary and Hodge didn't see that," Deep Voice told him. "Because it hadn't happened yet when they went back to intervene in Second's life at the FBI headquarters."

"But he was *twenty-six* then," Jordan said. "He was only—what? Thirteen?—when we saw him disappear."

It seemed perfectly logical to him that Second would be twenty-six *after* he was thirteen. But maybe Jordan shouldn't rely on that, considering how old his own parents were right now.

"Second grabbing Jonah's Elucidator is probably going to make it so that none of what you just saw actually happens," Deep Voice said, waving his arm in the general direction of the screen. "The changes just haven't been released yet, so we can still see what would have been."

Jordan saw Jonah and Katherine exchange glances. Was there something they didn't want to say in front of Deep Voice and the others?

"Where did Second go with Gary and Hodge's Elucidator?" Katherine asked, as if she was trying to distract the adults. "Where did he go when he stole Jonah's? Was it the same place? Was he the same age when he got there?"

"That's what I'm looking for right now," Doreen said,

bending over a keyboard that seemed imbedded in the table in front of her.

"And why didn't JB or anyone else at the time agency know where Second had come from, when he worked for them?" Jonah asked. "Or—*did* they know?"

"That one we can answer without research," Tattoo Face said, smirking. "Who do you think always did JB's intelligence work for him?"

"Second," Katherine said.

"So don't you think it was really easy for him to determine what JB saw and what he didn't see?" Tattoo Face added.

"But after Second—" Jonah began.

Jordan saw Katherine dig an elbow into Jonah's side.

What's that about? Jordan wondered. *What's she trying to keep him from saying?*

All three of the grown-ups were hunched over the keyboard, so they probably didn't notice.

"This says Gary and Hodge took Second to a time before the time agency had all its regulations in place," Doreen said. "So he was never registered as a time immigrant. And . . . Gary and Hodge were the ones who set Second up to work at the time agency. He was supposed to be their spy. Their source of insider information."

"Second was working for Gary and Hodge from the

very beginning?" Katherine asked, sounding stunned.

"That's what Gary and Hodge thought," Doreen said. Her eyes flickered, as if she was scanning large amounts of information. "But it appears that Second only ever works for himself."

Jordan saw Jonah and Katherine glance at each other again.

Hello! He wanted to say. *Include me! Don't act like I'm not even here!*

He didn't have the slightest idea what Jonah and Katherine were trying to telegraph with their eyes.

Deep Voice looked up from the keyboard, and Jonah and Katherine instantly put on innocent, bland expressions.

"So Second vanishing from the moment of the time crash rather than the FBI office might actually heal one potentially devastating time-travel rip in the twenty-first century," Deep Voice said. He sounded like he was just throwing out theories. "As he says, no one would have missed him disappearing from that rock in the gully. But that put him on the loose in time with an Elucidator of his own."

"A parental-controls Elucidator," Jonah reminded him. "That Elucidator Mr. Rathbone gave us was set up only to do what he wanted us to do."

"Um, no offense, but I'm pretty sure Second would have been able to override the controls," Tattoo Face said.

"Hey, we probably could have too!" Jordan protested. "Eventually, I mean! If we'd had enough time!"

Now it was Doreen, Deep Voice, and Tattoo Face exchanging glances. But before any of them had a chance to speak, a booming voice spoke from outside the lab.

"Attention, all Interchronological Rescue employees!"

Jordan guessed the sound came from speakers just outside the lab door.

"All employees are required to attend a mandatory meeting in the fifth-floor conference room in five minutes," the voice continued. "I repeat, all employees must attend a meeting in the fifth-floor conference room in five minutes. Your actual presence is required. No virtual show-ups."

Deep Voice moaned. "Do they know what I did?" he asked. "Am I going to be publicly shamed for unauthorized time travel? Is Rathbone going to make an example of me in front of the entire company? Will the police be there?"

Jordan remembered what Deep Voice had said on their trip together through time: *It's possible I'll be arrested when I get back. . . .*

Tattoo Face clapped Deep Voice on the back.

"We covered for you, man," he said. "You know that. You're safe. Stop freaking, or you'll give yourself away."

Deep Voice didn't look particularly comforted. He had such a massive face that the worry lines on his forehead seemed as deep as trenches.

Doreen looked toward the three kids.

"We have to go to this," she said. "We'll be back, but you need to *stay here*. You step one foot out of this room and your presence will be detected instantly. Better to let Rathbone think you're trapped in the past than that you returned without completing his task. Better to keep him in the dark."

"How do we know we can trust *you?*" Katherine challenged.

Points for boldness there, sis, Jordan thought.

He was still feeling dizzy trying to figure out everything that was going on. Or maybe the dizziness was just a little residual timesickness. Or even a remnant of the illness that seemed so minor now, which had kept him home sick from school back in the twenty-first century.

Regardless, it made it hard for him to think.

Doreen narrowed her eyes at Katherine as if she was seriously considering the question.

"We'll set things up so you can see what's going on in that conference room," Doreen said. "You'll see Markiel, Liam, and me go in; then you'll see us come out. And if we're not back here five minutes after that, then . . . then . . ."

"Then we're on our own," Jonah said grimly. "All deals are off."

Whoa, harsh, Jordan thought.

He waited for one of the grown-ups to say, *No, no, you wait for us here, no matter what.* He waited for them to say, *Of course we wouldn't leave you completely on your own. Of course you can count on our assistance, regardless of what happens next.*

But none of the adults said anything. They just left.

Maybe Jordan and Katherine and Jonah really were all on their own already?

THIRTY

Oddly, as soon as the door closed behind the last grown-up, Jonah turned beseechingly toward Jordan.

"Please tell me," Jonah began, "that in that other dimension you lived in, Mom and Dad never limited your time on the computer, and you became some genius programming-hacking expert. Please tell me you don't have the same friends I do, and, I don't know, you've been hanging out with Dushaun Ross the past three years. And maybe learned everything he knows?"

Dushaun Ross was a kid in Jordan's class who had probably been born clutching a laptop. Jordan could remember only one conversation he'd ever had with Dushaun Ross: Once, in fifth-grade computer class, Jordan's computer had frozen up. When Jordan raised his hand to ask the teacher for help, Dushaun had reached over and hit some magical combination of keys that made the computer work again. The whole time, his eyes never even left the screen of his own computer.

Come to think of it, that hadn't actually been a conversation.

"I'm not friends with Dushaun," Jordan admitted. "And I'm not a computer expert."

"*Hello*, what about me?" Katherine asked. "Couldn't *I* have been a computer expert in one of the other dimensions?"

"Are you?" Jonah asked.

"No," Katherine admitted. She tilted her head, considering. "I think, up until the moment we started traveling through time, I was exactly the same person in both dimensions where I had a brother."

Jordan couldn't decide if he should find that comforting or not.

"But then time travel changed you?" he asked.

Katherine darted her eyes toward Jonah.

"Of course," she said.

"What about the dimension where you were an only child?" Jordan asked.

"I don't know," Katherine said, squinting off into the distance. "It's like that's been almost entirely replaced in my mind."

"Okay, okay, this is not all about you, Katherine," Jonah

said, walking toward the table where the three grown-ups had stood. As far as Jordan could tell, the area where the keyboard had been was nothing but a smooth table-top now. "I want to find out about Second, and what he's doing now—both versions of him, if there really are still two versions. But I don't think even Dushaun Ross could figure out how to hack into a computer system that's so far ahead of what we're used to."

"Maybe it's just, like, idiot-proof now?" Katherine asked, going to stand beside him. "Maybe computers are actually *easier* than we're used to?"

Jonah snorted. "Yeah," he said. "Like how Elucidators are so easy to operate."

Jordan wanted to ask the other two a lot of questions before the grown-ups came back. But before he could say anything, the screen that had shown the empty FBI office back in the twenty-first century suddenly went blank. A moment later it flashed to life with a different scene: some sort of futuristic auditorium. A man in an ivory-colored robe walked across the stage.

It was Mr. Rathbone.

"I have sad news to impart to all of you," he announced, bending his head down in a way that made Jordan think that the man was trying hard to look sad, but proba-bly wasn't. "I have just learned that two of our longtime employees have lost their lives in a time-travel accident. I have summoned you all together to honor the memories of our good friends, 'Gary' Giuseppe Payne and Mikhail Grantley Hodge."

Katherine gasped. "Mr. Rathbone went through with his plans to fake their deaths?" she whispered. "Or—could this be true?"

Jonah muttered, "I never even thought about them having full names. . . ."

"They told us first and last names at the adoption conference, remember?" Katherine said. "But that was so long ago. . . ."

Jordan felt an odd stab of shock. What if this was true? It wasn't as if he'd ever met the two men—not that he remembered, anyway—but he'd just seen them a few moments ago on the screen. And the screen was so crystal clear and lifelike, he'd felt like they'd been right there in the room with him.

But that could have been centuries ago, Jordan reminded himself. *Time travel messes up everything. They could have stayed alive for just five minutes after I saw them on the screen, and then died traveling home, or they could have lived decades more and died of old age.*

A "time-travel accident" wouldn't be dying of old age. It was something that could happen to Jordan, Katherine, or Jonah. Or Mom and Dad.

Words appeared at the bottom of the screen, below Mr. Rathbone's feet: DOREEN K'ADU'SUPADRE SMITH HAS AUTHORIZED YOU TO SEE HER THOUGHTS AT THIS MOMENT. HERE THEY ARE: RATHBONE IS LYING. HE'S RECEIVED NO CONFIRMED INFORMATION ABOUT GARY AND HODGE BEING ALIVE OR DEAD. WHAT ARE HIS MOTIVES FOR ANNOUNCING THIS?

"Whoa," Katherine breathed. "Computers can do that now? Let people share their thoughts with each other?"

On the screen a small glow appeared above one of the heads in the audience standing before Mr. Rathbone. Jordan realized that the computer was showing where Doreen was in the crowd. If he'd looked closely, he could have picked her out anyway, because she was right beside Deep Voice, and he stood a full head taller than anyone else.

"What made Mr. Rathbone decide to make an announcement now about Gary and Hodge?" Jonah murmured behind Jordan. "If they didn't actually die, then what else changed?"

"He sent us back in time and Second stole the Elucidator Mr. Rathbone gave us," Katherine said. "That's what changed."

"So does Mr. Rathbone know that happened?" Jonah asked.

"He doesn't know where we are now," Jordan said. "Doreen and Deep Voice and Tattoo Face said so."

Jonah shot Jordan a look that made Jordan feel really young and childish, almost as if he'd piped up to say, *Santa Claus and the Easter Bunny are going to take care of us.*

On the screen Mr. Rathbone finished his dramatic pause and looked back toward the audience.

"Giuseppe and Mikhail believed in the mission of Interchronological Rescue above all else," Mr. Rathbone said, his voice ringing with conviction. Or faked conviction. Jordan really wasn't sure. "At times their zeal was interpreted as . . . well, shall we say, criminal intent by certain agencies that had other, less noble goals of their own."

Below Mr. Rathbone's feet, more words appeared, giving Doreen's thoughts: THAT'S HIS ATTACK ON THE TIME AGENCY, IN CASE YOU COULDN'T TELL. HE HATES THE TIME AGENCY.

"In their selflessness, Giuseppe and Mikhail gave me letters of resignation from Interchronological Rescue before their last, most dangerous trip through time," Mr. Rathbone continued. "They were most concerned that nothing they did might reflect badly on our company."

Jordan could see that Doreen had a completely different thought: THEY WERE MOST CONCERNED WITH PADDING THEIR OWN POCKETS AND PROTECTING THEIR OWN SKIN. IF THEY CARED SO MUCH ABOUT INTERCHRONOLOGICAL RESCUE, WHY DIDN'T THEY JUST AVOID DOING ANYTHING WRONG?

"Of course, we all know that their intentions—and actions—were always pure, but the time agency tends to misinterpret," Mr. Rathbone said. "Even in their last moments, Giuseppe and Mikhail wanted to protect Interchronological Rescue and our mission. Which we will resume as soon as the time agency ends its foolish restrictions. We will do so remembering two good and faithful servants to the cause. In their honor, you may have the rest of the afternoon off. Go, in their memory."

Doreen's thoughts showed up on the screen again: HE'S TRYING TO CLEAR OUT THE BUILDING THIS AFTERNOON? WHY? WHAT DOES HE WANT TO DO HERE WITHOUT ANY WITNESSES?

Mr. Rathbone walked off the stage.

"We've only got a few minutes before Doreen and Deep Voice and Tattoo Face come back," Jordan said. Somehow he couldn't keep the panic out of his voice. "Can we trust what *they're* telling us? Can Doreen really make the computer tell us what she's thinking, or is that just another trick?"

Katherine shrugged. "It seems like *they* think they're telling us the truth," she said.

"But I think there's a lot they don't know," Jonah added.

On the screen everyone filed out of the auditorium. Mr. Rathbone stood in the doorway, shaking hands. Behind his mask of grief, he seemed to be watching people's reactions very carefully.

When Doreen's turn came beside the CEO, Mr. Rathbone held onto her hand a moment longer than he had anyone else's.

"Wait—you were one of the background investigators for Giuseppe's and Mikhail's trips, weren't you?" he asked.

Doreen looked over her shoulder toward Deep Voice and Tattoo Face.

"Yes, sir," she said. "Markiel and Liam were too."

"But only at the lowest levels," Deep Voice added, dipping his head humbly. "We can claim no credit for their accomplishments." He hesitated. "Sir."

"Then I am sorry for your loss," Mr. Rathbone said. "I know it's difficult to lose both your friends and your job."

Doreen gaped at him. "What? You're *firing* us?" she asked.

"No, no, just . . . shifting you to other departments," Mr. Rathbone said. He smiled as if he thought he was being exceptionally kind and Doreen should thank him profusely. "You'll get your new work assignments tomorrow."

"Oh," Doreen said.

She pulled her hand away from Mr. Rathbone and turned toward the door.

"Where are you going?" Mr. Rathbone asked.

"Upstairs?" Doreen said. "To get my things?"

"That won't be necessary," Mr. Rathbone said. "I've already had the robot movers clear out your desks and box it all up. You'll find all your personal items over there."

He pointed to the side. The camera angle was wrong for Jordan to be able to see any boxes.

"Ah," Doreen said, clearly flustered. "Um, thanks."

"I want everyone to be able to clear out and get to their transports as quickly as possible," Mr. Rathbone said. "So they can grieve in the privacy of their own homes."

"You're too kind," Doreen said. She hesitated, then lurched awkwardly toward Mr. Rathbone. She patted him on the back. "I am sorry for *your* loss too, sir. I know you thought very highly of Gary and Mr. Hodge."

The words showing her thoughts appeared at the bottom of the screen again: DON'T PANIC. JUST KEEP WATCHING. AND STAY IN PLACE. WE NEED YOU AS WITNESSES.

"What does that mean?" Jordan asked. "Didn't they say they'd be back in five minutes? And what does she think we're going to witness if everyone's leaving?"

Neither Jonah nor Katherine answered.

But a few moments later, after Mr. Rathbone finished shaking hands and started back toward his own office, Jordan understood. The view on the screen seemed to follow him in a tight little bubble, almost as if a camera hovered over his head and periodically darted in front of or behind him.

"Do you think it's like Doreen put a spy camera on him when she patted his back?" Katherine asked. "I bet she did! Wow! She was smart!"

"So do you think that's what she wants us to witness? What Mr. Rathbone does when everyone else is gone?" Jonah asked.

Jordan, Katherine, and Jonah were all lined up now, staring at the screen. Mr. Rathbone climbed stairs. He stepped into his office. He sat at his desk. He looked at the wall. He lifted a golf club that was sitting beside his desk and swung it. He swung it again. And again.

"Um, do you think all of us have to watch the whole time?" Jordan asked. "Could we maybe just take turns? Like, have one of us watch at a time, and the other two of us can see if we can find another computer that could tell us where Second took Mom and Dad?"

"That's actually a good idea," Jonah said, as if he were surprised.

Katherine looked at both boys and rolled her eyes.

"I'll keep watching," she said. "My attention span lasts longer than two minutes."

"But this is important, too!" Jordan protested. "Don't you want Mom and Dad back?"

"Don't you want to figure out how to fix their ages—and save all of time?" Katherine retorted.

Jordan made a face at his sister's back. She was totally facing the other way, but she called out, "I saw that!"

"Sisters," Jordan mumbled to Jonah. And for a moment it almost did seem like they were twins, like they were thinking the same thing. Then Jonah sighed.

"I usually mess up Elucidator commands, so I'm not sure how much I'll be able to figure out on one of these computers," he said.

"I don't even know how you're supposed to tell which part of the table is a keyboard and which part isn't," Jordan agreed. He walked over to the table behind the one Doreen had stood at, and ran his hand across the smooth, dark surface. Nothing, nothing, nothing . . .

Suddenly words glowed in the air above his hands: "Access denied. This unit unlocks only for Mikhail Hodge or Gary Payne."

"Figures," Jonah said.

Jordan shot him a sidelong glance.

"Are you *sure* they're not dead?" he asked.

"I'm sure the time agency didn't kill them," Jonah said. "They wouldn't have done that. But . . . Jordan, there were a lot of ways to die in history. And I don't know where the time agency put the baby versions of Gary and Hodge."

"We don't know where Second went either," Jordan

grumbled. "After *any* of the times we saw him. With Mom and Dad or without them."

He felt a little like sniffling, but held it back, because he didn't want Jonah to think he was a total baby. He turned the sniff into a cough instead.

"This day has kind of tied my brain in knots too," Jonah said. "But . . . I think something did change, with Second stealing our Elucidator and escaping our time period when he was thirteen instead of just when he was twenty-six. Maybe that fixed something even the time agency didn't know was broken."

"Second still hasn't brought Mom and Dad back," Katherine pointed out from across the room.

"I didn't say it fixed everything!" Jonah argued.

Katherine gave him a dismissive wave without even turning around. Jordan wondered if Katherine was staring so fixedly at the screen because she didn't want Jonah to see her being emotional about Mom and Dad either.

"I still don't understand," Jordan admitted. "How could we have seen Second escape as a teenager *and* as a twenty-six-year-old? How could both things happen?"

"I think it has to do with the different dimensions of time that existed before I smashed them all back together," Jonah said. "Remember? I'm not sure the Interchronological Rescue workers understand this, but Second's escape happened so close to the time of our plane's crash landing. The three versions of it, I mean. I bet time split into three dimensions of what happened to Second down on that rock, too."

Is that why Jonah and Katherine kept giving each other those looks when Deep Voice, Tattoo Face, and Doreen were talking about Second? Jordan wondered. *Because they were trying to keep the dimensions secret?*

Jordan didn't ask, because Jonah was still explaining.

"In one dimension," Jonah said, "Second fell on that rock, and his so-called friends ran away and never told anyone, and Second must have died. In another, we went down to that rock, and Second stole our Elucidator and got away. In the third dimension, the FBI found Second and rescued him, but then kept him like, I don't know, a pet or something—until Gary and Hodge helped him escape. And that would have been the worst dimension, because it would have done the most damage to time."

"And I guess Second had to stay in a wheelchair for thirteen years," Jordan said.

"Right," Jonah said. "So maybe Second was trying to get us to replace what happened in that version of time. Or maybe he wanted there to be two of him running around even after the dimensions merged again. . . . It's so frustrating. No matter how much I thought I was outsmarting him, he must have known that I'd end up going to Mr. Rathbone and Mr. Rathbone would send us back in time."

Jordan thought about all of this. He could kind of keep track of the three dimensions if he pictured the Venn diagram Katherine had drawn back in the Skidmore family kitchen.

"So Second was in a wheelchair in your dimension of time," Jordan asked. "What happened to him in mine?"

Jonah tilted his head.

"I guess it could have been either of the other two possibilities," Jonah said. "But I'm not always so great at figuring out the ins and outs of time travel, or all the changes. I used to mostly just try not to think about it."

"Jonah wants you to believe that what he's good at with time travel is the action-hero stuff," Katherine said, turning around from all of Mr. Rathbone's golf swings long enough to make a face at both boys.

Jordan thought about how Jonah had gotten them through flames and a bear attack and crushing ice. Maybe it had all been a simulation, but it had felt real. Jordan's heart had pounded with real fear.

Would he sound like a total suck-up if he defended Jonah to Katherine?

Katherine had already turned back toward the screen. Then she reeled back and gasped.

"Jonah! Jordan! Look—now!" she cried.

Mr. Rathbone was no longer standing alone in his office, idly swinging a golf club.

Second was standing on the carpet in front of him. And the golf club was broken between them.

THIRTY-ONE

Jordan and Jonah rushed over beside Katherine. All three kids leaned toward the screen.

"Those two are working together now?" Katherine moaned.

"I don't think that golf club broke on its own," Jordan told her.

Second and Mr. Rathbone seemed to be staring each other down.

"You," Mr. Rathbone cried. "You—you—you're the one who ruined everything!"

"I think your two employees Gary and Hodge did a fine job of ruining things all by themselves," Second observed calmly. He looked down at his hands as if he had nothing more to worry about than a possible hangnail.

"*If* you had stayed at the time agency like you were

supposed to, *if* you had followed instructions, *if* you had helped us—" Mr. Rathbone began.

"If all of that had happened, we would all be so, so bored, wouldn't we?" Second asked, waving his hand carelessly.

"What if the time agency never reinstates our license?" Mr. Rathbone fumed. "What if they never permit the retrieval of time-rescued children again?"

"Our lives would go on anyway," Second said, shrugging. He cocked his head thoughtfully. "Or would they? What if too much damage has already been done? Back in the past—"

"I don't care about the past!" Mr. Rathbone exploded, pounding his fist on his desk.

"And . . . that would be the problem with everything you've done at Interchronological Rescue," Second said. "You don't actually care about anything except making money. How many billions have you acquired on the backs of poor children from the past?"

"We've saved hundreds of children," Mr. Rathbone said. "We've rescued them from certain death. And from desperate, destitute eras. The money was only . . . a sidelight."

"And that's why you started faking children's identities," Second said.

Beside Jordan, Jonah made a sound deep in his throat that might have been a moan. Katherine patted his arm.

Meanwhile, Second went on listing Mr. Rathbone's crimes: "And that's why you started reselling certain children more than once, when they failed to be as . . . *amenable* to their new families as their parents had hoped."

"It's not my fault that the kind of parents who are most impressed by having, shall we say, name-brand children are not always the ones who are best at actually raising those children," Mr. Rathbone defended himself. "Or that modern parents are more willing to help a starving child from the past if he has a famous name or a famous heritage."

Second gave a scornful snort.

"You know the time agency is coming for you, don't you?" he asked.

Mr. Rathbone glanced around frantically.

"You're lying," he said. "And anyhow, they can't pin anything on me. What my underlings did—how was I to know they didn't follow the rules?"

Second picked up the two pieces of the broken golf club and laid them gently on Mr. Rathbone's desk.

"Unfortunately, you're right that the time agency won't be able to prove your guilt," Second said. "You have been clever at hiding your crimes, if nothing else. But I know what you've done. I've seen the evidence. And so I will be the one to judge you. I will mete out your punishment."

"What?" Mr. Rathbone said, sounding jarred. "What are you talking about?"

"It's time," Second said, extending his arm.

In the next instant, both of them disappeared.

"What was that all about?" Jordan asked. "Why's Second so mad at Mr. Rathbone? Didn't Mr. Rathbone kind of *help* Second, by sending us back to rescue him?"

Neither Jordan nor Katherine answered. Both of them were staring past the screen, which had gone dark. Jordan had to crane his neck to see what they were looking at. For a moment Jordan thought the screen had just reactivated in a different spot. Then he realized what had actually happened: Second was now standing right in the lab with them. And he was holding a long swath of ivory cloth that looked suspiciously like the robe that Mr. Rathbone had been wearing only a second ago.

"Did you . . . vaporize Mr. Rathbone?" Jordan asked, his voice breaking.

"No, look, there's something moving inside that robe," Katherine said. "Did Second just *shrink* him or something?"

It was Jonah who figured it out.

"You turned Mr. Rathbone back into a baby too?" he asked.

THIRTY-TWO

Um, okay, I know everyone keeps saying it's possible to turn someone back into a baby, Jordan thought. *I know Jonah said it happened with Gary and Hodge. But . . . Second is just tricking us again, right? Right?*

Jonah and Katherine didn't look like they thought this was a trick.

"Why?" Jonah asked Second. "You could have killed him, doing that! You could have given him brain damage, or, or—"

"Or given him a chance to grow up this time as a better person?" Second asked. "This is no more than *he's* been doing to other people."

"You mean because all the rescued children from history were turned back into babies before they traveled through time?" Jordan asked. He moved just close enough to Second to see that there was indeed a baby nestled inside all that ivory cloth. The baby had silky reddish hair and chubby cheeks. He didn't look like he would grow up to be a CEO.

But then, what baby did?

"Rathbone has started supplementing his baby-smuggling income with selling his un-aging expertise," Second said, shrugging. "Rich parents who have, say, an unruly thirteen-year-old have been paying Rathbone's company to un-age the kid back to whatever age he supposedly went off the rails. There's been a rash of 'new babies' in families where teenagers have vanished. . . . Oh, it's always explained perfectly well, so no official ever gets suspicious. Sometimes there's an accident that no one witnesses, sometimes the kid supposedly runs away and can't be found . . . I'm sure you can imagine some of the more creative excuses."

"Then he should be arrested," Katherine said. "Not . . . this."

She gestured toward the baby and made a horrified face.

"Oh, yuck," she said, wrinkling up her nose even more. "Don't they have deodorizer diapers in the future? Or . . . didn't you let him have a diaper?"

Second put the baby Mr. Rathbone down on the floor,

which at least put more distance between Jordan's nose and the stench.

"I'm insulted," Second said as he stood back up. "I thought you would be glad that I'd eliminated Rathbone as a threat. And . . . I thought you'd be honored that I'm coming to the three of you to decide what should happen to this baby next."

"Seriously?" Jonah asked. He looked as disgusted as Katherine. "Now you're going to act like you're giving us a choice about anything?"

"I am," Second said. "Tell me what to do with this baby and that's what will happen."

Jordan watched Second's face. The man seemed perfectly calm, his expression placid.

If we said, "Kill him!" would Second actually do that? Jordan wondered.

His stomach twisted. He didn't say anything.

Katherine and Jonah glanced quickly at each other.

"Send this baby to a time hollow," Jonah said. "Until everything else is straightened out."

"Done," Second said, snapping his fingers.

Jordan looked down at the baby again, but he was too late—the infant version of Mr. Rathbone had already vanished.

"Of course," Second said thoughtfully, "you may have

just condemned that child to be stuck in a time hollow forever. Because when in life do we ever have everything straightened out? When do we have every little thing resolved, every problem solved?"

"You know what I meant!" Jonah protested. "I was talking about just until we have our parents back, and they're the right age, and time is safe again, and—"

"And why won't you just *help* us instead of playing all these games?" Katherine asked. Her voice had that tone it always got right before she started crying. "Why do you have to be so mean?"

"You said you wanted to fix time, not ruin things all over again," Jonah agreed. "Just give us our parents back and let us get in touch with the time agency again and—"

"The two of you have become so tiresome," Second complained. He shook his head. "You know what? I find myself not wanting to listen to your whining anymore. Adios!"

"Don't—" Jonah and Katherine both cried. And Jordan couldn't tell if they were going to say, *Don't kill us!* or *Don't leave us here!* or *Don't be such a jerk!* Before either of them could say another word, both of them vanished.

And Jordan was left alone with Second.

THIRTY-THREE

Did Second keep me here because I wasn't talking? Jordan wondered. *Just because I was too scared to say or do anything?*

He felt even more frozen now.

Second chuckled. "Oh, don't look so terrified," he said, rolling his eyes. "I didn't *hurt* them. I just sent them to a time hollow. And it was even a different time hollow from that reeking baby, so there could be no charges of cruel and unusual punishment."

Would stinky babies keep stinking in a time hollow? Jordan wondered nonsensically. Why was his brain working so badly?

Was it because he was alone with a psychopath?

"Did you send Katherine and Jonah to be with Mom and Dad?" Jordan asked, his voice coming out in a squeak.

Second laughed again.

"The fate of all time hangs in the balance, and *that's* what you ask about?" he said. "Are you jealous? Or just worried that everything will end for you, and Jonah will get to keep the family you thought was yours?"

"I—" Jordan began.

He couldn't defend himself. He was afraid of losing his family. He was afraid of never seeing Mom, Dad, or Katherine again. And somehow it would be even worse if Jonah got to keep what Jordan had lost.

"Jonah and Katherine aren't with your parents," Second said.

"Then send me to be with Mom and Dad," Jordan whimpered, as pathetic as a little kid crying, *I want my mommy. I want my daddy.*

"Ennh," Second said, making the same kind of *Wrong answer!* buzzer noise he'd used before on Jonah. "Try again."

Should Jordan be encouraged that Second seemed to be trying to give Jordan a choice now, too?

"Then . . . send me to be with Katherine and Jonah," Jordan said.

Katherine and Jonah at least had a lot more experience than Jordan did with all this time-travel craziness.

But Second made the "ennh" noise again.

"Think," he said. "Jonah and Katherine are in time-out. Your parents are clueless. Why would you ask to be put out of commission as well? Why would you want to be powerless?"

Aren't I powerless now? Jordan wanted to protest. *I'm a kid. I'm from the twenty-first century and I don't even understand the computers in this room. I'm standing beside a man who can turn people back into babies—and he might do that to me if I annoy him.*

"Well?" Second said.

Powerless, Jordan thought. *Clueless.*

But Second seemed to be offering Jordan some sort of power, some sort of control over what happened next. Was he offering Jordan a clue or two as well?

"Send me . . . ," Jordan began. "Send me . . . someplace I can make a difference."

"Bingo," Second said.

In the next instant Second disappeared, and Jordan was sailing through time. When he landed again, he blinked furiously, trying to figure out where he was.

Blank, bland walls . . . , he thought dizzily. *Nondescript floor . . . Is this another time hollow?*

He looked around for the baby version of Mr. Rathbone or—though he didn't think it was likely—Katherine or Jonah or Mom or Dad or just about anybody he'd ever known in his life. But the room around him was empty.

Yeah, right, I can make a difference here, Jordan thought bitterly.

Then there was a thud behind him.

Jordan turned, squinting, trying to get his eyes to focus.

Messy blond hair . . . torn shirt . . .

It was Second again. But it wasn't the adult Second lying on the floor before him.

It was the teenage Second who'd stolen the Elucidator from Jonah.

THIRTY-FOUR

"You?" Jordan cried.

The teenage Second blinked up at Jordan.

"You left after me but got here first?" the boy asked. "Is that proof—or evidence anyway—that time travel really is possible? Like the note said?"

Was the teenage Second delirious or just suffering from timesickness?

Or am I just too stupid to understand what he's talking about? Jordan wondered.

The teenage Second squeezed his right hand tightly shut and pressed it into his armpit, as if he was trying to hide something from Jordan.

"I'm not giving it back," he snarled. "The note said I deserved to have it."

Jordan realized Second was talking about the Elucidator he'd stolen from Jonah.

What if I lunge for it and snatch it back before this kid knows what I'm doing? Jordan wondered.

But the teenage Second was already thinking about Jordan grabbing the Elucidator. And Jordan wasn't even particularly good at snatching away a basketball from an opponent out on the basketball court, let alone something the size of a watch battery that another kid was clutching tightly and hiding out of Jordan's sight. Right now Jordan couldn't even tell if the Elucidator looked totally futuristic and tiny or older and bigger.

And if Jordan tried to steal the Elucidator back but failed, what was there to stop the teenage Second from simply ordering it to take him someplace else? That would leave Jordan alone and useless again in the empty time hollow.

"I'm not here to steal that back from you," Jordan said cautiously. He was mostly just trying to get the other kid to stop staring at him so suspiciously.

The teenage Second narrowed his eyes even more.

"You can't steal it 'back,'" he said. "Because I didn't steal it in the first place. The note said three kids would deliver something to me when I was in need, and it would be rightfully mine. And the note said it would be two boys who looked exactly alike, and a girl with them—and that's what you were, right? Thanks a lot for waiting so long— I've been 'in need' my whole life!"

He said the last part with such a bitter tone that Jordan took a step back.

Jordan really did not have a thief's instincts.

"I—" Jordan began. Then he shifted tactics. "Who did this note come from? When did you get it?"

A certain craftiness slid over the teenage Second's expression.

"What's it to you?" he snarled, then pressed his lips together to make it clear he wouldn't give a serious answer.

Was it Mr. Rathbone? Jordan wondered. *No—he wouldn't want Second wandering around on his own, as a teenager. Mr. Rathbone just wants babies he can sell. And control.*

In his mind Jordan saw the adult Second holding the baby Mr. Rathbone—the CEO rendered powerless in the blink of an eye. Jordan held back a shiver. What if the teenage Second knew how to do that to Jordan?

"Time travel can be a little . . . confusing," Jordan said, pronouncing each word carefully, like someone inching forward along a dangerous cliff. "I just want to make sure that I'm doing things right. That I understand who I'm helping."

The teenage Second fixed him with a dead stare.

"I don't think it's confusing," he said. "If *you* could reach back in time and rescue yourself from being trapped, wouldn't you do it?"

Did Second mean that his adult self had sent him a note telling him to steal the Elucidator?

Jordan knew almost nothing about time travel, but he kind of thought the time agency would object to something like that. He started to say, *Um, aren't you worried about messing up time?*

But just then the teenage Second twitched, and a panicked look came over his face.

"I—I can't get up," he gasped. He hit his hand against his jeans. "I can't feel my legs!"

He lifted his right hand toward his mouth, and Jordan saw a glint of silver—the edge of the Elucidator.

"Fix my legs!" the teenage Second demanded, shouting into the Elucidator. "Right now!"

He twitched again, but only the top half of his body moved.

"This has to work!" he screamed. "Fix! My! Legs!"

Nothing changed.

"Um, that was kind of a limited Elucidator," Jordan said, because it was awful watching the other boy's anguish.

"The note told me how to unlock it and get it to do anything I want," teenage Second said, barely looking at Jordan. He was struggling to lift his neck enough to gaze down at his unmoving legs and feet.

"Aren't you afraid all that trying to move might hurt you worse?" Jordan asked. "Wouldn't it make more sense to . . ."

He stopped, because his brain skipped ahead to the

next thought. He'd been about to say, *Wouldn't it make more sense to have the Elucidator send you to some hospital in the future, where they know how to cure people like you who have fallen off cliffs? So you don't end up in a wheelchair this time around too?*

But if the teenage Second got the Elucidator to take him to the future, that would leave Jordan alone in the time hollow again.

Powerless again.

The other boy's eyes widened, and Jordan guessed that he'd just figured out exactly what Jordan was about to say. The teenage Second put his right hand even closer to his mouth and hunched over, like he didn't want Jordan to hear what he was going to say into the Elucidator.

Jordan dived for the other boy and grabbed for his arm.

A split second later, everything in the time hollow vanished.

THIRTY-FIVE

I did it! Jordan wanted to scream. *I outsmarted Second and made him take me with him!*

But there was already someone screaming a hundred times louder than Jordan could have. It was actually a little surprising that Jordan could hear his own thoughts.

"Shh," Jordan said, which was crazy, of course, because there was no one to hear him except the teenage Second, and he was the one screaming at the top of his lungs.

"The pain!" Second screamed. "The pain!"

And then, even as Jordan clutched the other boy's arm, Second slumped over in what seemed to be a dead faint.

The darkness of time travel zoomed past them in utter silence.

Is he still alive? Jordan wondered. He reached over and felt for Second's pulse at his neck—it was faint but definitely there.

He passed out from the pain, Jordan realized. And yet the boy hadn't seemed to be in pain at all in the time hollow. *Oh, right, because people don't feel hunger or thirst or pain or anything like that in a time hollow. But coming out of it just shredded him.*

Jordan reached over and eased the Elucidator out of Second's grasp.

"Now who's the genius?" Jordan said aloud, gloating.

The Elucidator gleamed at him as he held it up. Oh, wait, it was actually gleaming *words* at him: YOU WOULD LIKE TO SEE A LIST OF ALL CERTIFIED GENIUSES SINCE THE BEGINNING OF TIME? YES OR NO?

"No, no, I don't need that," Jordan said quickly. "I was just . . . thinking out loud."

A REMINDER: I AM SET ON VOICE COMMANDS AND WILL FOLLOW YOUR ORDERS ACCORDINGLY appeared above the Elucidator screen now. PLEASE BE CLEAR IN YOUR INSTRUCTIONS.

"Right," Jordan said.

Why couldn't he enjoy even one moment of gloating before somebody—or, well, in this case, some*thing*—was telling him off?

The emptiness around him seemed to zoom by at an even faster rate.

Um, maybe I don't have time for gloating anyway? he thought.

He held an unlocked Elucidator in his hand, which, as

far as he knew, would be able to whisk him off to any time or place he wanted. He could go find Mom and Dad on his own; he could be the hero who rescued Katherine and Jonah.

But his other hand was holding on to the arm of a limp, unconscious teenager who had apparently broken his back and leg.

He's just going to turn into that nasty Second when he grows up! Jordan's brain screamed at him. *Or he already did grow up into Second, or he will or he could or—whatever! He's not my problem!*

But Jordan didn't let go of the teenage Second's arm. He could see in his mind the way his parents would look at him if he told them he'd abandoned some hurt, unconscious kid in the middle of nowhere—even if Jordan felt he had to do that to rescue them. The corners of his mother's mouth would sag, and his dad would avoid Jordan's eyes, and maybe they wouldn't actually say, *We're so disappointed in you; that's not how we raised you*, but he would feel it.

"But he tried to abandon me back at the time hollow," Jordan protested aloud, as if he needed to defend himself.

TIME HOLLOW? DO YOU WISH TO RETURN TO THE TIME HOLLOW? the Elucidator glowed up at him.

"No!" Jordan cried quickly, because what if the Elucidator turned them around and the teenage Second woke up again in the time hollow?

If he did, he'd probably figure out a way to outsmart me this time around, Jordan thought.

And would that be a good enough reason to abandon Second?

No, Jordan thought.

He sighed. "I have to take care of teenage Second before I go anywhere else," Jordan told the Elucidator. "Where exactly did he tell you to take him?"

HIS INSTRUCTIONS WERE IMPRECISE the Elucidator spelled out in glowing letters. HE SAID, 'TAKE ME WHERE I CAN BE CURED.' SO I'M TAKING BOTH OF YOU TO THE NEAREST HOSPITAL IN THE NEAREST TIME PERIOD AFTER 2035, WHICH IS WHEN MEDICAL EXPERTS FIGURED OUT HOW TO HEAL THE KIND OF SPINAL INJURIES HE HAS.

"That sounds okay for Second," Jordan said.

All Jordan would have to do was leave the teenage Second on the doorstep of some hospital, and he'd be taken care of. And then Jordan could go wherever he needed to go.

But Jordan's stomach twisted. If he were Second, would he really want to be treated in the *first* year they knew how to handle his type of injuries? And . . . what was that thing Jonah and Katherine had talked about, saying people couldn't be duplicated in time without creating serious problems? What if Second was already supposed to be alive in 2035?

Forget Second—wouldn't I be alive myself in 2035? Assuming I get back from all this time travel safely? Jordan wondered.

"Wait, no—don't send us there," Jordan told the Elucidator. "Take us to a time period where doctors know how to solve Second's problems, but after any time when Second and I might already be alive. I mean, if we survive this trip."

SO BE IT the Elucidator glowed back at Jordan.

Jordan liked an Elucidator giving him that kind of answer. He slipped it into his back pocket and held his hand over it so there was no danger he'd lose it traveling through time.

They seemed to speed up instantly, zooming toward lights far off in the distance. Jordan's thoughts became jumbled: *Mom . . . Dad . . . Katherine . . . fix time . . . make Mom and Dad the right ages . . . .* Then he hit the moment of time travel where he couldn't think.

The next thing he was aware of, he and the teenage Second were tangled together on a soft carpeted floor. Someone was screaming above him, "Time travelers! Unauthorized time travelers! You're under arrest!"

THIRTY-SIX

Jordan actually thought, *What would Jonah do?*

All those time-travel disasters Jordan and Jonah had dealt with back in the futuristic lab—hadn't Jonah navigated each of them almost perfectly?

Because they were all disasters he'd already lived through, Jordan thought. *And maybe even he didn't do so well the first time around. . . .*

But thinking about Jonah made him want to at least not shame himself too badly. Even though his head swam and his vision and hearing still swung in and out of focus, he forced himself to sit up. This made the teenage Second slump down even lower against the floor. He was still unconscious; his eyelids didn't even flutter.

Jordan realized that the person screaming "You're under arrest!" was not some sort of police officer or other law enforcement expert—not unless those officials in the future wore uniforms that looked like candy-striper volunteers in twenty-first-century hospitals.

The person glaring at Jordan looked to be, at most, high-school age. She had pigtails hanging down on either side of her face.

"I'll have you know, I am a time traveler authorized by the Interchronological Rescue agency," Jordan said, trying for the same confident tone that Jonah had used with the medieval monks back in the lab at Interchronological Rescue. And it wasn't like he was even lying—Mr. Rathbone had authorized him and Jonah and Katherine to rescue the teenage Second. This was just . . . a detour.

What if Interchronological Rescue has been shut down in this time period? Jordan wondered. *What if those time-agency rules about not bringing anyone back from the past are already in effect here?*

Jordan decided to ignore his own brain.

"What kind of a hospital is this, where you're more concerned about yelling at people than treating seriously injured patients?" he asked. "We've just escaped from, uh, extreme danger in the past. This boy has a spine injury. Aren't you going to help him before he dies?"

The girl jumped.

"Oh! Oh—of course," she said. "I'm so sorry. Of course patient care is our first priority."

She glanced anxiously toward a corner of the room—toward some sort of video camera, maybe? Could it be that everything was going to be recorded in the future? And maybe people at hospitals were punished for any mistake?

She lifted her wrist toward her mouth.

"Stretchers!" she called out. "Emergency personnel! Stat! Spinal injury in the lobby!"

Would people in the future have microphones imbedded in their wrists, so they could call anyone they wanted, anytime they wanted?

Jordan decided that must be the case. Before he even had a chance to blink away the last of his blurry vision, people in scrubs and face masks were swarming around him and Second. Voices went in and out:

". . . located site of damage . . ."

". . . into spinal-reconstruction surgery immediately . . ."

"Are you injured too?"

Jordan realized this last question was directed at him.

"No, no," he said quickly. He didn't think he could manage standing yet, but he made himself sit up a little straighter. "I'm fine. Just bringing, uh, Kevin there in for treatment."

He thought "Second" or that other name Jonah and Katherine had said—Sam Chase?—might be recognized.

And thanks to Gary and Hodge, Jordan knew that Second really had been called "Kevin" as a teenager.

"Let me show you to a private waiting room, then," someone replied. Jordan realized it was the candy-striper girl. "It will probably be about fifteen minutes before your friend is back on his feet."

Fifteen minutes! Jordan thought. *That's all?*

He guessed that meant they were far into the future, long past the time when doctors had first figured out how to fix spinal injuries like Second's. Er—Kevin's.

Jordan decided to just start thinking of the other boy as "Kevin." It made him seem less scary. And less likely to hunt Jordan down when Jordan left him behind.

"Here's a detox suit, so you're not bringing in any germs from the past on your clothes," the girl said, handing him a thick wad of rubbery material. It didn't seem to have any openings in it.

Oh, great, Jordan thought. *How would somebody put this on? She's going to know I'm lying when I can't figure it out!*

But it was like the detox suit had a mind of its own: It unfurled and then slipped around Jordan's body, somehow covering his T-shirt, sweatpants, and tennis shoes completely.

"Don't worry—that's one of the newer models that just breathes up an area of sterile air around your head," the girl said. "It won't cover your face like the old models used to."

Jordan nodded, pretending he understood. He tried not to show panic at the thought of thick rubber covering his face. But she was right: The detox suit stopped at his neck. He glanced around quickly. He didn't see anyone else wearing this kind of dark rubber suit, but maybe that just meant that he was the only person here who'd just traveled through time.

The only other person besides "Kevin."

"This model works faster too," the girl said. "It will finish and completely disintegrate by the time the other boy is out of surgery. Of course, his clothes will have to be detoxed separately. . . . Does your friend work for Interchronological Rescue too?"

"Oh, no," Jordan said, thinking of the older Second in Mr. Rathbone's office, the broken golf club between them. And then—Second turning Mr. Rathbone back into a baby. "Kevin is . . . a kid rescued from the past."

That seemed like the easiest story to use. And it was sort of true. Even if Kevin had mostly just rescued himself.

But the girl's eyes widened, gazing at Jordan with even more interest.

"Which famous historical kid is he?" she asked. "The tsarevitch from Russia, maybe? Though I heard rumors about some problem rescuing him—"

"You wouldn't have heard of Kevin's original identity," Jordan said quickly. "It's not like he's famous here."

Jordan hoped that was true.

And . . . have I done enough now to take care of Kevin? Now can I just zap my way out of here and go rescue the rest of my family? Even with this stupid detox suit on?

Could he just say, *Get me out of here!* to the Elucidator, and then give better directions as he was floating through time?

Before Jordan had a chance to do that, the girl wrapped her hand around Jordan's arm and tugged him to his feet. If Jordan said, *Get me out of here!* now, the girl would end up going with him.

Jordan tried to shake her hand off his arm.

"No, no, I've heard that time travelers get timesickness sometimes, and may have trouble walking," the girl said. "Let me help you."

"Um, I need to go to the bathroom," Jordan said.

Surely she wouldn't follow him there.

"Don't worry," she said, still holding on tightly. "There's one in the waiting room. You can't use the restroom until the detox suit's done anyhow."

Jordan remembered how she'd yelled, "You're under arrest!" just a few moments earlier. Maybe he needed to play along with all this just to keep from attracting even more attention, and having the time agency come after him for real. He wouldn't mind being a little steadier on his feet before he made any dramatic moves. He could walk into that waiting room she was talking about, then go to the bathroom and disappear from there.

Jordan let the girl pull him down a hallway and into an elevator. It didn't seem to move at all, but a split second later the door opened and a cheerful-sounding voice said, "Twenty-third floor."

Don't act spooked, Jordan told himself. *If you really worked for Interchronological Rescue, and you were really from this time period, you'd probably expect elevators to move that fast.*

When they stepped out of the elevator, Jordan didn't let himself look too closely at anything around him. If he was really from this time period, wouldn't he act like he took everything for granted?

And it's not like you have to pay attention to know how to escape, he reminded himself. *You've got the Elucidator in your pocket. All you'll have to do is ask it to zap you away to find the rest of your family and fix everything.*

They got to a door, and the girl waved some sort of authorization card at it. Or maybe she just waved her hand—maybe it was reading her fingerprints or DNA or something like that. The door slid open.

The room that appeared behind it held two beds rather

than the couches or chairs Jordan would have expected in a waiting room. But what did Jordan know? Maybe that was typical for hospital waiting rooms in whatever time period they were in. Jordan stumbled across the threshold, and the door swooshed shut behind him.

"Where was that bathroom?" he started to ask. He'd figure out some way to get the detox suit off if he had to.

But the girl's expression had changed so much it frightened Jordan. She was smirking at him the same way soccer or basketball opponents did when Jordan's teams lost by huge margins.

"I brought him in," she said. "I tricked him into coming with me without making a scene. Nobody thought I could do something like this, but I did."

"This is highly unusual," a man's muffled voice said from behind them. Jordan hadn't realized there was anyone else in the room, but apparently someone was standing beside the door, in a corner Jordan hadn't glanced toward. "And it's suspicious. Are you sure—"

The man broke off the instant Jordan glanced his way. And Jordan knew why.

The man by the door was JB.

THIRTY-SEVEN

JB! Jordan started to shout.

But JB's eyes went all wide and panicked and he shook his head quickly during the moment the girl turned toward Jordan.

Jordan swallowed his exuberant *JB!* and turned it into a cough. The girl looked back at JB, and JB instantly smoothed out his expression and stopped shaking his head.

"Interchronological Rescue is getting desperate, and desperation makes them dumb," the girl said scornfully.

"Perhaps," JB said. He seemed to be trying to hide a strain in his voice. "Or perhaps something else is going on. Why don't you let me interrogate the suspect, and then we'll draw conclusions."

Suspect? Jordan thought. *Wait—they're treating me like a criminal? So . . . I really am under arrest?*

The girl's smirk collapsed.

"*I* brought him to this room," she said forlornly. "I thought I could do the follow-up."

"Cira, believe me, you'll get full credit for this," JB said. "You are an excellent undercover agent. But so much is hanging in the balance right now—I'm sorry, but I'm going to have to pull rank on you on this one."

Undercover agent? Jordan thought. *Do undercover agents dress like candy stripers?*

JB patted the girl on the back. She didn't exactly look comforted.

"I'd let you sit in and help, but there may be information revealed that's beyond your security clearance," JB said, sounding truly sorry.

"I know, I know," the girl muttered. "Follow procedure. Everything in its own time. I'll finally be allowed to do the fun jobs with the agency by the time I'm eighty and on the verge of retirement."

Jordan almost felt sorry for her.

Though, geez, do people really wait until they're eighty to retire in this time period? he wondered.

Dejectedly, the girl turned and walked out the door.

As soon as the door shut behind her, JB called out, "Set security screens at highest levels."

Then he grabbed Jordan by the shoulders.

"What are you doing back here so quickly? What happened? Are you all right?" JB cried.

"Um . . . ," Jordan said, because his brain wasn't quite catching up. Why did JB look so worried? And what did he mean by "back here"? How could Jordan be back in a place he'd never been before? And "so quickly"? It'd been forever since Jordan had last seen JB.

Oh, wait, Jordan thought. *With time travel, it could be that for JB, we were together just a moment ago, even though I've been all over the place since the last time I saw him.*

Time travel really messed things up. And it still didn't explain the "back here" part of what JB had said.

"You were just here," JB said, like he was trying to prompt Jordan to agree.

"No, I wasn't," Jordan said irritably. Because if Jordan could figure out all that about time travel, wouldn't an actual time *agent* know it, too?

JB dropped his hands from Jordan's shoulders and took a step back. He seemed to be making a great effort to stay calm.

"I just sent you and Gavin home," JB said. "You just left. That *wasn't* the last time you saw me?"

"No," Jordan said with great scorn. "The last time I saw you, you were in my kitchen. This morning. I don't even know . . ." He was about to finish with *who Gavin is.* But something jarred in his brain.

Back home, back in my own kitchen, didn't that Chip kid say something about someone named Gavin? Jordan remembered.

It'd been when Chip was asking if Jordan and Jonah were famous. And then he'd listed people who were royalty, or the children of famous people, or people who were going to be famous in the future.

Gavin was someone Jonah knew. Maybe he was even one of the other kids who'd been on the plane with him.

Does JB actually think I'm Jonah? Seriously? Again?

Maybe if Jordan and Jonah had grown up together their whole lives, Jordan would have gotten used to people getting them confused. Maybe if they'd always been brothers, Jordan wouldn't mind it.

No, I think it would make me mad regardless, Jordan thought.

He opened his mouth to really yell at JB, to demand, *Can't you see my chin dimple's in a different place from Jonah's?* But in a flash JB clamped his hand over Jordan's mouth, keeping him from saying anything.

"Stop," JB said. "We have to be careful. You've seen me since the last time I saw you, so there's a huge danger of paradoxes. You *know* this."

Probably time-expert Jonah knew it, but Jordan was a little iffy on what was dangerous in time travel and what wasn't.

No, I know—everything is dangerous, Jordan thought.

"I'll admit, things worked out when we were dealing with the sixteen hundreds, and you and Katherine gave me information out of the proper sequence of time," JB said cautiously. "And then I was able to change a situation you'd already lived through. It was practically a miracle we didn't ruin everything. The odds against us being able to do something like that again—they're astronomical."

He really does think I'm Jonah, Jordan thought.

What if it was dangerous for JB to find out that Jordan wasn't Jonah? What if he was seeing JB in a time period before JB had even heard of Jordan?

But this is the future! I know this is after my time in the twenty-first century. . . .

Jordan's brain was inching toward a weird thought: Because of time travel, something in the future could happen *before* something in the past. Maybe this moment had happened in JB's life before JB had seen him in the twenty-first century, or even in the nineteen thirties.

Jordan remembered how Deep Voice and Mr. Rathbone had seemed not to recognize Jordan. Maybe they'd just been psyching him out, trying to make him feel worthless, but maybe they really hadn't known about him. Maybe it was because of the different dimensions. So could there be danger in JB recognizing Jordan now? Even if JB knew Jordan existed, even if there was lots of information available in this time period about Jordan, maybe JB wasn't supposed to know everything about him yet.

But clearly JB in this time period had already met Jonah. So would it be less dangerous if Jordan just acted like Jonah?

Now Jordan started worrying that maybe JB would notice Jordan's chin dimple being in the wrong place.

Jordan lifted his hands and shoved JB's away. Then Jordan made a show of keeping his own hand over his mouth and chin, as if he were only trying to show JB he would be careful not to blurt out anything that could ruin time. Really, he was hiding his chin dimple.

"Good," JB said. "You understand. Think carefully before you answer these questions. You being here . . . was that on purpose? Did you *plan* to come here, right now, or did somebody set you up?"

Was that *supposed* to be a trick question?

Jordan lowered his hand a little, so it covered only his chin.

"You mean, did anybody set me up besides that candy-striper undercover agent?" he asked. "I came to this time period on purpose, just not to this exact room."

"Whose Elucidator did you use?" JB asked, then waved his hands frantically, as if trying to erase his own words. "No, no, don't answer that. Too much potential for paradoxes."

"Could you . . . ," Jordan began. But he was lost. What if *anything* he asked JB might ruin time?

"I'll just go," Jordan said. "I'll go back to my own kitchen a split second after I last saw you, and if I talk to you there—I mean, then—that won't create any paradoxes."

Could he do that? Jordan hadn't liked JB much back when all of this mess first started. But Jordan really liked the idea of handing off responsibility to some trustworthy adult. If Jordan explained everything, surely JB would want to help. And he had to have a better idea of what to do than Jordan did.

But JB was shaking his head.

"You've been arrested here and now," he asked. "There's a whole time-agency file being put together automatically. We're just lucky Cira didn't recognize you, because she's so new on the job. I've delayed things a little by setting up this private interrogation, but as soon as we step out of this room, we'll both face an official investigation into how and why you got back here."

"Fine," Jordan said. "I'll just leave without stepping out of this room. Tell that girl she imagined everything about seeing me and arresting me. It's not like she has any proof."

Even as he spoke, he was pretty sure he was wrong. Probably every step he'd taken through the hospital had been captured on some sort of security camera. For all he knew, that girl might have a security camera embedded in her wrist along with a microphone.

There might even be some kind of tracking device in the stupid detox suit he was wearing. It felt weightless and unnoticeable, but who could say what it was capable of?

JB was still shaking his head.

"Don't you remember?" he asked. "This room is a dead zone. Nobody can time-travel directly into or out of this room. We set it up specially to protect you and Gavin while you were healing."

Just what happened with Jonah and this Gavin kid that they had to take so many precautions? Jordan wondered uncomfortably. *What were they healing from?*

"And Cira confiscated your Elucidator, anyhow," JB added.

"No, she didn't!" Jordan protested, reaching for his back pocket, where he'd stowed the Elucidator for safe-keeping while he and Kevin were traveling through time. Somehow the detox suit was flexible enough that he could still dig into his pocket.

He shoved his hand deeper and deeper. He twisted around and reached into his other back pocket, just in case he'd gotten confused.

Both of them were empty.

"How could she . . . ?" he began. "Did the detox suit . . . ? I didn't notice anything!"

"It may only be Cira's first week on the job, but she was

first in her class in Elucidator Recovery Training," JB said wryly.

Jordan stopped trying to dig into his pockets.

"Then give me your Elucidator," he said. "I'll run out the door before Cira notices, I'll yell for that Elucidator to take me . . . uh . . . someplace else . . ."

JB shook his head at that, too.

"My Elucidator is an agency-issued model that would be completely traceable," he said. "You and I would both end up in time prison before we had a chance to blink. I'm already on thin ice over that trick with giving Katherine access to my Elucidator so she could go back to 1918. Nobody believes that was an accident."

Jordan realized he'd heard Katherine talking about that same episode back home. Right before Jordan himself had snatched JB's Elucidator and soared off toward the future with his whole family and Jonah.

"We've got to plan this out before we take any action," JB continued. "Was there . . . was there anything specific you wanted to tell me first?"

Jordan remembered the problems he'd gotten his family into. Could he just make it so they never happened in the first place?

"Take a working Elucidator with you when you go back to the twenty-first century the morning of November, uh . . ." Would Jordan mess up everything just because he couldn't remember the exact date he'd stayed home sick from school and everything went crazy?

"I'm a time agent," JB said, as if he were offended. "I always take a working Elucidator with me when I travel through time."

"Not—" Jordan began. But JB cut him off.

"I promise, I'll double- and triple-check from now on," JB said quickly. He winced. "Jonah, where you came from—the time you came from—were you in danger?"

Jordan had to hold back an instant retort: *I'm not Jonah!* But he considered JB's question.

I don't even know where the real Jonah and Katherine are, he thought. *Or Mom and Dad. And I know I don't trust Second. Or Kevin.*

"Yes," Jordan said. "And it's not just me. All of us are in danger."

"All the missing children from history?" JB asked.

Before Jordan could say, *No, I mean all of us Skidmores,* a loud buzzer went off and a mechanical voice intoned, "Agent in peril! Your assistance is urgently needed outside!"

JB slammed his hand against the wall.

"Shields down!" JB screamed. "Let me see what's going on!"

The door slid away.

Cira the candy striper/undercover agent was down on the floor, wrestling with someone in a futuristic-looking close-fitted hospital gown.

Kevin? Jordan thought in amazement. *The teenage Second? He healed that fast?*

Kevin was facing away from Jordan, so he couldn't see the boy's face. But the shock of messy yellow hair looked right.

"Help! He's trying to steal the Elucidator!" Cira yelled.

"Use the evasive tactics you learned in your training!" JB called to her.

Jordan wasn't quite sure what happened next—maybe time travel was involved. But the next thing he knew, Cira stood triumphantly over Kevin, one foot on his back.

"I got it," Cira told JB. "I knew what to do. I just hadn't done it yet."

"Of course," JB said wryly, as if he didn't quite believe her.

Jordan took a step closer to Cira. She seemed a little distracted trying to convince JB that she'd done everything right. Jordan could see the outline of an Elucidator—*his* Elucidator, small and round and battery-like—in the front pocket of her candy-striper smock. What if he just grabbed it himself and screamed, *Get me out of here!* Wouldn't that solve his problems? *His* Elucidator wasn't a time-agency one with all the tracking info. It had come from Mr. Rathbone.

Jordan slid his right foot just a bit closer, ready to launch himself at Cira and the Elucidator.

And then something—no, some*one*—slammed into Jordan. It was Kevin, springing up from the floor.

"Everybody freeze!" Kevin screamed, as he wrapped his arms around Jordan's shoulders. "Give me that Elucidator or I'll snap this boy's neck!"

THIRTY-EIGHT

"I saved your life!" Jordan protested. "Or—at least your spine! You passed out from the pain and I brought you here! This is how you thank me?"

"Sometimes life sucks," Kevin mumbled in Jordan's ear.

The boy cowered behind Jordan's shoulder. Jordan recognized this pose from a million TV shows and movies: Kevin was using Jordan's body as a shield. Kevin wasn't even showing his face. So JB and Cira wouldn't dare try to shoot Kevin, because Jordan was in the way.

"Slide the Elucidator across the floor," Kevin demanded. "Right to me."

He stuck out a foot, making it clear that that was where he wanted to catch the Elucidator.

They can't even shoot him in the ankle because . . . what are those, army boots under his hospital gown? Jordan wondered.

Or is that just part of the hospital outfit in the future?

It was horrifying how much Jordan didn't know. And how powerless he felt right now. How paralyzed.

"You think taking a hostage is the best approach?" JB asked in a cautious, measured tone that sounded like every hostage negotiator Jordan had ever heard on TV or in the movies.

"Seems to be working so far, doesn't it?" Kevin taunted. "Quick! Give me that Elucidator!"

Cira eased the small, silver Elucidator from her pocket. She held it high, as if to show Kevin that she was doing exactly what he wanted.

And then she screamed, "Think again, time primitive!" and aimed the Elucidator right at Jordan and Kevin.

Jordan didn't hear anything—not even a ping—but suddenly Kevin slumped toward the floor, pulling Jordan down with him.

"He didn't know our stun gun setting can work on the *second* body it encounters," Cira crowed triumphantly. "It's so fun dealing with time primitives!"

"Uh . . . are you sure you didn't knock out *both* boys?" JB asked, a bit too loudly.

Even as he spoke, JB strode across the floor. Jordan could hear the footsteps. Then the toe of JB's shoe nudged Jordan's shoulder in a way that didn't seem accidental.

Is he trying to tell me something? Jordan wondered.

He couldn't figure out what it was, so he just lay still a moment longer. He seemed to be covering Kevin's body; Kevin sprawled facedown and apparently totally unconscious beneath him.

JB grabbed Jordan's arm and yanked him away from Kevin.

"Keep your eyes closed, but be ready." JB leaned close to whisper in Jordan's ear. He pressed his fingers against Jordan's neck—was he covering by pretending to check Jordan's pulse?

"This one doesn't seem injured, but he is unconscious," JB said loudly, clearly talking to Cira again. "You checked out that Elucidator you confiscated and determined it would be safe to discharge in an emergency like this, correct? And you had it set for voice commands only for the person touching it?"

Why's he asking about that? Jordan wondered. *Is he trying to tell me something? Does he expect me to leap up and wrestle the Elucidator from Cira and actually get away?*

He decided to wait for Cira's answer.

"Of course," Cira said. Her voice shook. "I followed procedure."

"I'm sure you did," JB said soothingly. "But . . . let me see that Elucidator myself. The one you took from this boy and used just now."

He's definitely setting something up, Jordan thought. *But how will I know when whatever I'm supposed to be ready for is going to happen?*

He dared to open one eye just a crack, enough to see Cira reaching over him to hand JB the Elucidator.

"Got it," JB said. "Oh—oops!"

Something hit Jordan's stomach: the Elucidator. JB had dropped the Elucidator on Jordan.

He did that on purpose, didn't he? Jordan wondered. Then he told himself: *Who cares? It happened! This is my chance!*

Jordan wrapped his hands around the Elucidator.

"Get me out of here!" he screamed.

JB, Cira, Kevin, and the hospital hallway all vanished instantly.

THIRTY-NINE

Jordan spun through time. It seemed to go on and on and on, just him and the darkness and the spinning.

"Where are you taking me?" Jordan asked the Elucidator.

YOU JUST SAID "OUT OF HERE" the Elucidator glowed back at him. I'M NOT TAKING YOU ANYWHERE AT THE MOMENT.

Jordan realized he was just spinning in place. No wonder he was starting to feel sick to his stomach.

"Take me to my family," he said, and it felt so good to say those words.

SECOND TOLD YOU THEY WEREN'T ALL IN THE SAME PLACE, REMEMBER? the Elucidator glowed again.

How could a mere glowing light actually look snarky?

Jordan remembered the wording Second had gotten him to use. This time he was going to add to it a bit.

"Take me where I can make a difference—in a way that leads to rescuing my family," he said.

IF YOU INSIST the Elucidator flashed back.

Jordan began to speed forward. Now he could see lights in the distance that seemed to be moving closer.

Jordan thought of something else to worry about.

"That girl Cira couldn't follow me, could she?" he asked. "I mean, because you're not a time-agency Elucidator. Or would there be tracking in the detox suit? Should I—"

He tried reaching for the collar of the suit, to pull it off, but it seemed to have vanished.

IT'S GONE the Elucidator assured him. IT FINISHED DETERIORATING WHEN YOU WERE SPINNING. SO DON'T WORRY. NO ONE FROM THE TIME AGENCY CAN TRACE US.

Jordan didn't quite trust the way the Elucidator put that.

"Can Second?" he asked. "Can the teenage Second—or Kevin, or whatever his name is?"

But before the Elucidator could answer, Jordan hit the point of time travel where he felt like all the tiniest particles of his body were coming apart. He stopped being able to think.

The next thing he knew, he was lying on his back on a hard floor.

Back in the futuristic lab again? he wondered. *Or back in the time hollow? Or back home again in the kitchen? Or somewhere with at least one of my family members?*

Dizzily, he sat up and blinked until his eyes started coming into focus.

Blank walls again. Featureless floor and ceiling.

"I'm in the time hollow again? Or is it a different one and I just can't tell?" he asked the Elucidator.

DOES IT MATTER? the Elucidator flashed back at him. MOST TIME HOLLOWS ARE PRETTY INTERCHANGEABLE.

Jordan tried to look around a little more carefully. He really couldn't tell if it was the same place he'd been before.

His senses came back a bit more, and he remembered the teenage Second landing on him the last time he was in a time hollow.

"So who's going to fall on me this time?" he asked. "What should I be prepared for?"

DON'T WORRY the Elucidator flashed back. YOU'RE ALONE HERE UNTIL YOU MAKE A DIFFERENCE.

Jordan snorted.

"How do I make a difference in an empty room, all by myself?" he asked.

YOU THINK. YOU LEARN. YOU GROW glowed above the Elucidator. AND MAYBE YOU'RE NOT AS ALONE AS YOU THINK. YOU NEVER ARE.

Jordan snorted again.

"That sounds like something Mom would say," he complained.

He didn't want to think about Mom right now, not even about her annoying him.

JUST BECAUSE IT SOUNDS LIKE YOUR MOTHER, THAT DOESN'T MEAN IT'S WRONG the Elucidator retorted.

Jordan swallowed hard.

"Can you at least . . . show me where Mom and Dad are right now?" he asked. He remembered how useless that question had been when he'd asked the same thing about Gary and Hodge. "Or at least . . . where Second took them after the last time I saw them?"

YOU'RE GETTING BETTER AT ASKING QUESTIONS the Elucidator complimented him.

And then the wall in front of Jordan lit up with such a clear image that Jordan felt like the wall must have disappeared, and he was looking into another room.

There were the teen versions of Mom and Dad, standing absolutely still.

"Mom! Dad!" Jordan yelled, scrambling up and running toward them at top speed.

His face smashed into the very hard, very real wall. Even if he couldn't see it, the wall was still there.

"Let me *through*!" Jordan demanded, turning his smashed face toward the Elucidator. Nothing hurt, probably because he was in a time hollow, but what if he'd actually broken his nose? He had to run his fingers over it to make sure it was still okay.

YOU WANT TO BE IN THE DARK EMPTINESS OF OUTER TIME

AGAIN? the Elucidator glowed back at him. It hurt to squint at the words. Maybe he'd broken his eye sockets.

"I want to be in that other room with Mom and Dad!" Jordan said. "The one just on the other side of this wall!"

THERE'S NOT A ROOM ON THE OTHER SIDE OF THE WALL. YOU ARE JUST WATCHING A—WHAT WOULD YOU CALL IT IN YOUR TIME?—A VIDEO OF YOUR PARENTS the Elucidator told him. DO I NEED TO EXPLAIN THE CONCEPT?

Jordan frowned. He was acting like a little kid who thought the people on TV were really inside the screen. And he'd seen this kind of thing before, back in the time hollow he'd landed in with Mom, Dad, Katherine, and Jonah.

It was easier to be fooled now that he was alone.

"They just looked so real," he mumbled. "It confused me."

He took a step back from the wall and peered toward the image of his parents. Now that he knew it was just an image, they seemed impossibly far away.

"You say this is *video*? Why aren't they moving?" Jordan asked. "They're still alive, right?"

Even as he asked the question, he wasn't actually that worried that they were dead. His parents were standing as still as wax statues, but they looked completely real, completely alive.

SECOND PUT THEM IN SUSPENDED ANIMATION, the Elucidator glowed back at him.

Motionless, both of his parents looked even younger than they had back home in their own kitchen or in the lab or time hollow they'd been in before. Dad looked like a middle-school boy who'd just heard a fart joke. Or was about to tell one. Mom's hair flipped out in a goofy way that she never would have allowed as a grown-up, and everything about her was so childish that it didn't seem weird that she was wearing Katherine's sparkly CHEER! sweatshirt.

Jordan remembered how, when Second had first taken his parents away, he'd wanted them back to fix all his problems. He remembered how, when he was a little kid, he'd thought they could do anything. He'd thought they were superheroes.

"Rescue me," he whispered, too softly for the Elucidator in his hand to hear.

Right now, his parents didn't look like they could rescue anyone. They were the ones who needed him.

Jordan cleared his throat.

"Show me where Second sent Katherine and Jonah," he asked, trying to sound authoritative.

WOULD YOU LIKE TO SEE A SPLIT SCREEN, WITH THEM AS WELL AS YOUR PARENTS? the Elucidator asked.

"Sure," Jordan said.

Instantly it was like another window opened up on the wall, showing another pair of Skidmores. Katherine and Jonah stood just as motionless as their parents. But there was something fiercer and more defensive about their stance, as if they'd been trying to fight back against Second in the moment before he froze them in place.

"Let me guess," Jordan said to the Elucidator. "Suspended animation again?"

YES the Elucidator glowed back at him.

"Why?" Jordan asked. "What was Second trying to accomplish, freezing all of them?"

YOU ARE NOT READY TO HEAR THAT EXPLANATION the Elucidator told him.

"Why not?" Jordan asked.

THAT IS NOT FOR ME TO ANSWER the Elucidator glowed back. YOU'LL UNDERSTAND WHEN THE TIME COMES.

"Oh, thanks a lot," Jordan said sarcastically. "Can't I time-travel to wherever and whenever the time comes?"

He felt really smart saying that, but the Elucidator just flashed back at him, NO.

Evidently, the Elucidator didn't have much of a sense of humor.

Jordan spent a moment longer peering at his parents and Katherine and Jonah. Somehow it was Jonah his eyes kept returning to.

Take a selfie—it'll last longer, Jordan told himself. Except for the old-fashioned clothes and the placement of the chin dimple, Jonah really did look almost exactly like Jordan. No wonder people kept confusing them.

But the longer he stared at Jonah, the more differences Jordan saw. Jonah wasn't just Jordan's mirror image. In a way Jordan couldn't even put his finger on, Jonah looked braver. Also steadier, more composed, and better prepared.

So why is he the one frozen and I'm the only one who can do anything? Jordan wondered.

He took a deep breath and turned back to the Elucidator.

"Okay," Jordan said. "Tell me how I can rescue all of them without Second finding out."

THAT IS NOT WHAT YOU SHOULD BE CONCERNED ABOUT the Elucidator told him.

"Yes, it is," Jordan insisted. "I have to rescue my family!"

YOU DON'T KNOW ENOUGH FOR THAT YET the Elucidator replied.

"Then tell me! Show me! Whatever! Let me do what I need to do to get ready!" Jordan exploded.

ALL RIGHT the Elucidator flashed back. WATCH AND LEARN.

Its slow, steady light seemed maddeningly calm.

The images of Jordan's parents and Katherine and Jonah vanished from the wall, replaced by a familiar scene: JB and Cira standing over Kevin's unconscious body in the hospital hallway Jordan had just left.

Am I seeing what happened immediately after I left? Jordan wondered.

"We're both going to be in so much trouble for that," Cira was saying. She kept turning her head toward the spot where Jordan had been lying, as if she expected him to come back. So probably he had just vanished.

Cira cleared her throat, as if she was trying very hard to sound and act professional.

"Can you trace that Elucidator?" she asked.

JB was looking down at something cupped in the palm of his hand—probably his own Elucidator.

"No luck," he said in a clipped voice. "Look, I'll make it clear in my report that I was the one who dropped that. None of the blame will reflect on you. Since it's my mistake, I'll do what I can to pursue the boy who escaped. You take care of identifying and processing that time criminal."

He pointed at Kevin, who was still facedown.

I bet JB doesn't even realize who that is, Jordan thought. *He probably never got a glimpse of Kevin's face.*

Cira and Kevin and the hospital melted away, and Jordan watched JB floating through time.

"Can't you just summarize this a little, so I only see the important parts?" Jordan asked the Elucidator.

OF COURSE I CAN the Elucidator replied. YOU HAVE ALL THE TIME IN THE WORLD IN A TIME HOLLOW. I THOUGHT YOU WOULD WANT TO BE THOROUGH, BUT IF NOT . . .

"I don't want to die of old age waiting for your video to get to the important parts," Jordan complained.

TECHNICALLY, NO ONE COULD DIE OF OLD AGE IN A TIME HOLLOW the Elucidator said.

"You know what I mean," Jordan said.

Evidently, the Elucidator did, because the next thing Jordan saw was JB and a tall, beautiful African-American woman riding in a car together. The woman looked vaguely familiar, and Jordan couldn't figure out why. Then she winced as if deeply worried, and Jordan recognized her.

Angela? he thought. This had to be the girl who'd shown up at his house with the teenage versions of his parents. Only in this scene, she was an adult.

She'd been really pretty as a teenager. As an adult, she was intimidatingly gorgeous. If Jordan had been JB, he would have been stammering and blushing and having trouble putting two words together.

JB was just slamming his hand against the dashboard.

"Yes, I'm certain that something's going to happen this morning!" he shouted. "I can't tell you the nature of the warning we received—it's incredibly complicated—but all the missing children from the plane are in danger! We've got to make sure Jonah and Chip are okay!"

Why does he think all those kids are in danger? Jordan wondered.

Could it possibly be because of what Jordan told him?

When Jordan actually meant that his whole family was in danger?

Jordan started to say, *Elucidator, is there any way I can get a message to JB, so he at least worries about the right things?* But just then Angela and JB both jerked back, as if they'd been hit by some mysterious force. The camera's focus narrowed to Angela. By the time she'd straightened back up to her original position, everything had changed. She was a teenager again, crying out, "Why can't I reach the gas pedal anymore? What happened?"

A kid suddenly sitting beside her yelled, "I'll help! I'll hit the brake!"

He dived down for the pedals at Angela's feet.

"No!" Angela yelled back at him. "You're going to make me crash! I just need to scoot down a little! I've got it! Stay back!"

She took one hand off the steering wheel and grabbed the kid by the shoulder, shoving him so forcefully that he slammed against the door on the opposite side of the car.

Shouldn't he have knocked into JB instead? Jordan wondered. *JB was on that side of the car.*

His brain was just slow catching up. This was like some logic problem they'd hand out in school: *A man and a woman are riding together in a car. Suddenly the woman turns back into a teenager. There's a teenage boy sitting beside her now, and the man is* missing. *What happened to the man? Where did the teenage boy come from?*

No, that was way too strange to be a logic problem they'd hand out in school. But Jordan knew the answer: The adult JB had turned into a kid again too. Now that Jordan was thinking that way, he could see the resemblance between the adult JB and the gawky, skinny kid sitting beside teenage Angela.

Jordan took a step back from the images spread before him on the wall.

"Explain!" he yelled at the Elucidator. "JB was turned back into a teenager again, but there was a cure for him when there wasn't one for Angela or my parents? Why? Why can't whoever helped JB help Mom and Dad, too? Why isn't this problem already solved?"

The Elucidator seemed to be taking forever to answer. Then it flashed two words:

KEEP WATCHING.

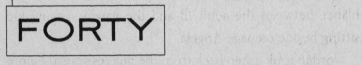

FORTY

At first it was excruciating for Jordan to force himself to sit down and pay attention to the continuing scene playing out on the wall. JB and Angela were in a panic over turning into teenagers . . . they were arguing over who was safest driving the car . . . they were turning corners recklessly . . .

Come on! Jordan thought impatiently. *Show JB changing back so I know how it can work for my parents!*

Then Jordan realized Angela and JB were speeding down the streets of his own neighborhood. Moments later they were face to face with . . .

That's not me, Jordan had to remind himself. *That's Jonah.*

Jordan was kind of impressed with how forceful Jonah was with JB, demanding help for Mom and Dad and a vanished Katherine.

So this was after Katherine was kidnapped by Charles Lindbergh, Jordan realized. *Jonah doesn't know yet that she's going to come back, safe and sound and sassy as ever.*

Jordan didn't let himself think about how quickly she would vanish again, kidnapped by Second this time.

Keep watching, he told himself. *Keep watching.*

On the screen JB and Angela, and now Jonah, too, were running around in a panic, then speeding away in a car with an unconscious—and teenage—Mom and Dad. Seemingly just moments later JB, Angela, and Jonah were dangling from the side of an old-fashioned airplane, high above an endless stretch of water.

Okay, I guess Jonah really did have to endure a lot of problems, traveling through time, Jordan thought grudgingly.

He found himself watching in awe as Jonah endured more time-travel dangers, lost JB and Angela, and had to face off against Gary and Hodge all by himself. Meanwhile, the young JB seemed to be slipping into madness, overcome with guilt and worry.

Jordan himself showed up on the screen as an infant, and Jordan watched as Jonah struggled to deliver Jordan to their parents.

Would I have worked so hard to do that, faced with all the same odds Jonah faced? Jordan wondered.

Now Jonah was challenging Charles Lindbergh. Now

Lindbergh was leaving Jonah with a planeload of babies, the fate of every single one of them—and time itself—in Jonah's hands.

I'm glad it was him and not me! Jordan thought.

Jonah sent the planeload of babies away from the nineteen thirties. And then the scene shifted back to teenage JB, who was sitting in a car, staring off at nothing, his expression blank. Jordan could tell it was the same car JB had been in with Angela, but it seemed to be parked in a cave now, and JB was alone.

Suddenly a hooded figure appeared beside the car door and leaned in through an open window toward JB.

"JB, I'm going to take care of you," the figure whispered. "The time agency must never find out. You and I both know they wouldn't approve."

And then, before Jordan's eyes, JB turned into an adult again. The figure slipped something into JB's hand: a familiar-looking cell phone.

Could that be the exact same cell phone JB had in our kitchen? Jordan wondered. *The one I stole, that was actually a faulty Elucidator?*

Being an adult again seemed to startle JB out of his blankness. He glanced down at the cell phone/Elucidator in his grasp. His gaze seemed to linger on his own hand, as if he was figuring out that he wasn't a teenager anymore.

"Angela?" he called. "Jonah?"

He turned his head to the right, toward the hooded figure standing beside the car. Jordan was eager for JB to see the figure, maybe JB would know who it was. Maybe he'd call out the person's name, and Jordan could go find that person and get him or her to cure Jordan's parents, too.

The figure spun away from JB, his motion exactly synchronized to JB's. At the instant JB's head turned far enough that he would have seen the figure, the figure vanished completely.

But not before Jordan got a view of the figure's face. Not before Jordan got his biggest surprise of the day— which was really saying something, given that his day had included so many surprises.

Because Jordan knew the person who had returned JB to his proper age.

It was Second.

FORTY-ONE

"This doesn't make sense!" Jordan screamed at the Elucidator in his hand.

WHY NOT? the Elucidator asked. But the words sounded aloud, as well as glowing above the Elucidator. Either the Elucidator had reset itself, or someone behind him had also asked, "Why not?"

Jordan whirled around. The adult Second was standing right there. Second dropped a hood from his head, revealing his familiar shock of bright blond hair. Jordan guessed he was wearing the same hooded cloak he'd had on when he'd helped JB.

Jordan took a step back, but that only meant he was trapped against the wall.

"Aren't . . . aren't you and JB enemies?" Jordan stammered. "Aren't you on opposite sides? Why would you help him?"

Second tilted his head thoughtfully.

"Is it possible for you to see the, shall we say, multiple dimensionality of this situation?" Second asked. "I know your recent experiences—and your siblings' prejudices—have convinced you to think of me as a villain. But what if I'm capable of being a hero, too?"

"Why would I trust you?" Jordan asked, his back against the wall.

"I know how to cure your parents," Second said.

Jordan could feel the wall digging into his spine. Or his spine digging into the wall. Whatever.

See, I can see the—what did Second call it? The multiple dimensionality?—of this situation, Jordan thought.

He had a choice of how to answer Second. He went for the default mode of a seventh-grade boy: sarcasm.

"Oh, right, and you're the only person in the whole world who can do that," Jordan said.

He was about to add, *So, thanks, but I'll find someone else to do that. Someone I really can trust!*

But Second wasn't reacting in a predictable way. The corners of his mouth turned up into a slow, sad smile.

"You could twist yourself into knots over the exact definition of 'only' in that sentence," Second said. "But yes, that's pretty much the sum of it. I am the only one who can help your parents."

Was he lying? Telling the truth? Just trying to trick Jordan?

Jordan decided the last option was the likeliest.

"Oh, yeah?" he said. "Then why didn't you just help them right from the beginning? Why didn't you change them at the same time you changed JB?"

Second didn't move a muscle, but somehow his smile looked even more forlorn than before.

"Remind me—what did Jonah and Katherine tell you about me?" he asked.

"That you're their worst enemy," Jordan said, and it felt strangely good to say that out loud. "That you rearranged time and split it and created some other dimension. You almost ruined everything. And then you taught Gary and Hodge how to mess things up too."

"And you trust Jonah and Katherine's opinions," Second said. He toyed with the button on his cloak.

"Are you trying to convince me I shouldn't trust them?" Jordan asked. "You think I'm more likely to trust you than my own . . ."

He stopped.

"Were you about to say 'brother and sister'?" Second asked, leaning closer. "Have you grown to feel that way about Jonah?"

"Are you trying to manipulate that, too?" Jordan asked, trying to distract Second.

He *had* been about to say *brother and sister.* Did he really think of Jonah that way? When had that happened?

Second confuses me too much for me to know what I think, Jordan told himself.

Second didn't answer Jordan's question.

"Jonah and Katherine have good reason to despise me," Second said instead. "I did . . . push them to the brink. Mostly just for my own entertainment. I nearly destroyed all of time just because I was curious about what would happen without all the time-agency regulations. I craved that knowledge beyond all reason."

Jordan didn't know what to say.

"A well-educated young man might point out that I'm describing my errors—my sins, you might say—in very recognizable ways," Second said. "I was Pandora, bound and determined to open that box. I was Adam and Eve, unable to resist the temptation of eating from the Tree of Knowledge of Good and Evil."

"I *have* heard of Pandora and Adam and Eve," Jordan said. He wasn't going to admit that he hadn't been thinking about any of them. He'd still been thinking about Katherine and Jonah.

"You probably think I'm confessing," Second said. "You probably think I'm trying to convince you to tell Jonah and Katherine to forgive me."

"Then will you help my parents?" Jordan asked. "Then can we all just go back to normal life?"

He'd seen the expressions on Jonah's and Katherine's faces every time they'd encountered Second. He didn't think it would be easy for them to forgive Second. But maybe they would do it to help their parents.

Or maybe we could just trick Second into thinking they'd forgiven him? Jordan wondered.

Second sighed. "Let me show you something," he said, turning to the wall where Jordan had just watched JB return to his proper age.

Jordan stepped back from the wall and away from Second as the man ran his fingers in a careful pattern against the wall. Jordan guessed he was programming in some sort of command.

"You know from Jonah and Katherine that I created my own dimension, my own little world," Second said. "This is what it ended up looking like."

On the wall, a scene sparked to life: two men in heavy wool coats leaning over the edge of a boat.

"You—" one man said.

Then both men vanished. The wall was blank for a moment, then the scene came back. This time one of the men had his coat drawn higher over his ears.

"You—" the man said again.

"Let's try another time period," Second said.

Now it was a man and a woman sitting at a table.

"Should—" the woman said.

The scene flashed out of sight again.

"I think your Elucidator is broken," Jordan said. "Or your TV or computer or whatever's showing those images."

"No, it's my world that's broken," Second said sadly. "That's all that's left of it. Flickers of existence, and then it's gone. I ruined everything. I destroyed it all."

FORTY-TWO

Jordan believed him.

It was weird: He didn't like Second, and he still didn't trust him. But somehow he was certain that Second was telling the truth.

About this, anyway.

"Well, um, the real world's still okay, right?" Jordan asked. It was almost as if he were trying to comfort Second. "Real time, I mean. If you just created that other dimension to play around with—and if it was dangerous to real time—then who cares if it broke?"

For some reason, he found he had a lot more to say to Second about this topic.

"Maybe you should think of your other dimension like . . . like a video game or a movie or a book," Jordan said. "It seemed real to you while you were playing it or watching it or reading it. Whatever. It *felt* like it mattered. But it really didn't. So . . . no problem. Let it go. Move on."

Maybe Jordan didn't have a great future ahead of him as a guidance counselor or a therapist or anything like that. Second's expression just got sadder and sadder with every word Jordan spoke. The corners of his mouth drooped more and more.

"Don't you want to know *why* my world failed?" Second asked.

Jordan was so tempted to say no. He didn't want any part of the sadness that was clearly weighing Second down.

"I think you're going to tell me, whether I want to know or not," Jordan said.

This at least earned Jordan a rueful head shake from Second.

"You can accuse me of hubris," Second said. "You can accuse me of playing God. You can—"

"I don't want to accuse you of anything," Jordan said. "I just want—"

"I know, I know," Second said. "You just want your family back. You just want your life to be normal again. Who are you—Dorothy in Oz? She goes to an incredible place like the Land of Oz, and the whole time she's there all she wants to do is go home?"

Jordan didn't like that comparison. He wasn't some girl

in a gingham dress and stupid sparkly shoes. He didn't even have a dog. Still, he felt compelled to defend Dorothy.

"She was worried about her family," Jordan said. "Auntie Em and, well, whatever her uncle's name was. If she'd had them with her—or just known they were okay—she would have been really happy to hang out with the Munchkins and all, and enjoy Oz. Not so much the Wicked Witch, though."

He cast a worried glance at Second. Was Second as much like the Wicked Witch of the West as Katherine and Jonah seemed to believe? Or was he more like the Wizard of Oz, someone hiding behind a fake image?

What if Second was just trying to trick Jordan again, trying to get him to think that anything about his situation was like Dorothy's in Oz?

"Can we skip the language arts lesson and go back to talking about rescuing my parents?" Jordan asked.

Second sank to the floor. Jordan felt weird towering over him, so he crouched down beside the man.

"You *can* help my parents, can't you?" Jordan asked.

Second stared fixedly at a point on the floor a few feet from Jordan's knee.

"The time agency always thought time travel itself endangered reality," he mumbled. "They thought, if any human can travel through time and change the past or watch the future, doesn't that alone destabilize the space-time continuum?"

"Does it?" Jordan asked.

Second glanced up and let his eyes meet Jordan's for the briefest of instants. Then he went back to staring at the floor.

"The truth is, time travel is hard, and people are lazy," he said. "It twists your brain in knots, and after a few experiences of unintended consequences, most people will choose lives of comfort over constant exploration and change. From the very beginning of my new world, humanity disappointed me."

"Why? Because the people in your world did what *they* wanted instead of what *you* wanted them to do?" Jordan asked. He wasn't sure why Second was making him so mad all of a sudden. "Why didn't you just stay home and play Sims? That lets you control people!"

Unexpectedly, Jordan's outburst earned him a grin from Second.

"See, you *are* going to accuse me of playing God," he said.

"I mean—" Jordan began.

Second waved away his interruption.

"Truthfully, I deserve that accusation," he said. "I thought I was smarter than God. I thought the world I created would be better than the original world."

"Gary and Hodge pretty much told you you were the smartest person ever," Jordan said, remembering the scene he'd watched in the laboratory at Interchronological Rescue. "Though, did that really happen after all, since Katherine and Jonah and I went back and rescued you as a thirteen-year-old?"

Second didn't answer that question. He went back to staring at the floor.

"In the original world, time travel had built-in limits, even without the limits the time agency added," he said. "Time is very good at protecting itself against paradoxes."

"So why does the time agency worry so much?" Jordan asked. "JB just about freaked out when I . . ."

Should he tell Second what had happened with JB at the hospital?

Was there any chance that Second didn't already know? He *had* been able to follow Jordan to the time hollow, when the Elucidator said no one could do that.

No—the Elucidator said no one from the time agency could do that, Jordan remembered. *It never answered the question about whether Second could do that.*

Jordan gasped. "Are you the one who's been controlling the Elucidators from the very beginning?" he asked. He remembered wondering about the Elucidator Second had left with JB. That had to be the same faulty Elucidator JB had had in the Skidmore family kitchen, didn't it? The one Jordan swiped?

Jordan looked down at the Elucidator he was clutching in his hand at this very moment. It was the Elucidator Mr. Rathbone had handed Jonah at Interchronological Rescue. The one that teenage Second had stolen right out of Jonah's hand.

"So you were the one who set up Mr. Rathbone, too, to send us back to rescue you at a younger age," Jordan said.

Second started shaking his head so forcefully that his messy hair trembled.

"No," he said. "No. I *did* have control over the Elucidator I gave JB. He needed to think he was in contact with the time agency, but I needed to keep the rest of the agency in the dark. That was a necessary deception."

"But this one—" Jordan held up the Elucidator that had come from Mr. Rathbone.

"I *wish* I'd had total control of that one," Second said, lifting his own hands in a show of innocence. "I'm just lucky I could do anything with it. I could track it and follow you here."

Second's voice held so much pain that Jordan hesitated.

"But you thought . . . I mean, the teenage version of you thought . . . that he'd gotten a message from his older self about how to unlock this Elucidator," Jordan said. "He thought the instructions had come from you!"

Second just stared at Jordan.

"You saw Mr. Rathbone program that Elucidator," Second said. "It was based on information he'd gotten from Gary and Hodge. Because all three of them wanted the idea I had in my head even as a thirteen-year-old. The idea that destroyed my world. And that will destroy your world unless we stop it."

"Okay, okay, let's stop it!" Jordan snapped.

Second just stared at Jordan. The man's eyes seemed sadder than ever.

"Don't you understand yet?" he asked. "It's the same idea that you want to use to rescue and fix your parents. Saving your parents means destroying the world."

FORTY-THREE

For a moment, Jordan could only gape at Second.

"Are you saying they have to stay teenagers forever?" he finally asked. "Or, well, just grow up alongside Katherine and me? And, uh, Jonah? And Angela?"

For a moment he tried to imagine this: his normal life along with a new twin brother and his parents always the same age as him. They'd have to have someone come and stay with them to act like actual adults. Maybe their grandparents? And he guessed someone would have to figure out the whole money thing, so they could afford food and everything else. And . . .

"No, I'm not saying they'd have to stay teenagers forever or grow up with you and Katherine and Jonah," Second said irritably. "Don't you see what a huge disruption in time that would be, to have your parents consistently thirty years too young for the rest of their lives? And remember, it's not just them. The ages of some sixty other adults were knocked back at the same time. Time can't survive that big of a change for very long."

"So if we change my parents and the others back to their right ages, the world ends," Jordan said. "And if we don't change them back, the world ends. Isn't there another choice?"

Second's eyes bored into Jordan's.

"I think you're ready to hear what went wrong with the alternate world I created," he said softly.

Jordan nodded, but Second didn't launch into his story right away.

"What's the best thing about time travel?" Second asked. "Or, I should say, what would you have said the best thing was before you actually traveled through time?"

Jordan considered this question seriously.

"Getting to see the future," he said. "And . . . getting to see my own future."

It was kind of disappointing that in all his travels through time, he hadn't yet had a chance to look at his own life when he was, say, twenty-five. Or whenever he'd be all grown up and doing whatever he was supposed to do as an adult. Maybe he'd be a professional basketball player by then. Maybe he'd have made a million dollars somehow. Maybe . . .

"Okay," Second said. "So what if you see your own future and you're *not* rich and famous? What if your future's not even mediocre? What if it kind of sucks?"

"Then you go back in time and make it so you are rich and famous in the future. Or . . . whatever your goal is," Jordan said, just so Second didn't think he only cared about being rich and famous.

"Right," Second said. "That, I've found, is how most people think. Or if their present sucks, they want to go back to the past to fix that. The principle's the same."

"So that's what messed up your world?" Jordan asked. "People kept wanting to go back and forth in time to change things?"

"No," Second said. "That's not what ruined everything. Because it's still hard. People can't duplicate themselves in time, so they'd have to figure out a work-around for that. And they'd have to be willing to go through a potentially dangerous un-aging process to go back to whatever age they were when they could make a difference. Then they'd have to do all the hard work of, say, practicing the bassoon for six hours every single day for twenty years so they'd be champion bassoonists. Or athletes, or whatever they were aiming for. With time travel, a lot of people did learn from their mistakes and changes their lives the second or third time around. But a lot of people . . . didn't."

"So people ruined your world because not enough of them wanted to work hard enough to become champion bassoonists?" Jordan asked.

That made Second chuckle. But it was a sad chuckle.

"No," he said. "People ruined my world because I remembered something I started thinking about when I was a thirteen-year-old climbing a fence. It was about a way to skip over the unpleasant parts of life. Without consequences."

Jordan remembered wishing he could use time travel to skip the boring parts of school.

"You mean, like, your body would feel like you'd eaten your spinach, but you didn't ever have to taste it?" Jordan asked.

Second wrinkled his nose.

"In my case, as a teenager, it was that my father would feel he'd had the satisfaction of beating me, but I didn't ever have to experience it," he said. "But yes, I think you have the general principle."

"Everybody would want that," Jordan said.

"Right," Second said. "The problem is, if people skip too many parts of their lives, they're constantly the wrong age. Others can tell they've stepped out of time. And, well, that they've cheated, and haven't actually earned anything they accomplished."

"But if everyone's doing that, who cares?" Jordan argued.

"Time cares," Second said. "Time makes barriers to that. So I thought I was fixing everything when I made it possible for people to readjust their ages any time they wanted. Time travelers knew almost from the very beginning how to do that with kids. But it was always seen as an impossibility with adults. Before my brilliant idea."

There was still some pride in his voice—pride at his own brilliance. But somehow it was mixed with shame.

Jordan waited for Second to explain what happened next. But the man seemed strangely out of words.

Jordan tried to figure it out for himself.

"I guess . . . I guess if anybody can change anything they want, anytime, and be any age they want, anytime, then nothing's stable," Jordan said. "Nobody's reliable. Nobody could count on anyone or anything."

"Exactly," Second said. "And so my world ended. And kept ending every time I restarted it. Just like your world—the real world—would end if I made your parents the right age again."

Jordan shoved back a lock of hair that had fallen into his eyes. He couldn't believe Second was giving up.

"Oh, come on—this is *easy*," he said. "You were able to change JB back to the right age without the secret destroying the whole world, right? All you have to do is change my parents and Angela and the other messed-up adults. And then you don't ever change any other adult's age. And you don't share your secret with anyone."

Second's expression didn't change. No, wait—it did. He looked sadder than ever.

"It's already too late for that," he said.

"What?" Jordan asked. "No, it's not! What were you just telling me? The way you can mess around with time and adults' ages—doesn't that mean it's never too late for anything? Anything can change anytime?"

Second lowered his head.

"Certain things are final," he said. "You should have watched every single second of what happened after I made JB the right age again. You need to know that I couldn't even manage to keep that secret."

"What are you talking about?" Jordan demanded. "Who found out? The time agency?"

"No," Second said. "The person who killed me."

"Killed you?" Jordan repeated numbly. "But . . . you're still alive! You're sitting right in front of me! Or do you mean . . . someone is *going* to kill you? Have you seen your own future? If it hasn't happened yet, you can still stop it!"

Second shook his head mournfully.

"Jordan, you are entirely too trusting," he said. He

reached out as if he intended to grab Jordan's hand. Jordan jerked back, but he was already trapped between Second and the wall. He decided to shove Second away instead.

Or he tried to. His hands kept going forward. They slid right through Second's cloak. Then they slid right through the middle of Second's body.

"What the—?" Jordan gasped, pulling his hands back and cowering against the wall.

Second gave him the saddest smile of all.

"See?" Second said. "Now you know the truth. I'm not actually alive. I'm just a hologram of the person who used to be Second Chance."

FORTY-FOUR

Even with the wall behind him, Jordan was so shocked he fell over.

For a moment, he just lay there, too stunned to sit back up.

"Holograms can't talk," he said. "I mean, not to answer questions and . . . have a conversation."

"Don't you see how my responses could be pre-programmed, based on certain key words?" Second—or the hologram of Second—asked. "Words like, 'answer questions'?"

Jordan winced. Was this why the whole conversation had felt so odd?

"Holograms are always kind of . . . see-through," he muttered. "You can always *tell*."

"With holograms in *your* time—the twenty-first

century—you could always tell they weren't real," Second corrected him. "Just like you can always tell what's not real with twenty-first-century virtual-reality role-playing games. Holography and VR are still in their infancies in your time period. But—"

"But they're going to improve," Jordan moaned. "People are going to perfect those things, so people like you can always fool time primitives like me."

"Why do you automatically assume *I* did this?" Second asked. "How could I have set up my own hologram after I'm dead? And why are you so sure it's just a trick?"

"Because you fooled me," Jordan said. He managed to prop himself up on his elbows. "So is it a trick, too, what you said about knowing how to help my parents?"

"A hologram of a dead man can't reveal information he never revealed in real life," Second said, shrugging. "But remember, I did start figuring everything out when I was thirteen. When I was climbing a wall."

"You mean, when Katherine and Jonah and I saw you fall," Jordan said. "When you stole our Elucidator. You're saying the teenage version of you knows your secrets! The version that's still alive!"

"Yes, he knows," Second said. "Even though he himself may not know he knows."

Maybe it was just Jordan's imagination, but now that

he understood it was just a hologram in front of him, the man seemed to be fading slightly around the edges.

What were you supposed to do, talking to a hologram of a dead man, when a younger version of that man was still alive? Should you offer condolences?

Jordan decided that really wasn't necessary.

"So you're saying I can just go ask the younger version of you to help," Jordan said. "And, tell him to keep his secret after that. And . . . maybe avoid whoever killed you."

"I don't think you'll actually have to . . . go anywhere for that," Second said, his voice going all vague and wispy. "Once I leave, the Elucidator is set up to . . ."

It wasn't Jordan's imagination that the hologram was fading away. Jordan blinked, and when he opened his eyes again, he could definitely see through Second. He could see every chink in the wall behind Second.

"Wait!" Jordan cried. "You never told me who killed you! You never told me who to watch out for! You never told me—"

Second was gone.

"Told you what?" a voice said behind Jordan.

Jordan whirled around. Kevin was standing right behind him, in the same fitted hospital gown and boots he'd been wearing the last time Jordan had seen him.

Jordan laughed in relief.

"*That's* why I didn't have to go anywhere to find you," he said. "The Elucidator was set up to summon you here! It was all arranged for you to come help me!"

"*Help* you?" Kevin repeated. "Are you kidding? I'm here to take back the Elucidator you stole!"

And then he reached out to grab the Elucidator from Jordan's hands.

FORTY-FIVE

Jordan had never had quick reflexes. That had always been his problem with basketball and soccer and other sports: Even when he knew the moves he needed to make, he could never make them fast enough. But maybe he just needed to play against an opponent who had recently recovered from serious spinal injuries and traveled through time.

Jordan jerked the Elucidator back and out of Kevin's reach.

"No, you won't!" Jordan yelled.

Rather than tackling Jordan and trying to yank the Elucidator away, Kevin just started laughing.

"Are you kidding?" he said. "My IQ's, like, a hundred points higher than yours. You're not going to outsmart me. Now that I'm not in pain or paralyzed anymore, you don't have any advantages!"

"Freeze Kevin completely in place!" Jordan screamed.

Instantly Kevin stopped moving. A strand of hair swung down into his eyes, and he couldn't even shove it away.

"Who's got the advantage now?" Jordan couldn't help gloating. "Maybe you're smarter than me, but I've got more experience with Elucidators and time travel."

Kevin didn't reply. It took Jordan a moment to realize that that was because Kevin's mouth was frozen, too.

Should I keep Kevin like this until I've had a chance to talk him into helping me? Jordan wondered.

Even without moving, Kevin's eyes were taking on a glaze of rage.

I'm just going to make him mad if I don't let him talk or ask questions or brag about how brilliant he is, Jordan decided. He remembered how Second had dealt with the entire Skidmore family in a different time hollow.

"Okay, let Kevin move his head," Jordan said aloud, to the Elucidator. "Just not any other part of his body."

"Wow, aren't you nice," Kevin exploded sarcastically.

"Look, I'm not doing this to be mean or anything," Jordan said. His voice came out as pleadingly as if he were the one frozen and Kevin were the one in control.

Which, if you think about it, is true, Jordan thought. *Because he's the one who knows how to help Mom and Dad.*

"I promise, I'll set you free as soon as I've explained everything and gotten your help," he continued.

"Right," Kevin sneered. "Why don't you just make me your slave, while you're at it?"

"That's not what I . . . ," Jordan began. One look at Kevin's face made him give up explaining. Kevin would never just decide to trust Jordan. Not without seeing some things for himself.

"Don't you want to know who killed you in a different version of time?" Jordan asked instead. "So you know who to watch out for?"

Kevin didn't say yes. But he didn't say no, either.

"Elucidator, show us both what happened to Second when he, um, died," Jordan said.

He looked back at the wall where he'd seen his parents and Katherine and Jonah. Nothing happened.

"Stupid, all the action's over there," Kevin said, pointing with his chin.

The Elucidator was projecting a scene on the wall facing Kevin.

Oh, the Elucidator's being nice to Kevin, so he doesn't have to watch the whole time with his head turned all the way to the right, Jordan realized.

He turned his body so he was also watching from the most comfortable position.

In the image on the wall, the grown-up Second was standing beside JB and the car again. JB looked awestruck as he peered down at his hands, newly restored to adult size. Second was turning away from JB and the car. But somehow the camera angle was ever so slightly different this time. The camera focused in tightly on Second's face and neck, following his every move. This time Jordan saw something small and metallic fly past the folds of Second's cloak and jam into Second's neck, right at the jugular. Second winced—a wince Jordan hadn't noticed the last time. Then his face smoothed out.

The last time Jordan had seen this scene, all he could think was, *That's Second! Second was the one who helped JB! So Second could help my parents!* Jordan had been too stunned to notice anything else. But this time he wondered at the slackness of Second's expression, the way his jaw drooped and his eyelids lowered.

Then, just like before, Second vanished.

"Was that it?" Jordan asked. "Did we just see Second die, right before he disappeared? Because of that silver thing on his neck?"

He looked down at the Elucidator he was still holding. The word YES glowed red on its screen.

"But where did the silver thing come from?" Jordan asked. "Who sent it? And why?"

The Elucidator projected its words onto the wall this time: IT WAS AN UNTRACEABLE ASSASSIN DRONE. SO YOU CAN'T SEE WHO SENT IT OR WHY.

"It could have come from any time or any place or any person," Kevin snarled. His face was red and furious. "It could have come from you, for all I know. I could be watching my own future!"

"No, no, this is a different version of you, from a different dimension . . . ," Jordan started trying to explain. Kevin didn't look the least bit comforted. Jordan tried a different tack. "I promise, I've never killed anyone. I don't *want* to kill anyone."

"But that doesn't mean that you won't kill anyone in the future," Kevin said. "You froze me in place. You could do anything to me!"

"Can't we just work as a team?" Jordan was ashamed of how much he sounded like he was begging. "You help me, I help you—everything's good?"

Kevin gave his head an angry shake. Jordan had the feeling that if the boy could move the rest of his body right now, he'd beat Jordan up.

"You just showed me proof that someone wants me dead," Kevin said. "And it could be anyone from any time or place. And you think that's going to make me want to trust *you*?"

"I took you to the hospital when you passed out," Jordan said. "I didn't have to do that. I—"

He'd been thinking about asking the Elucidator to show them Second's last moments again, or to show where his body vanished to, or something like that. But if it wasn't possible to see who had sent the attack on Second, none of that would do any good. And watching the murder again would hardly put Second into a more trusting mood.

"What do *you* want the Elucidator to show us?" Jordan asked.

Kevin narrowed his eyes into slits.

"Everything connected to you or me that afternoon I fell," he said. "Or those other two kids who were with you. Starting—I don't know—let's say five minutes before I climbed that fence."

"Okay," Jordan said.

Instantly the wall glowed with multiple images. It was like watching a bank of security videos. At first, the only action was in a scene where Kevin stood with a group of guys in hoodies and jeans.

"Yeah, sure, we look like people who fly on airplanes," one of the boys mocked the others. "You think the security guards are going to let any of us pick up a suitcase?"

Jordan got distracted because suddenly something happened in one of the other scenes: He, Katherine, and

Jonah appeared sprawled out on the ground, cowering beneath an airplane coming in to land. Katherine and Jonah blinked back the effects of time travel and started looking cautiously around as soon as possible; Jordan on the screen seemed groggy and dazed, barely able to move.

"It's really easy to tell you and your brother apart," Kevin taunted.

"Hey, he had hundreds of years more experience with time travel than I did," Jordan said.

Kevin ignored him and went back to watching intently.

On the screen, Jordan finally sat up.

"How about we just grab whatever kid we're supposed to grab and get out of here?" Jordan heard himself ask.

"You were there waiting to *kidnap* me?" Kevin asked. "And you think I'm ever going to *trust* you?"

"No, no—we didn't actually know it was you we were there for!" Jordan said. "And—listen to what else we're saying. . . ."

On the screen Jonah demanded, "Do you *see* any kid anywhere around here? Any kid who looks endangered and in need of saving?"

"See?" Jordan told Kevin. "We were there to *rescue* you!"

He thought about backing up the scene to show the directions Mr. Rathbone had given them, but then he reconsidered. He couldn't remember exactly what Mr.

Rathbone had said, or what they had agreed to just because they were desperate.

"You've got to see everything from the start, to really understand," Jordan said. "Right after we rescue you, a plane will land that's full of babies—you have to see that."

Kevin gave a skeptical snort, but he didn't say anything else.

On the screen Kevin started climbing the fence. He fell; his friends ran away; Jordan, Jonah, and Katherine ran to help.

Jordan resisted the urge to say, *See? See? We risked our lives to rescue you!*

The action on the screen continued. Kevin snatched the Elucidator from Jonah; the three Skidmores climbed back up toward the fence (Jordan couldn't quite let himself watch that part); Deep Voice appeared and whooshed them all back toward the future.

Jordan realized that the screen was showing only what had happened to Kevin directly, not what had happened in the other versions where the boy died on the rocks or where Second worked for the FBI for thirteen years before escaping to the future.

Is that because the Elucidator doesn't think of those other dimensions as being connected to Kevin anymore? Jordan wondered.

"What were you saying about a planeload of babies?" Kevin asked.

"Show him," Jordan told the Elucidator.

WHICH DIMENSION? the Elucidator asked.

"All of them," Jordan said, because he was curious about this too. "Show us everything."

Now there were three views of what seemed to be the exact same scene: rows of babies sleeping on a plane.

"So one of the dimensions has an empty seat on the plane and the others don't," Kevin observed. "What's that mean?"

"Um, I'm not sure," Jordan said. "Different babies came from the past in the different dimensions, but . . ."

It struck him that that the empty-seated version of the plane might have led to the dimension where Katherine was an only child. But he didn't feel like explaining that to Kevin.

Before Kevin could say anything else, the camera angle shifted in each scene. Now Jordan could see into the cockpit of each version of the plane. In the first version, Gary and Hodge were sitting in the pilots' seats. They looked younger than Jordan had ever seen them, but it was hard to tell because they were screaming in terror.

"The time agency found us! What should we do?" Gary cried as he frantically swiped through screenfuls of information on the instrument panel before him.

"Don't worry—they won't shoot us down! But—evade! Evade!" Hodge yelled back.

A disembodied voice spoke over their heads: "You are being arrested under Time Code section 503972, paragraph 48913. You must instantly land in the nearest time hollow and disembark. Repeat . . ."

The rest of the message was drowned out by Hodge screaming, "We've got to get out of here! Bail! Now!"

"What about the babies?" Gary asked, casting a glance over his shoulder. "They're worth a fortune!"

"We'll come back for them later!" Hodge bellowed back.

And then both men disappeared.

Jordan saw that they were missing from the other two scenes of cockpits as well. He wasn't sure if they'd ever been in those cockpits, or if those planes had been on autopilot the whole time.

"Anybody you know on any of those planes?" Kevin asked lazily, as if he really didn't care.

"Me," Jordan said. "And Jonah. And, I guess, this other kid I met once, Chip . . ."

Neither of them said anything else as the planes landed safely in all three scenes. In each case, the plane pulled up to the airport and came to a stop.

In one version, none of the babies were taken off the plane, and it flew on with Charles Lindbergh in the pilot seat.

Jordan waited for Kevin to ask about that, but he didn't. Probably he was too distracted watching the other two scenes.

Jordan realized he'd already seen this part of the middle scene before. Once again, Gary and Hodge removed the baby version of Jordan from the plane and left him with the teenage Jonah, stranded and desperate.

Kevin didn't ask any questions about that either, and Jordan turned his attention to a scene he'd never seen before. An adult version of Angela stepped cautiously onto the plane and saw all the babies. And then dozens of people swarmed in behind her, carrying the babies out into the airport.

Finally Kevin spoke. "Let me guess—none of that was supposed to happen, right?" he asked.

"I don't think so," Jordan said uncomfortably.

"Where'd all the babies come from in the first place?" Kevin asked.

"Um, history?" Jordan said, wishing he could sound more certain.

"Show me," Kevin said.

And then they watched scenes of Chinese princesses from the fourth century and English settlers on the coast of North America in the fifteen hundreds and Albert Einstein's daughter in 1903. They watched the stories of all the babies from the plane, endangered and kidnapped and returned and rescued again. Jordan saw everything that Katherine and Jonah had done, sweeping in and out of time. Where he'd been jealous before, now somehow he was only proud. He had to bite his tongue not to brag to Kevin, *That's my sister and brother doing all that! Don't you see what heroes they were?*

When they'd finally worked through the last frame of the last kid's story, the wall went dark.

Is now a good time to ask Kevin again to help my parents? Jordan wondered.

Kevin didn't look mad anymore. But he also didn't look particularly friendly.

"Let me see you and Jonah and Katherine growing up," Kevin said.

"It wasn't together," Jordan told him. "I mean, I was with Katherine, and Jonah was with Katherine, but Jonah and I weren't in the same dimension. And then there was even a dimension where Katherine was alone. . . ."

Kevin didn't ask for more of an explanation. He just grunted.

Jordan told the Elucidator to start showing every version of the childhoods of all three Skidmore kids. In the dimension where Katherine was an only child, Jordan couldn't believe how many pink, frilly clothes and toys she had.

But he also saw her staring plaintively out the window as a preschooler, complaining, "Why aren't there any other kids to play with in this house? Why don't I have any brothers or sisters?"

She really was lonely in that dimension, Jordan thought. *She wasn't just making that up.*

He started paying more attention to the dimensions he or Jonah had been in. Shown side by side, they were practically identical. Birthday parties and Cub Scout meetings and Christmas pageants at church. A parade of identical Halloween costumes and trips to the zoo. Mom helping each of the boys with homework; Dad teaching each of the boys to swing a bat.

Jordan had to look away. He pretended he needed to double-check something on the surface of his Elucidator.

"Hey, why did one of you get a new neighbor and the other one didn't?" Kevin asked, his gaze still fixed on the wall. "That's kind of a big difference."

Jordan squinted up at the scenes before him. Jonah was playing basketball in the driveway with Chip, the kid Jordan hadn't met until right before Chip kissed Katherine. In the same scene showing Jordan's life, Jordan was dribbling the ball in the driveway all by himself.

"It's because Chip was one of the babies on the plane with Jonah, I guess," Jordan explained. "All the babies came off the plane in their dimension. I was the only one off the plane in mine. So in my world, Chip was somewhere else. Or sometime else."

"Huh," Kevin said.

Jonah and Chip seemed to be playing a lot of basketball together.

Is that how Jonah got better at it than me, and might actually be a starter on the team when I'm not? Jordan wondered.

Then Jonah and Chip started getting mysterious letters hinting at their origins. Jonah and Katherine and their parents went to meet Mr. Reardon at the FBI; Jonah and Katherine and Chip met Angela. All the missing children from the plane gathered back together; JB fought with Gary and Hodge to determine the fates of all the kids.

And then Jonah and Katherine took their first trip through time, and the same scenes Jordan and Kevin had seen before began to repeat.

"It's all a loop, isn't it?" Kevin asked. "Interconnected."

"I guess," Jordan said. "I wasn't really part of it. I missed almost all the excitement."

He'd glanced at scenes of his own life only a few times after Jonah's dimension started taking such dramatic turns. Jordan already knew that his life had been completely ordinary until the morning he came down to find identical Jonah sitting in his living room.

"Excitement?" Kevin asked. "Is that what you want?"

Jordan thought about how the hologram of Second had made fun of him for being like Dorothy in Oz—someone who got to go on a great adventure, but spent it all just wanting to go home. Put that way, he did sound kind of pathetic.

But he told Kevin the truth anyway. "What I want most is for my parents to be all right," he said. "And for time to be all right."

"Huh," Kevin said.

"Maybe it's hard for you to understand," Jordan said. "It sounds like you don't really like your parents. Or your dad, anyway. And maybe you had to go live with foster parents you didn't like, either. But my parents . . ."

He wanted to say, *They love me. I love them. They'd do anything for me. And I'd do anything to save them.* But there was no way he could force those words past the lump in his throat. And anyhow, it would seem kind of mean to say that to Kevin, who evidently hadn't had such great parents. It would be like bragging, *I got a good family and you didn't!*

"What do you want?" he asked Kevin instead. "Really?"

Kevin didn't let his eyes meet Jordan's.

"You say you want to help me, right?" Kevin asked. "Would you help me like you'd help your own family?"

Jordan squinted at him in confusion.

"I guess," he said. "Sure."

"Promise?" Kevin asked, and now he peered straight at Jordan, his eyes drilling into him.

"Uh, yeah," Jordan said. "I mean, yes. Exactly the same."

"Well, then, put the Elucidator up against my mouth so I can whisper into it and tell it my idea for fixing your parents," Kevin said. "I think that's the only way we're ever getting out of this time hollow."

Jordan jerked the Elucidator back, so it was farther away from Kevin.

"That's crazy!" he said. "How do I know you're not going to just say something like, 'Unfreeze me and get me out of here with the Elucidator, and leave Jordan behind'?"

Kevin looked like he wanted to laugh.

"You could always tell the Elucidator not to follow any instruction from me unless it fixes your parents," he said.

"Oh," Jordan said. "Right."

He didn't move at all for a moment, because his mind was racing.

Kevin's a lot smarter than me, and what if he's still trying to trick me? Jordan wondered. *What if there'd still be some way he could get around my instructions?*

"Why don't you just tell me your secret, and *I'll* tell it to the Elucidator?" Jordan asked.

"Then whoever wants to kill me might want to steal the secret from you and kill you, too," Kevin said. "Is that what you want?"

"Oh," Jordan said. "No."

He'd never felt so stupid in all his life. He did fine in school. He did fine on all those standardized test kids had to take all the time. But this felt like a test no one could pass. Even the genius Second Chance hadn't been able to understand and navigate everything about time travel; even he hadn't been able to anticipate and avoid whoever wanted to kill him. The kid standing frozen before Jordan right now was just an earlier version of Second—a not-yet Second Chance.

Or should Jordan see him as a Third Chance?

What if he thinks he's helping me but he really isn't? Jordan wondered. *Or what if he's just tricking me, and I'm too stupid to figure it out?*

Jordan felt as paralyzed as Second.

Oddly, it was something Mom had told him about taking multiple-choice tests that floated into his brain: *When you don't know the right answer, try to eliminate all the choices you know are wrong. Then pick from what's left.*

Jordan didn't want to be stuck in this time hollow forever.

He didn't want Mom and Dad frozen and thirteen forever.

He didn't even want Jonah and Katherine to be frozen forever.

And he didn't want to ruin time.

"Don't follow any orders from Kevin unless he's helping Mom and Dad and the other un-aged grown-ups," Jordan mumbled into the Elucidator.

Then, slowly, he reached the Elucidator out toward Kevin's mouth, to touch the side of his face.

Kevin whispered something.

Instantly both boys began whirling through time.

FORTY-SIX

"What did you tell it?" Jordan screamed at Kevin. "You weren't supposed to say anything about traveling through time! It wasn't supposed to follow any extra orders from you!"

"I didn't tell it anything extra! I swear!" Kevin screamed back as they both spun dizzily through time.

Somehow Jordan believed him.

"Then where's it taking us?" Jordan screamed. "And why? Elucidator, take us back to the time hollow! Or, no—take us to be with Mom and Dad, so we can see if they're the right ages again!"

ALL FURTHER COMMANDS FROM THE TWO OF YOU ARE SHUT OUT the Elucidator informed him. SORRY.

"What?" Jordan screamed. "What's it talking about? Kevin, what's going on?"

Kevin shook his head.

"I . . . feel funny," he said.

"You don't look so good either," Jordan snapped.

Kevin had prickles of sweat along his hairline. The only light nearby came from the glow of the Elucidator, but even that was enough to show that the color had drained from Kevin's face.

Kevin held his hand in front of his face and stared like he'd never seen it before.

"Oh," he said. "I see. I see how this is working. It's even faster than I thought."

"What?" Jordan demanded. "What do you see? What's faster than you thought?"

Kevin turned his head to peer directly at Jordan.

"I don't think there's time to tell you," Kevin said. "You'll figure it out if you think hard enough. And you need to think that hard. But you should know this. I really did try to help your parents. I did what I could. Everything is up to you now. Remember your promise."

"*Why* is everything up to me now?" Jordan asked. "You're right here with me—wherever we're going, we'll be there together. Right? We can work as a team now, can't we?"

Kevin smiled sadly.

"Keep telling yourself that," he said.

But something had happened to his voice. It had lost its defensive huskiness—lost its low register, too. By the word "that," Kevin's voice came out sounding as sweet and childlike as an elementary school kid's.

And . . . was Kevin actually *smaller* than he'd been a moment ago?

Jordan reached out and grabbed Kevin's arm. Jordan's fingers circled the bicep easily, with room to spare.

Was his arm so spindly before? Jordan wondered.

Kevin's hospital gown seemed much too large all of a sudden. The top part of it started sliding off one shoulder, and he had to tug it back up. Then he had to clutch the bottom part of it to keep it from doubling over and getting tangled in his legs.

How was there suddenly so much extra cloth in the gown? Hadn't it ended right at Kevin's ankles before? Right at the top of his boots?

One of Kevin's boots slid off and fell into the darkness. Then the other one did too.

"What's happening to you?" Jordan demanded.

"Can't you tell?" Kevin asked with a sad smile that revealed huge gaps where teeth were missing.

Kevin had all his teeth a minute ago, Jordan thought. *Didn't he?*

Kevin slipped his hand into Jordan's, and it felt so small and fragile and bony that Jordan worried that it might break.

"I'm scared," Kevin said. "What if we see the bogeyman?"

Kevin sounded like a kindergartner. Jordan lifted the Elucidator so its dim light shone more directly on Kevin's face: Kevin looked like a kindergartner too.

"You're getting younger," Jordan gasped. "You're turning into a little kid."

Little Kevin scowled at him in a way that made Jordan think that Kevin/Sam Chase/Second Chance had certain expressions that fit on his face no matter what age he was.

"You're stupid," little Kevin said. "I'm not going to stop there. Watch."

He was practically lisping. A moment later, he opened his mouth, and maybe he wasn't even capable of speaking anymore at all.

But Jordan couldn't listen to anything Kevin said anyway. Just then they hit the phase of time travel where everything sped up, and Jordan felt like his body was being torn down to its smallest particles. To the extent that Jordan's brain could function at all, he just kept thinking, *Hold . . . on to . . . Kevin's . . . hand . . . . You . . . promised . . . promised . . . like . . . family . . .*

And then everything stopped. Jordan's senses began to wake up again.

What am I holding? His brain sputtered. *Holding . . . Am I still holding on?*

His brain was so pathetic. He couldn't quite remember who or what he was supposed to be holding. But he kept trying to remember, kept trying to double-check, even though his eyes were still too blurry to see anything, and the nerve endings of his fingertips were still too numb to feel.

He fought harder against the timesickness than he ever had, trying to come out of it as soon as possible.

Right hand? He thought. *Right hand holding . . .*

It was something small and smooth. The Elucidator?

Okay, I'll think about that later. If it won't take commands from me or Kevin, it's not going to do me much good. Left hand?

His left hand seemed to be empty, the fingers extended. But there was something soft pressed against his left wrist and the inside of his left elbow. No—he was cradling something.

Jordan summoned the energy to lift his head and look.

He was cradling a baby wrapped in an oversize hospital gown against his left arm.

Jordan had managed to hold on to Kevin. But Kevin had turned all the way back into a baby.

"So what do you think you're going to do now?" a voice asked above him.

FORTY-SEVEN

Jordan blinked frantically, trying to get his eyes to see beyond the baby cradled in his arms.

"Who's there?" Jordan asked.

Someone chuckled just outside his range of vision. All he could see was a blur.

"You should be able to recognize me by now," the voice said. Whoever it was made a *tsk-tsk* noise. "It appears you're prone to lengthy spells of timesickness. So you're not a very good time traveler."

The voice was familiar. Jordan had the feeling he would have recognized it if it hadn't seemed to be coming from a million miles away.

The blurry shape came closer. A face loomed above him.

"Mr. Rathbone?" Jordan cried.

The face swung in and out of focus. The chuckle came again.

"Shouldn't that be 'Mr. Rathbone, I presume'?" the voice asked. "Oh, well, never mind. I'm sure you don't get the reference."

"Someone looking for a lost explorer in Africa a long time ago . . . ," Jordan mumbled. "'Dr. Livingston, I presume . . .' My mom likes talking about stuff like that in history. . . ." He didn't want to talk about his mom in front of Mr. Rathbone. "But I don't understand. Why are you here? I thought Second . . ."

Maybe it wasn't too smart to talk about what he'd seen Second do to Mr. Rathbone. Maybe that hadn't happened yet.

Mr. Rathbone chuckled once more. The man seemed much happier than he'd been the last time Jordan had encountered him.

Jordan didn't like that.

"You thought Second . . . what? Completed his betrayal of Interchronological Rescue by turning me back into a baby?" Mr. Rathbone asked. "And then by allowing you and your puerile siblings to decide where my baby self should be stowed?"

His chuckle turned into a full-on laugh. It was a horrible sound, triumphant and gloating.

"You actually fell for that?" Mr. Rathbone asked. "Even after you found out that Second was a hologram in the time hollow, you never once thought, *Could he have been a hologram the last time I saw him too?*"

"He . . . he touched things," Jordan said. "He carried . . ."

"A hologram version of me as a baby?" Mr. Rathbone said scornfully. "A hologram man can carry a hologram baby. Neither has any substance."

Jordan wanted to keep protesting: *But Second broke your golf club! He pressed buttons on the wall of the time hollow! He made my family vanish! He said he put a button in a cubicle for me to push!*

But all of those could have been more illusions. Illusions or tricks or lies—or things that Mr. Rathbone himself had arranged.

Maybe Second had been a hologram every single time Jordan had seen him. It wasn't like *any* conversation with the man had ever seemed normal.

Mr. Rathbone was still talking, using his words like a club to beat up Jordan even more.

"You actually chose to believe that Second defeated me?" Mr. Rathbone ranted. "Me—the CEO of Interchronological Rescue? When, actually, I had a plan that would get me everything I ever wanted?"

Jordan's vision seemed to be totally back now. He could see every line of the gloating expression on Mr. Rathbone's face. Jordan sat up woozily and darted his eyes around, trying to look past Mr. Rathbone.

Big desk, long walls . . .

It appeared that Jordan and baby Kevin had landed back in Mr. Rathbone's office at the Interchronological Rescue headquarters.

Is this where Kevin told the Elucidator to take us? Jordan wondered. *And did he* want *to be a baby again?*

That seemed ridiculous. And Jordan had done his best to shut out Kevin from commanding the Elucidator to do anything but help Jordan's parents.

But this Elucidator came from Mr. Rathbone from the very start, Jordan remembered. *Did Mr. Rathbone have it programmed to ultimately turn Kevin back into a baby and bring us here?*

Mr. Rathbone had probably also sent Kevin the message Kevin thought was from his older self. It was that message that had made Kevin grab the Elucidator from Jonah.

Jordan's brain hurt, trying to figure everything out. And he could hardly think past the bigger question looming in his mind: *Regardless of what Mr. Rathbone planned or didn't plan . . . how do I get out of here?*

Mr. Rathbone watched Jordan's eyes dart about. It felt like he was watching Jordan's thoughts, too.

"Don't even think you could escape," Mr. Rathbone said

with a snort. "Interchronological Rescue has a top-notch security system. All automated, of course. I control it all. I can see everything going on in the entire headquarters."

"Really?" Jordan taunted, just because Mr. Rathbone was so annoying. "But there are parts of the headquarters away from the security cameras. You didn't know when Katherine, Jonah, and I landed in the lab that Gary and Hodge used."

Scorn flickered in Mr. Rathbone's eye.

"Actually I did know about that," Mr. Rathbone said. "I just didn't choose to let you know that I knew."

Is he lying? Jordan wondered. *Did he know anything about Deep Voice and Doreen and Tattoo Face helping us?*

There was no way Jordan could ask without giving everything away.

"Perhaps my employees gave you a different impression?" Mr. Rathbone sneered. "Not that I think someone like *you* would ever be a CEO, but I'll give you a little hint. Sometimes it's helpful to let your worthless underlings think you're a little more ignorant than you really are. So you can see who might deceive you, given the chance. Or what they think is a chance."

Okay, Mr. Rathbone knew all along what Deep Voice, Doreen and Tattoo Face were doing, Jordan thought. *He knew about the camera Doreen put on him. He knew . . .*

Mr. Rathbone gave a slow, evil smile.

"You're finally figuring it out, aren't you?" he asked. "I won. I won everything. Nobody can touch me now."

Jordan struggled to hold baby Kevin up a little. The baby whimpered at the change.

"You won one more stinking baby from the past to sell to some rich family," Jordan said. "So what? You're already rich. What does it matter if this baby makes you very, very rich? Who cares?"

Mr. Rathbone started shaking his head.

"You really aren't very bright, are you?" he asked. "You still don't know what you're talking about. I bet your brother and sister would have understood by now."

"Why didn't you set up my brother or sister to be the stork delivering your baby, then?" Jordan asked. He tried to sound like he didn't care.

Mr. Rathbone laughed as if he was genuinely amused.

"Maybe I thought I needed someone ignorant and stupid like you," he said. "So Second—or, should I say, Kevin?—wouldn't worry about anyone outsmarting him."

Jordan could tell that Mr. Rathbone meant this conversation to hurt him. Probably he meant it to make Jordan's brain shut down in shame.

Maybe he doesn't know how many people have already called me ignorant and stupid so far today, Jordan thought. *It's not like I'm not used to it.*

He had been kind of ignorant and stupid both, that morning he'd walked down the stairs in his own house, back in the twenty-first century, the last time he'd thought of himself as someone absolutely ordinary, with one ordinary mom, one ordinary dad, and one ordinary sister.

With no brother at all, and no secret background involving time travel and life-or-death decisions.

But he'd seen a lot since then. He'd learned a lot.

And really, now I've seen and heard and learned everything Jonah or Katherine saw or heard or learned, Jordan thought. *Because of watching everything in the time hollow, I've witnessed everything they did. No—I've witnessed more, because I had the extra time with Kevin. . . .*

"Pay attention," Mr. Rathbone snapped, and Jordan saw how much the man hated being ignored.

Mr. Rathbone shoved his face closer to Jordan's.

"I'll explain, because I don't want to waste any more time on you," Mr. Rathbone said. "You brought me two payoffs. One was that Elucidator that contains the secret for re-aging adults. The secret to completely separating time from aging, as it were. And life from its consequences."

Jordan felt a tremor of panic deep in his gut.

"But Second said that secret ruined his world!" he protested. "I mean, I know he was just a hologram when he told me that, but—what he said was true, wasn't it?"

"Second ruined his own world," Mr. Rathbone said scornfully. "But I won't ruin ours. In his world, Second gave out his secret freely, to everyone who wanted it. He said he wanted everyone to have a chance to fix their mistakes, as quickly and easily as possible."

"But . . . shouldn't that be a good thing?" Jordan asked.

Mr. Rathbone laughed scornfully.

"Don't worry—I won't make the same mistake," he said. "I'll keep control of the secret always. Even when I'm selling temporary access to the highest bidders."

Mr. Rathbone reached out and yanked the Elucidator from Jordan's hand.

Belatedly, Jordan realized he should have held the Elucidator hostage, refusing to hand it over until Mr. Rathbone gave Jordan what he wanted.

No, that would have just gotten me killed, Jordan thought. *Or, at best, thrown into some sort of prison. Mr. Rathbone is holding all the cards right now.*

Wasn't he?

Something tickled at the back of Jordan's mind, something his brain seemed to think Jordan should pay attention to. But Jordan couldn't figure out what it was.

Reflexively, Jordan tightened his grip on baby Kevin. Mr. Rathbone's eyes seemed to follow the action.

"Oh, you think you're going to be able to hold that baby back from me?" Mr. Rathbone asked. "You think there's anything you can keep from my power? Wouldn't you be better off begging me to deal with you kindly?"

"You've already told me I'm stupid and ignorant," Jordan said. "I know I'm too stupid and ignorant for you to want to turn me back into a baby and sell *me* to the highest bidder. Anyway, I'm not a famous missing child from history."

Mr. Rathbone shook his head, his eyebrows arched in scorn and amazement.

"You *still* think this is about famous missing children from history?" he asked. "That was the old business model. With Gary and Hodge gone, with the time agency making new rules right and left . . . that's over. But the key to business success is adaptability. You look at your assets and figure out what they're worth in the changing business environment. That baby you're holding might very well be the smartest human who's ever lived. You think selling him—I mean, adopting him out—is the best use of something like that? When there are so many other possibilities?"

Now that he wasn't holding the Elucidator anymore, Jordan placed his right arm over his left, adding another layer of protection to baby Kevin.

"He's not a thing," Jordan said. "He's a baby. A human being."

Mr. Rathbone rolled his eyes.

"The other versions of Samuel Kevin Chase were a little too human—too rebellious, anyway," he said. "I think the life he lived his first thirteen years left him with no loyalty to anyone. Second Chance betrayed Gary, Hodge, Interchronological Rescue, JB, the time agency, and time itself. The boy I sent you and your siblings to rescue betrayed me. He was supposed to come straight back here, not go off to time hollows and hospitals. Fortunately, I anticipated that problem and embedded commands in the Elucidator that forced him back here anyhow."

"As a baby," Jordan said flatly. This was proof, then. The Elucidator had been set up to zap Kevin back to babyhood and off to Mr. Rathbone the minute he confided his secret idea. Even Kevin hadn't been brilliant enough to know that that would happen—or how to stop it.

"Right," Mr. Rathbone said, nodding. "And now I can raise the child to adore me and tell all his brilliant business ideas to me."

Jordan had seen Kevin/Second Chance/Sam Chase at various ages, and neither the teenager nor the man had seemed like the loyal, adoring type. Maybe it was because of the way he'd grown up; maybe it wasn't. Jordan didn't know how Mr. Rathbone's experiment would turn out.

But it kind of sounded like Kevin/Sam Chase/Second

Chance would once again have a miserable childhood.

"How do you know Kevin's idea about re-aging adults even works?" Jordan asked, because he still wanted to taunt Mr. Rathbone. That seemed to be the only power Jordan had left. "Maybe Second Chance knew what he was doing, but you killed Second. Right?"

Mr. Rathbone barely shrugged.

"He was expendable," he said.

Jordan winced. He wished he hadn't brought up anything about Second dying. Did he really want to know for sure that it had happened—and that Mr. Rathbone had caused it? A cruel voice in his head whispered, *If that was how Mr. Rathbone dealt with Second, who was a genius, what's going to happen to me? What hope do I have?*

"You don't see the precautions I took?" Mr. Rathbone asked. He still seemed to want to brag. "I made sure I had proof, of course. Using guinea pigs, you might say."

Jordan didn't understand. Probably his face looked completely blank, because Mr. Rathbone sighed.

"Your parents?" he hinted.

Jordan's body seemed to catch on before his brain did. He clenched his fists, which was hard to do while still holding baby Kevin.

"You used my parents as guinea pigs?" Jordan exploded. "Like, like lab rats?"

Mr. Rathbone favored him with a thin, triumphant smile.

"Them, and JB, and some sixty other adults," he said. "It was a bit larger of a sample than I intended. But that's what happens when you're using untested technology."

"You used untested technology on my parents?" Jordan screamed. Baby Kevin whimpered at the noise.

Mr. Rathbone glared at Jordan.

"Now, now," he said. "*Somebody* had to be first. And we couldn't alert the time agency in any way. As it was, we had them convinced that the whole experiment was a mistake, a simple error caused by Charles Lindbergh ignorantly fiddling around with an unfamiliar Elucidator."

Jordan wished he were holding almost anything in his arms besides a live baby. It would have been so satisfying to throw something at Mr. Rathbone—preferably something huge and heavy and pain-inducing. It would have been so satisfying to punch the man.

"My parents should never have been guinea pigs!" Jordan yelled. "They're *people*. So were the other adults you changed—"

Maybe Jordan was screaming too loudly. Maybe, in his fury, he'd started squeezing baby Kevin too tightly. Either way, something set the baby off, and he began to wail.

"Now you've done it," Mr. Rathbone said, frowning.

He reached behind him to the desk and picked up something small and silver. He pressed it into baby Kevin's arm.

Instantly the baby stopped crying. His body went limp in Jordan's arms.

"Sedative," Mr. Rathbone said. "Very useful. Should I use one on you, too?"

Jordan decided not to answer that question.

But what would it matter? Jordan wondered. *Mr. Rathbone's probably going to kill me in a few moments anyhow.*

Somehow that thought made him reckless.

"Are you going to keep Kevin sedated his whole childhood?" Jordan asked. "I don't think that's how people turn out to be geniuses. I bet he won't grow up to have any brilliant ideas for you at all."

Mr. Rathbone narrowed his eyes.

"What made you such an expert on raising kids?" he asked.

"Watching my parents," Jordan said. He was just trying to taunt Mr. Rathbone again, but somehow this struck him as an incredible truth. He'd just watched a repeat of his entire childhood—and Jonah's and Katherine's entire childhoods. Living through it, of course, Jordan had been just a kid. He'd taken his parents for granted. They were so ordinary. Normal. But seeing his life in reruns—while his parents' lives hung in the balance—made him realize just how great his parents had been. How patient, how kind, how loving.

How extraordinary.

Maybe watching his and Katherine's and Jonah's childhoods a second time around had actually made him wise.

Mr. Rathbone snorted. "You and Jonah and Katherine didn't turn out to be geniuses," he said. "None of you did."

"But we turned out to be pretty good people," Jordan countered. "That's what my parents were aiming for."

He thought about his dad putting up tents in the rain at Boy Scout campouts. He thought about his mom setting the alarm to get up early to take him and Katherine to Sunday school. He thought about his parents wiping tears and tying shoes and hugging all three of their kids, again and again and again.

"Look," Jordan said, pushing his words past a huge lump in his throat. "I know you're going to kill me. But can't you give my parents a good life? Send them back home as adults, like they're supposed to be. And you could give Jonah and Katherine back to them, and maybe you could make it so that they don't even remember that they ever had another son. . . ."

He couldn't go on talking. But this seemed like the best he could hope for.

Mr. Rathbone laughed, and the sound echoed cruelly.

"Such melodrama," he said. "And such idiocy. You *still* don't understand anything. Look. Here's a replay of something else that happened when Kevin whispered into the Elucidator."

He tapped the Elucidator sitting on the desk behind him, and the wall nearest Jordan lit up, turning into a floor-to-ceiling screen. On that screen Jordan saw one of the images he'd seen back in the time hollow: his parents, frozen as thirteen-year-olds. And then, as he watched, they unfroze. In the blink of an eye, they grew up. It was a little bit like watching an Incredible Hulk transformation, because as adults they were too big for Jordan's Ohio State T-shirt and Katherine's CHEER! sweatshirt. Seams ripped; Dad's paunch stuck out below the bottom of the T-shirt. His bony ankles stuck out at the bottom of the jeans.

But Mom and Dad looked at each other and laughed joyously. And then they hugged each other.

"Shall I go on?" Mr. Rathbone asked, his finger hovering over the Elucidator. "Shall I let them keep aging—until they're ancient and infirm and struggling with dementia and incontinence and arthritic joints? Shall I take them to the brink of death from old age?"

"No!" Jordan shouted. "Don't do that!"

He squeezed baby Kevin too tightly once again. Even sedated, the baby let out a soft whimper of complaint.

Mr. Rathbone laughed again.

"It's so easy to torture you," he said. "It would be so much fun to keep you here, and keep showing you images that make you scream."

Would that be better or worse than dying? Jordan wondered.

It kind of seemed like, as long as he was alive, there was still hope that he could fix things.

"You . . . ," Jordan began, trying to figure out how to work that out.

"Oh, stop," Mr. Rathbone said, his voice thick with disgust. "*Think.* Remember all the revelations you witnessed back in the time hollow. Much as I would like to keep you here to torture, there are certain requirements for keeping time alive."

Jordan looked at him blankly once again. Mr. Rathbone saying "think" and "remember" only reminded Jordan of what Kevin had said, spinning through time: *You'll figure it out if you think hard enough. . . . I really did try to help your parents. I did what I could. Everything is up to you now. Remember your promise.*

How could Kevin have thought anything could still be up to Jordan? Or that it should be? Kevin was a genius. He'd figured out how to outsmart an Elucidator the first time he'd touched one. How had he failed to figure out that Mr. Rathbone was going to turn him back into a baby?

Wait—what if he did know? Jordan wondered. *What if he couldn't stop it, but thought I would rescue him?*

Jordan was so stunned at that thought that he barely noticed Mr. Rathbone easing baby Kevin out of Jordan's arms.

But now Jordan's arms were empty.

Kevin would have known not to count on me for anything, Jordan thought. *Wouldn't he?*

Mr. Rathbone held baby Kevin carelessly in one arm. The baby's head lolled awkwardly, and he seemed about to fall. Maybe Mr. Rathbone wasn't used to holding babies. Maybe he was trying to taunt Jordan that there was nothing Jordan could do.

"It's exhausting to be around someone as stupid as you," Mr. Rathbone said, turning back toward the desk again. "But I'll be kind. I'll tell you you're actually going to get everything you wanted. Well, almost everything. Your brother saved time by melding his dimension and yours, remember?"

So Mr. Rathbone did know about the different dimensions all along, Jordan thought. *Or—at least he does now.*

How could Jordan still be so confused?

He forced himself to pay attention to what else Mr. Rathbone was saying.

"Because of the blended dimensions, I *have* to send you

and your parents and siblings back to the twenty-first century," he added. "Just so time continues normally, and so I get to have everything I want in *my* time."

Mr. Rathbone leaned over the Elucidator on his desk.

"Carry out the rest of my plan," he said. "Do it—"

Remember your promise pounded in Jordan's head. *Remember your promise.*

Jordan was usually terrible at multitasking, and not much better at thinking and acting fast. He didn't know if he had time for anything. But he was going to try. With one hand he lashed out at the Elucidator on the desk, trying to knock it to the floor.

With the other he grabbed for baby Kevin.

"—now," Mr. Rathbone finished.

FORTY-EIGHT

It felt like Jordan floated through time forever before he could tell if he'd succeeded at anything.

Without an Elucidator, he couldn't see a thing. But he frantically flexed his hands and pressed his arms closer against his body. . . .

Something was clutched in his hands and tucked between his arms and his body. It really was a baby. It really was baby Kevin. Jordan really had managed to grab him away from Mr. Rathbone.

Mr. Rathbone's just going to pull me back to his time, Jordan told himself. *I've just delayed this fight. I've just made him madder. I've got to plan my next step. . . .*

Jordan and the sedated baby Kevin kept floating through time.

Maybe the other part of what I did worked too, Jordan thought.

Maybe I managed to destroy that Elucidator, and it hit the ground right after Mr. Rathbone said his last word. Maybe right now Mr. Rathbone's huddled over a pile of broken Elucidator pieces on the floor of his office, and it's going to take him a minute or two to look for another Elucidator to yank me back. . . .

Jordan kept speeding forward. Lights rushed at him, and he braced himself for the feeling of being torn apart. He held on to baby Kevin as tightly as he could.

And then when you come out of the time travel, you're going to have to react as quickly as possible, he told himself. *None of this blinking and not being able to see or hear or feel . . .*

His mind blanked out. The next thing he knew, several people were leaning over him and exclaiming in such loud voices that Jordan's ears hurt.

". . . and now Jordan's back, too!"

"But what happened? How did it all work out?"

"And who's the baby?"

"How—?"

"Why—?"

Jordan struggled up to see three kids peering at him—Katherine, Jonah, and Chip—as well as four adults: JB, Angela, Mom, and Dad. So what Mr. Rathbone had shown Jordan was true. All the adults were the right age now.

The Skidmore family kitchen loomed behind them as Jordan's vision reeled in and out of focus.

"Hey, take it easy, sport," Dad said. "We're all okay now. You've got time to recover before you tell us anything."

"No, I don't!" Jordan exclaimed.

Did he have more than an instant? Could he possibly have a full minute? Or two?

"Grab on to me!" Jordan screamed. "Everybody grab on!"

A split second later, Jordan was floating through time again.

FORTY-NINE

"Ahhhhh!" someone screamed, so Jordan knew at least one person had managed to follow his instructions. It was too dark to see who it was, and Jordan was still too numb from the fast turnaround of time travel to be able to tell how many hands were clutching him.

"Mom? Dad?" Jordan called. "Katherine? Jonah?"

There was too much screaming for anyone to hear Jordan. He raised his voice.

"Everybody shut up and listen!" he screamed, louder than anyone. "In a minute we're going to be back in Mr. Rathbone's office. We have to overpower him. And he's got an Elucidator and we don't. . . ."

"Tell us what happened," someone said, and Jordan recognized the voice as JB's. That was good. It would help to have someone with time-agency training.

"I don't think there's time to tell anything," Jordan said. "But we've got to protect this baby. . . ."

He glanced around frantically. His eyes adjusted a little to the darkness, and now he could see at least shapes of other people around him. Were there five people around him? Six? Seven?

He squinted hard, trying to make out faces.

"Mr. Rathbone is going to expect me to be holding Kevin," Jordan said. "It'll be safer for the baby if he's in someone else's arms. . . ."

He looked for Mom and Dad. Both of them were great at dealing with babies. Jordan had seen that clearly, watching his and Jonah's and Katherine's early years.

But Kevin's going to need someone who's used to taking care of babies in the midst of danger, Jordan thought.

He thrust baby Kevin into Jonah's arms.

"Jordan, you and Jonah look exactly alike!" someone squealed—was it Mom? Katherine? Maybe it was both of them at once. "That's not going to change anything!"

"Mr. Rathbone can tell us apart," Jordan said stubbornly. "He knows what clothes we're wearing."

There wasn't time to explain the rest of Jordan's reasons.

"Who *is* this?" Jonah asked.

"Your worst enemy," Jordan said. "But take care of him anyway."

The rushing of time ripped the words from his mouth, and Jordan wasn't sure how much Jonah heard. Jordan wondered what else he should have said, what instructions he should have given. They were all going to be so numb when they landed. They would have to react so quickly. . . .

Jordan stopped being able to think. Flipping back and forth through time so quickly was evidently a bad idea. He didn't just feel as though he was being ripped to shreds; he also felt as though he was being pummeled down to nothingness. No—he was being reduced to less than nothing.

Then he was back in Mr. Rathbone's office, facing Mr. Rathbone.

Mr. Rathbone had a stunned look on his face. But he also had something in his hands. Something that had to be an Elucidator.

Was it a different Elucidator? Jordan desperately hoped so. He desperately hoped he'd managed to break the one holding Kevin's secret.

"You dared to defy me! Fool!" Mr. Rathbone roared at Jordan. "And you thought it would do any good to bring back this pack of *other* worthless, ineffectual people? Freeze in place for interrogation! All of you!"

If Mr. Rathbone had started with the order, instead of taunting Jordan first, there would have been no hope. All of them would have been stuck where they landed.

But by the time Mr. Rathbone hissed his command and the Elucidator followed it, just about everybody was already lunging for Mr. Rathbone, ready to rip the Elucidator from his hand. Jordan felt his body go stiff as he leaned forward, at a forty-five degree angle with the floor. Because he couldn't bring his leg around to support himself, he just kept falling.

Falling toward Mr. Rathbone.

Jordan couldn't have said who hit Mr. Rathbone first: Angela or JB or Jordan's dad. But it was like a giant pileup of a tackle in a football game. And it was such a hard tackle that it caused a fumble: Out of the corner of his eye, Jordan saw the small, silvery Elucidator fly out of Mr. Rathbone's hands and slide across the floor.

Jordan landed on the top of the heap, with Chip's elbow in his ear and Mom's knee in his eye.

"Get off me!" Mr. Rathbone screamed from the bottom of the pile of stiff bodies. "Get off!"

"That's not really possible, when you've immobilized us," JB said. This was Jordan's first clue that Mr. Rathbone had left them the ability to talk. That must have been what the "for interrogation" part of the order was about. So . . . had he frozen them only from the neck down? Would Jordan be able to turn his head?

Before Jordan had a chance to try this out, Mr. Rathbone

started demanding, "Elucidator, move all the interlopers' bodies to—"

"Scream!" Jordan interrupted. "Drown out Mr. Rathbone's words so the Elucidator can't hear them! AHHHH!"

He couldn't hear what Mr. Rathbone said next. Too many voices echoed in his ears: Mom's and Katherine's and Angela's, Dad's and Jonah's and JB's. Was Chip's in there too? And maybe baby Kevin, screaming as well?

There was a bass rumble from far below Jordan, probably Mr. Rathbone complaining about everyone screaming. And then the bodies beneath Jordan's began to shift. Mr. Rathbone seemed to have decided just to fight his way out.

Jordan slid left and right. Then he began slipping down the pile. He had no control over how his body fell. He hit the floor so hard he bounced.

And then his cheek came to rest on something small and round.

The Elucidator.

FIFTY

In the next instant Jordan saw Mr. Rathbone's flushed face staring at him from the bottom edge of the pile of bodies.

"Don't even think about it, Jordan," Mr. Rathbone said. Jordan kind of thought he was lip-reading more than actually hearing the man's words. Everyone was still screaming, and the sound was overpowering. "You're not going to be able to tell that Elucidator anything. You're, um, completely locked out."

He's lying, Jordan thought. *Why else would he be watching me so carefully?*

"Freeze Mr. Rathbone in place!" Jordan yelled.

Mr. Rathbone kept struggling out from the bottom of the pile.

"Give up," Mr. Rathbone said, his eyes boring into Jordan's. "There's nothing you can do."

But Mr. Rathbone is still wiggling toward me, Jordan thought. *He's acting like he thinks there's something I can do. Otherwise he'd be rushing off to find baby Kevin.*

Jordan could just barely see that Jonah was still holding on to baby Kevin. The two of them were frozen behind the pile of bodies. Jonah hadn't dived onto the pile to attack Mr. Rathbone. Jonah had protected Kevin, just as Jordan asked.

I've got to protect Kevin too, Jordan thought. *I promised.*

"Send all of us back to safety!" Jordan screamed. "Send us to . . . time-agency headquarters!"

That should be safe, shouldn't it?

Nothing happened.

Mr. Rathbone laughed as he dislodged his shoulder from under Dad's elbow.

"Jordan, you're never going to be able to figure out anything that would work," he taunted.

"Make it so JB is over here with his face on the Elucidator!" Jordan cried. "Let him give the commands!"

Mr. Rathbone seemed to be laughing so hard at that one that for a moment he stopped struggling forward.

"You think there'd be anything *JB* could do on that Elucidator?" Mr. Rathbone asked incredulously. "That's not the Elucidator you were using before. That's my personal Interchronological Rescue Elucidator. Naturally, anyone from the time agency would be shut out. Anyhow"—he turned his head mockingly—"JB's too busy screaming to do anything else."

Wasn't it a good thing that the Elucidator wasn't the same one Jordan had used before—and wasn't the same one that Kevin had entrusted with his secret? Did that mean that Jordan really had succeeded in destroying that Elucidator?

Jordan realized he didn't have time to figure out any of that. Because Mr. Rathbone was close enough now that Jordan was hearing his actual words, not just lip-reading them.

Which meant that Mr. Rathbone was close enough that the Elucidator could hear him too.

How much time did Jordan have before Mr. Rathbone figured that out? How much time did Jordan have before Mr. Rathbone just grabbed the Elucidator from beneath Jordan's face and shut off any chance for Jordan to do anything?

There's something about me touching the Elucidator that worries Mr. Rathbone, Jordan thought. *This is Mr. Rathbone's personal Elucidator—maybe there's some sort of emergency function it can follow even for someone who's not Mr. Rathbone. Is that what Mr. Rathbone's afraid of?*

Then Jordan knew what to try next.

"Can you summon Mr. Rathbone's employees into the office?" he asked the Elucidator. He didn't hear or see an answer, but he forged ahead anyway: "Bring Deep Voice and Tattoo Face and Doreen in to help!"

The words "I don't recognize those names as Interchronological Rescue employees" sounded in his ear. "I need first and last names."

Did that mean the Elucidator could bring them in if Jordan remembered the right names?

Mr. Rathbone had pulled his entire body except for his right leg out from under the pile of people. Now he was jerking his leg out too.

"Bring in, uh, Markiel Katun!" Jordan screamed. He couldn't remember Doreen's last name, or any part of Tattoo Face's. He hoped this would be enough.

Suddenly Deep Voice was standing over Jordan. But he just looked around in confusion. And Mr. Rathbone was away from the pile of all the other people. He lurched toward Jordan.

"Help!" Jordan screamed. "Stop Mr. Rathbone!"

Deep Voice swung his fist at Mr. Rathbone. But just then Mr. Rathbone screamed, "Freeze the intruder! The employee who's assaulting me!"

So Mr. Rathbone doesn't even remember his own employee's name? Jordan wondered. *Does that mean—?*

It didn't matter. Deep Voice froze in place, his fist a good three inches from Mr. Rathbone's jaw.

Mr. Rathbone spat in Deep Voice's face.

"You're fired," Mr. Rathbone said. A slow smile spread over his face. "Freeze the vocal cords of everyone in this room except me," he added.

Jordan opened his mouth to protest, but no sound came out. He could still move his head and face, but what good did that do?

Mr. Rathbone took a step back, putting even more distance between himself and Deep Voice's fists. He kicked Jordan's chest, shoving him away from the Elucidator that had been hiding under his cheek. Jordan's face came to rest on a cold, hard, marble section of the floor, but there was nothing he could do about it.

Mr. Rathbone bent down, picked up the Elucidator from the floor, and casually slid it into his pocket. Then he spun around, the only one able to move in the roomful of frozen bodies.

He seemed to be admiring everything he had done.

"I defeated all of you," he said. He peered at the pile of Skidmores, JB, Angela, and Chip. Then his eyes flicked toward Deep Voice and toward Jonah, standing helplessly with baby Kevin in his arms. Finally Mr. Rathbone's gaze came to rest on Jordan, helplessly sprawled on the floor. "It was nine against one, and I *still* came out ahead. Nine and a half against one, if you count the baby."

Jordan darted his eyes toward Mr. Rathbone's desk—at least he could still move his eyes.

And, from his new position on the marble tile, now Jordan could see that the Elucidator he'd pulled from Mr. Rathbone's desk was lying in pieces on the floor.

At least Jordan had managed to accomplish that.

"Yes, I see that too, Jordan," Mr. Rathbone said. But there was still an enormous amount of glee in his voice. "After everything else I've done, don't you think I'm capable of reassembling a mere Elucidator? Even . . ." His grin seemed even more malicious than ever. "Even the best Elucidator in the world?"

He went over and crouched down and began picking up pieces from the carpet.

"Repair mode!" he commanded.

Jordan was horrified to see the broken pieces fitting back together in Mr. Rathbone's hand.

"Victory!" Mr. Rathbone gloated. "Now I have everything I wanted!"

He glanced toward baby Kevin lying silent and still in Jonah's arms. Then he looked back at Jordan.

"And you actually thought you could defeat me?" he taunted.

There was something odd about his last word, "me."
It came out phlegmy and wobbly, as if spoken by a completely different man. A much older man, perhaps.

Mr. Rathbone put his hand to his throat, as if he had
noticed the difference, too. Just in the moment that it took
him to move his hand, it changed as well. It was suddenly
covered with loose, flappy, age-spotted skin. The skin of
his throat was loose and wrinkled too. So was his face.
And his hair had suddenly become sparse and white. And
then most of it vanished from the top of his head.

"What's happening to me?" Mr. Rathbone moaned.
"Stop it! Stop . . ."

He opened his mouth again, but no words came out. It
was like watching a skeleton try to speak.

And then Mr. Rathbone keeled over onto the carpet.

He was dead.

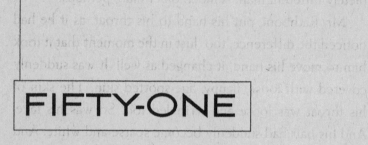

FIFTY-ONE

Nobody moved. Everybody in the room was frozen now: five adults, four kids, and baby Kevin because of Mr. Rathbone's commands, Mr. Rathbone because of his odd death. But Mr. Rathbone's body kept deteriorating. Now he *was* a skeleton.

Now he was dust.

In the last moments while Mr. Rathbone's hand still held together, it tilted forward, sliding away from the wrist as tendons and muscle and nerves broke down. The Elucidator Mr. Rathbone had reassembled fell through the bony fingers and rolled across the carpet, then onto the marble tiles.

It came to rest right against Jordan's forehead.

Oh, no! Jordan thought. *Is the same thing going to happen to me? Just because it's touching me?*

He tried to squirm away, since he'd been able to move

his head a little when Mr. Rathbone was still allowing everyone to talk. But he couldn't tilt his head back far enough. The Elucidator stayed against his skin.

Jordan stared down at his hands, motionless against the marble floor. Were they aging? Were they the hands of a fourteen-year-old now? A thirty-year-old? Was Jordan's death by old age going to be even more excruciating than Mr. Rathbone's, because it would take Jordan longer to get there?

Jordan stared and stared and stared, and his hands didn't change at all. He was fine, except for being frozen.

So that death was just for Mr. Rathbone, Jordan thought. *Second set it all up because somehow he knew what would happen.*

Did Second also know that Jordan would end up with the dangerous Elucidator right beside Jordan's face?

Jordan remembered his promise to Kevin, which he'd barely understood even as he was making it.

Is there still more that I need to do? he wondered.

Just then the door to Mr. Rathbone's office slid open.

"Markiel?" someone called cautiously.

Then someone else cried, "Oh, *my*! What happened here?"

It was Doreen, Tattoo Face, and . . . was that *Cira*? Cira the undercover time agent Jordan had mistaken for a candy striper at the hospital?

Cira waved an Elucidator toward all the frozen people.

"Unfreeze them enough that they can talk!" she commanded.

A jumble of voices rose in the air.

"*This* is your secret contact at the time agency?" Deep Voice exploded. "A little girl?"

"I'm not a little girl!" Cira protested.

"You were secretly working for them?" JB demanded.

"I was getting *information* from them to overthrow Interchronological Rescue!" Cira countered.

"Markiel, how could you have let Rathbone freeze you when you were carrying an Elucidator of your own?" Doreen demanded.

"I told you I'm not very good with Elucidators! That's why I needed you guys as backup!" Deep Voice replied.

"Jordan, Jonah, Katherine—are you all okay?" Mom and Dad called out, practically together.

Probably Jonah, Katherine, Angela, Chip, and even baby Kevin were shouting too, but Jordan lost track of all the individual voices.

He himself said nothing. Words were still ringing in his head: *Is there still even more that I need to do?*

He was no genius like Second/Kevin, and he'd never been inclined to make predictions about the future. Usually he didn't even bother thinking about the future.

But in that moment while everyone else was shouting, he could see exactly what was going to happen.

Everyone was going to unfreeze. And then JB and Cira were going to get all official and territorial and insist on examining everything that had happened ever since Jordan grabbed the glitchy cell phone/Elucidator out of JB's hands on that long-ago Tuesday morning in the Skidmore kitchen.

Probably Mr. Rathbone's entire office would be swarming with time agents inside five minutes.

In the midst of all that, Mom and Dad would find Jordan, Jonah, and Katherine and exclaim over them endlessly. They'd insist on making sure that none of them were hurt; they'd probably check all three kids' knees and elbows for injuries that even Jordan, Jonah, and Katherine might not have noticed.

And then Mom and Dad would want to gather all of them—probably even including Chip, JB, Angela, Deep Voice, baby Kevin, and whatever random time agent was nearby—into a some huge, happy Skidmore family group hug.

This time, Jordan would hug back. This time, Jordan would be as excited about it as his parents were.

But at some point in all that examining and exclaiming and hugging, someone was bound to decide to study the dangerous Elucidator that was currently leaning against Jordan's forehead. Probably the time agents would start cautiously, taking the pile of dust that had once been Mr. Rathbone as their warning. But eventually they'd lose that caution, because they'd just want to know. To understand. (In his head, Jordan could hear Second saying, *I was Pandora, bound and determined to open that box. I was Adam and Eve, unable to resist the temptation of eating from the Tree of Knowledge of Good and Evil.*) And then would Second and Kevin's secret come out, to destroy the real world and real time the same way Second had destroyed his own creation?

Or was there still a way for Jordan to stop that?

"Time-agency policy requires confiscating all Elucidators in the room," JB reminded Cira, his voice rumbling louder than everyone else's. "But—"

But I can't let that happen, Jordan thought.

He lifted his head as well as he could, straining his half-frozen neck to get an inch or two off the floor. The dangerous Elucidator stayed half up on its side and rolled forward, toward Jordan's ear.

Then Jordan brought his head down against the Elucidator as hard as he could. All he had to do was smash it into pieces like before. Surely no one would try to put it back together after what happened to Mr. Rathbone. Jordan heard the Elucidator crack. He felt it give way under his cheekbone; he felt it shatter. When he hit his head against it a second time, he could feel pieces of it dig into his skin along his jawline and on his cheek and all the way back by his ear. But he didn't stop. He kept bashing his head against the Elucidator and the floor as long as he could—until he could have sworn it was nothing but dust.

EPILOGUE

Back in the Twenty-First Century, Three Weeks Later

Jordan opened the front door.

"Jonah!" the girl standing on the Skidmores' porch said.

"Uh, no, I'm the other brother," Jordan said.

"Right," the girl said, blushing. "Sorry. I'm Andrea. I hear that you saved all of time too. Thanks." She peeked past Jordan, her braids swinging forward and her fluffy winter hat sliding down on her forehead. "Where is Jonah?"

"In there," Jordan said, tilting his head in the general direction of the family room, where a huge group was gathered.

Officially, the Skidmores were having a party for some "new friends" Katherine and Jonah had met at an adoption conference back in the fall, one day when Jordan was "sick." In reality, the party was for all the missing kids from history who'd ended up in the twenty-first century.

"These are kids you can just be yourself with," Mom had said when she and Dad had started planning this event. "They're the ones who actually know the truth about everything that happened."

She should have said they're the ones who know Jonah and not me, Jordan thought, watching Andrea scurry past him toward the family room.

It was weird knowing the background story of every single kid who walked in the door: He knew that Andrea had once been Virginia Dare; he knew that Antonio and Brendan had been such great artists in the sixteen hundreds that people traveled through time to steal their works; he knew stories about royalty and murdered inventors and shipwrecked children of celebrities. When he'd been in the time hollow with Kevin, Jordan had watched the most notable moments of all the kids' lives.

But the main thing the other kids knew about Jordan was that he'd spent most of his life in another dimension.

Even among the kids who were most like him, he was the outsider.

Rather than follow Andrea into the family room with the other kids, Jordan stepped out onto the front porch for a moment.

It was just starting to snow, and the Christmas lights of the other houses up and down the street twinkled and shimmered and reflected in the flakes. But what Jordan mostly saw, looking around his neighborhood, was history. History he hadn't been a part of.

That's where Jonah stood when he and Chip got their first mysterious letter. . . . That's where Gavin jumped out and kidnapped Jonah, Katherine, Chip, and Daniella. . . . That's where Jonah first saw JB and Angela after they'd been turned into kids. . . . That's where JB stood when . . .

Jordan blinked and realized he was seeing the present, not the past. JB really had just appeared out of nowhere on the front sidewalk. It was the adult JB, and Jordan was glad of that. But the time agent was wearing such an enormous winter coat that Jordan couldn't tell if JB looked the same as the last time they'd seen each other or if a lot of time had passed for JB and the man had gained an extra fifty or hundred pounds.

"Admiring the lights?" JB asked.

"I guess," Jordan said, shrugging.

"I still can't believe people in the twenty-first century go to the trouble of climbing up on ladders and roofs to put them up by hand," JB said, shaking his head.

"Why—how do people put up Christmas lights in your time?" Jordan asked, curious in spite of himself. "*Do* people still put up Christmas lights? That's something else I never got to see in the future!"

"I'll never tell," JB said, grinning in a way that took the sting out of his words. He brushed aside the snow on the porch step and sat down. "You know it really is just because I *can't*. Not without—"

"I know, I know," Jordan said, rolling his eyes. "You don't want to take any more risks with the space-time continuum. Katherine and Jonah and I already saw our lifetime supply of the future."

"You'll get to see more of the future—" JB began.

"Right—when we get there," Jordan finished for him, because he'd already heard that before.

This was something Jordan was a little bitter about. He'd helped save everyone and everything, and he still hadn't been able to go around sightseeing in the future. JB had even refused to tell him how far into the future he'd already been, those times at Interchronological Rescue and at the futuristic hospital.

How soon would it be before people invented time travel?

"Otherwise, is everything okay with you now?" JB asked, turning his head to look up at Jordan.

Jordan leaned against one of the porch pillars. How was he supposed to answer that?

"Mom and Dad are acting as much like adults as ever, if that's what you mean," he said. They'd started doing this annoying thing where they'd say, *You know, we do remember what it's like to be your age. Actually, we remember it much better than most parents of teenagers, because it was a lot more recent. . . .* But Jordan wasn't going to tell JB that.

"And you and Jonah?" JB asked. "How are the two of you getting along? Sharing a room and all?"

Jordan shrugged. "Fine," he said. It didn't seem worth mentioning that neither of them cared that much about the posters on the wall. Or who got which bunk. "We're not the problem. It's . . . everyone else. Like, when our basketball coach puts both of us in at the same time, he forgets we're two separate people. At our last game, the ref yelled at him and asked him if he knew how to count to five. And nobody can tell us apart."

"I think identical twins raised under normal circumstances have some of those same problems," JB said gently. "And time will keep healing the discrepancies. Your coach will figure out how to count to five again."

"Is everything really going to be okay with time now?" Jordan asked. "Are we done with all our time travel and people being weird ages? Done with all the adventure?"

Done with people aging into dust in the blink of an eye?

He didn't say that one out loud.

JB paused. He seemed to be watching the snowflakes gently floating down. They swirled in a way that made Jordan think the wind patterns were very odd tonight.

"Everything's fine," JB said, in a soothing voice that Jordan didn't quite trust. "Or . . . everything will be fine. With time travel, you know, verb tenses get a little confusing."

Jordan tilted his head, trying to figure out what JB was really saying.

"But that Elucidator I destroyed . . ." he began.

"It can never be reassembled," JB said. "By anyone. Ever. That electronic dust you left behind? There's not even a trace of it anywhere. We looked for it with every microscopic search technique we know. But it vanished completely."

Maybe that was meant to reassure Jordan. But somehow it just spooked him.

"And all the other changes . . ." Jordan tried again.

JB nodded, seeming more confident now.

"We released the ripple of changes from everything you were involved with—and for that matter, everything Jonah did connected to the nineteen thirties," he said. "Second tricked me before into thinking all of that had already been resolved. Now it really is. And everything's fine. You could say that between the two of you, you and

Jonah fixed everything in the end. You two . . . and Kevin."

Jordan squinted at JB. He didn't want to talk about Kevin yet. Or Second.

"So now if I went to the future, everyone at Interchronological Rescue would know who I am," Jordan said. Did he sound like he wanted to brag? "I mean, they'd know I'm Jordan Skidmore from the twenty-first century, not just some pitiful kid from the nineteen thirties."

"Yes—if there still *were* an Interchronological Rescue," JB said with a scornful snort. "We've shut it down completely. And time agents are combing through the records so we'll know how to prevent someone like Mr. Rathbone from doing what he did ever again. Some of the agents are a little upset that Mr. Rathbone is already dead, and they can't prosecute him and send him to time prison—he broke a lot of laws."

Jordan didn't want to talk about Mr. Rathbone's death yet either.

"I thought he said nothing could be traced back to him," Jordan said instead.

JB shook his head, the ghost of a grin on his face.

"A CEO can't treat his employees with contempt and still expect them to take the rap for all the CEO's crimes," he said. "Especially when he's dead and can't punish them anymore. Interchronological Rescue employees are lining up to give us incriminating information. And some of them were smart enough to keep very good records."

"Deep Voice, Doreen, and Tattoo Face," Jordan guessed, trying to match JB's grin. "Will I get to see any of them again? Will we even get to see *you* ever again?"

"I still have a few loose ends to tie up," JB said. "That's why I'm here tonight."

He stood up and brushed snow off his backside. The front part of his coat fell open while he was twisted around, and Jordan saw that JB hadn't gained a lot of weight. Instead, he had something tucked inside a large inner pouch of his coat.

No—someone.

"You brought baby Kevin with you to the party?" Jordan asked, stunned. "You still haven't turned him back to his right age?"

"What would his right age be?" JB asked. "Thirteen, the age he was when he stole the Elucidator from Jonah? Twenty-six, like he was when Gary and Hodge *gave* him an Elucidator? Thirty-nine, like when he created his ill-fated other dimension? Thirty-nine and a half, like when he rescued me and Mr. Rathbone murdered him for it?"

JB patted the baby's back. The baby kept its eyes closed. Jordan didn't know much about babies, but he guessed this one was soundly asleep.

"Also, we've learned there are . . . complications," JB said. "Some I need to talk to you about."

"Me?" Jordan repeated. "Not Jonah or Katherine? Or Mom and Dad?"

"You're first," JB said. "Because you were the only one there when Kevin gave his command to the Elucidator. The command that re-aged your parents."

"I didn't hear what he said," Jordan said. "So that information is gone. That's *why* I destroyed the dangerous Elucidator. I told you."

His voice came out strong and deep and defiant, and he was kind of proud of that.

JB looked down at the sleeping baby sheltered from the cold wind by the heavy winter coat.

"I'm not criticizing anything you did," JB said. "You saved us all. It was necessary. But . . . I'm trying to understand all the ramifications. The Sam Chase I knew was incredibly skilled at predicting what people would do. He would have known what to expect of both you and Mr. Rathbone. And . . . he would have known that Elucidators are practically indestructible under normal circumstances."

Jordan did a double take. This wasn't what he'd expected JB to say.

"Wait, you mean Kevin was able to tell the Elucidator something that re-aged Mom and Dad and everyone else *and* made the Elucidator self-destruct when I pulled it down to the floor? And then let me pound it into dust and nothingness after it killed Mr. Rathbone?" Jordan asked. He felt like JB was taking something away from him. Anger surged inside him. "You really think Kevin could have done all that in the three seconds he had to say anything? After I'd told the Elucidator not to follow any orders except to help Mom and Dad?"

Before JB had a chance to answer, Jordan thought of something else to ask: "And if Kevin could do all that—and *kill* Mr. Rathbone, too—then why didn't he stop the Elucidator from turning him back into a baby?"

JB gazed steadily back at Jordan.

"Maybe," JB said softly, "he was okay with being a baby again. As long as you kept your promise."

For perhaps the millionth time in the past three weeks, Jordan remembered what Kevin had made him promise, and the way Kevin had looked, saying the words. It was almost like Jordan had PTSD or something.

It's bad enough I have nightmares about watching Mr. Rathbone die and disappear, Jordan told himself. *Why does my mind also keep playing back Kevin's words: "Would you help me like you'd help your own family?"*

Had there been some kind of trick behind those words? Some trick that Jordan's brain was trying to tell him he'd missed?

"But—" Jordan began.

JB held up his hand, signaling for Jordan to wait.

"Most time hollows have . . . well, I guess you could consider them a type of recording apparatus," JB said. "That's a good enough explanation for now. All you really need to know is that we are able to figure out what Kevin said into that Elucidator."

"So the secret's out!" Jordan cried.

"No," JB said, shaking his head. "It's not. Kevin said nothing but 'Yes. I authorize the planned changes.'"

Jordan jerked his head back so hard he clunked it against the pillar.

"What?" Jordan asked. "But Mom and Dad and all the other adults changed back! How did they do that without Kevin providing the cure?"

"It's useful to look at where an Elucidator comes from," JB said. "And though Mr. Rathbone clearly believed that that Elucidator was a standard-issue Interchronological Rescue model, for him to program as he wished, its actual background was a bit more suspicious. It appears that Second Chance did the original programming on that Elucidator before he died. And somewhere in all that programming, he had a section that only his thirteen-year-old self was able to access."

"So . . . Kevin really did receive a message from his older self," Jordan said.

JB nodded. "Probably," he agreed. "And part of that message must have been a warning for Kevin about what Mr. Rathbone wanted from him. And . . . the Elucidator provided a way for Kevin—and you—to escape Mr. Rathbone without giving him what he wanted."

"But . . . but . . . that meant Second Chance knew I would grab Kevin away from Mr. Rathbone," Jordan stammered. "And that I would pull the Elucidator off the desk. And . . . probably that I would go back and get everyone else to help me. And that Mr. Rathbone would put the Elucidator back together, and it would kill him. And then I would destroy it."

JB shrugged. "Like I said, Second Chance was very good at predictions. He was good at knowing what holograms of himself to leave behind, too. To prepare you."

Jordan took a moment to absorb all of this. He thought about the many, many questions Second Chance had never answered. That was because Jordan had never seen the man as a real, living human being, in real time. Jordan had only ever seen him as a hologram—a hologram that Second Chance had set up before his own death. Even though he'd let Mr. Rathbone think that Mr. Rathbone controlled the holograms.

"Second talked to me about how he'd been tempted by the Tree of Knowledge and Pandora's box," Jordan said.

"But it's like Second wanted me to know enough to keep Mr. Rathbone from destroying the whole world with his own Pandora's box."

"That's not a contradiction," JB said. "Knowledge isn't evil, in and of itself. It's what people choose to do with their knowledge that makes the difference. I think it matters what you want knowledge *for*. And what you're willing to sacrifice to get it. There are trade-offs."

Jordan thought about how Jonah had told him that JB always talked to him about God and destiny and fate and free will. Was this all that JB was going to tell Jordan? Would Jordan have to figure out everything else on his own?

Jordan still had questions.

"But then . . . if Second could predict and arrange all that . . . why didn't he know Mr. Rathbone was going to kill him?" he asked. "Why didn't Second stop that?"

JB looked out toward the snow, which was thicker than ever.

"The time-agency experts say there's only one interpretation possible," he said. "Second wanted to rescue me more than he wanted to save his own life. He was loyal, in the end. And he thought he had to stop Mr. Rathbone once and for all, to save time."

"So Second was a good guy, after all," Jordan mumbled. "A good guy who *had* to kill Mr. Rathbone."

There. He'd touched on the one issue he hadn't let himself think about in three weeks.

JB kept staring out into the snow.

"I've been debating with myself about how much of this to tell you," he said.

"Well, you have to tell me now!" Jordan said.

That could have been taken as a joke, but JB didn't laugh. He turned to face Jordan.

"The best projectionists at the time agency have examined everything Second did, and everything he and Kevin set you up to do, from every angle," JB began, in a slow, hypnotic voice. "They say that, indeed, Rathbone had to die to save time."

It was amazing how relieved Jordan felt hearing that.

"But . . . ," JB went on. He swallowed hard. "It turns out there was one other way Second could have set things up that still would have saved time. He . . . he could have made it so *you* were the one who killed Mr. Rathbone."

Two thoughts exploded in Jordan's head at the same time. One was *I could have been the hero! Second stole that from me! Didn't he trust me to really do it?*

The other was *I could have been a killer! Second protected me!*

Would Jordan have wanted to live the rest of his life knowing he'd taken somebody's life? Even if it was somebody who needed to die?

Wouldn't Jordan have wondered forever if maybe, just maybe, there'd been some other way?

His nightmares about Mr. Rathbone's death would have been so much worse if Jordan knew he'd caused it.

"I . . . I think Second did the right thing," Jordan said.

"You do?" JB asked, almost as if he were surprised.

"Yes," Jordan said, and his voice was full of certainty now. "Except . . . would Kevin be a baby right now if Second had chosen the other scenario?"

JB bit his lip.

"No," he said. "He could have saved himself that. It appears that he thought paving the way for his younger version to have a good life was a reasonable trade for everything else."

Jordan looked down at the baby tucked inside JB's coat.

"But Kevin—I mean baby Kevin, now—the way things turned out, he doesn't have any control over his life," Jordan said. "He can't even control who changes his diaper!"

"Oh, but he exerted a lot of control over that before he un-aged," JB said. "He got an honorable person to promise to take care of him the same way he'd take care of his own family. The way he knew his whole family would take care of Kevin."

Jordan squinted at JB. JB stared steadily back. Then the man began nodding slowly.

"Yes," JB said. "He knew what you would do. And the rest of your family, too. How you'd take him in."

Jordan recoiled.

"Are you saying Kevin wanted my family to *adopt* him?" Jordan asked, his voice squeaking with surprise. "He wants Mom and Dad to have *three* thirteen-year-old sons, only one of them won't look like the other two?"

"No, we think Kevin wanted your family to adopt him as a baby," JB said in an even tone. "So he'll always be thirteen years younger than you and Jonah, and nearly twelve years younger than Katherine."

Jordan blinked.

"Second embedded an extra command into the Elucidator," JB said. "It appears to have been very precisely layered. And it seems that once your parents and the others were their proper ages again, it disabled every Elucidator in the world from ever un-aging or re-aging anyone. Even children. Even baby Kevin. That's a pretty clear message."

Jordan gaped at JB for a long moment. Then he thought of a loophole.

"Someone could always go back in time and steal an Elucidator that still works to re-age him," he said.

"Theoretically," JB said. "Except that, after tonight, the time agency is sealing off all time travel. We'll be able to watch the past and learn from it, but nothing more."

"But—" Jordan began.

"Time travel took us to the brink of total destruction multiple times," JB said. "It's like when the people of your time decided nuclear energy was too dangerous to . . . oh, wait, that hasn't happened quite yet. Sorry. There, I have given you one tidbit of information from the future."

Jordan's brain was reeling. He realized that he'd kind of thought that, now that the danger from Mr. Rathbone was past, he and Jonah and Katherine—and maybe some of their friends—could just zip off through time whenever they wanted. They could just play around with time travel, rather than having it always be something risky.

Instead it sounded like JB expected them to stay in the twenty-first century with a new baby brother who would be smarter than any of them when he grew up. And maybe he'd be dangerous, too.

"How do you know Mom and Dad even want another kid?" Jordan asked, shifting to the more immediate problem.

"Because they already offered," JB said. "That night in Mr. Rathbone's office. They were both worried about what would happen to Kevin. And of course we told them he wasn't going to stay a baby, because we didn't know everything else."

"Oh," Jordan said numbly.

"Everything worked out so, so precisely right," JB

said. "Even when I saw you in the hospital and I thought you were Jonah—do you know how many problems and paradoxes it would have created if I'd known who you really were?"

Jordan didn't answer that question. He didn't want to think about how close they'd been to disaster.

"And I thought you were giving me a warning about the missing children, when you were really talking about your family," JB went on. "And that set up Angela and me being nearby when Charles Lindbergh kidnapped Katherine . . . and then that helped Jonah save time, and set up everything for you and Kevin to stop Mr. Rathbone. . . . Everything that worked out just right so far makes us think that this is just right too."

Jordan felt frozen in a way that had nothing to do with the snow swirling around him.

"Here," JB said, slipping baby Kevin into Jordan's arms. "You take him on in to your parents. Would you send Jonah and Katherine out to talk to me?"

The baby was surprisingly light in Jordan's arms as he carried him in through the front door. Instantly a group of girls clustered around.

"Oooh! He's so cute!" one of them cooed.

Maybe having a baby brother wouldn't be such a terrible thing.

"Who is he?" one of the other girls asked.

Jordan realized this was an important moment. Should he tell them everything?

No, he thought. *Isn't that kind of the point of Second getting to be a baby all over again? So he really does get another chance?*

"This is Kevin," Jordan said. "My parents are adopting him."

Jordan had underestimated what the girls did and didn't know. Their eyes widened and they looked shocked. But then one of the girls—whose name, Jordan remembered, was Emily—reached out her hand and patted the baby's head.

"He's a lucky kid," she said. "He'll have the whole family watching out for him."

"Yeah, but this means Katherine won't be the baby of the family anymore," Jordan said.

He didn't realize Katherine had come up right behind him.

"I had my birthday last week, remember?" she said airily. "I'm *twelve* now. I'm not a baby anymore, no matter what."

"Hey, everybody, let's sing 'Happy Birthday' to Katherine," one of the other girls, Daniella, shouted.

Jordan remembered that Daniella had been Russian royalty in original time. Maybe bossing people around

was in her blood: She was really good at getting everybody to join in singing. Jordan used the cover of the song
to whisper to Jonah and Katherine that JB wanted to see
them. Then he took baby Kevin on into the kitchen, where
Mom was putting another tray of pizza rolls in the oven
and Dad was refilling the ice bucket.

"Jordan, could you—" Mom began without turning
around.

But Dad was staring at Jordan.

"Linda," Dad whispered. "I think . . . I think it's really
going to happen."

Then Mom turned around. Her jaw dropped. And
then she began laughing and crying all at once.

Suddenly Jordan realized why JB had wanted him to
deliver Kevin to his parents. Jonah had gotten to give
them the baby version of Jordan, and now Jordan was getting the same kind of experience.

"You don't know how he's going to grow up this time
around," Jordan warned, even as Mom and Dad circled
him and Kevin and started hugging them both.

"Silly, we didn't know how you and Jonah were going
to grow up either," Mom said. "Or Katherine. We just
hoped, and prayed . . . and loved you . . ."

"We brought Christmas cookies!" someone called
behind them, and Jordan was glad of the interruption.

He turned around to see the adult version of Angela and the bearded time agent that Jordan recognized as her boyfriend, Hadley Correo. But something really odd was going on tonight, because Angela and Hadley weren't just holding giant tins of cookies—they were also each holding a baby.

Jordan looked a little more closely. He'd seen those babies before . . . in a snippet of 1932 he'd watched from the time hollow with Kevin.

"You brought the baby versions of Gary and Hodge to the party?" Jordan asked incredulously.

"We're going to call them Gregory and Henry," Angela said evenly.

"It came through?" Mom asked eagerly. "The time agency accepted your proposal?"

Angela nodded. "We solved a lot of their problems," she said. "Gary and Hodge were kind of . . . orphaned by time and circumstances, and Second *didn't* do anything to re-age them, so . . . how do you prosecute babies for crimes they did as adults, in a totally different life? Hadley and I made the case that they deserved another chance. We're hoping growing up in a different time and place will make them different people."

She was looking at Jordan like she desperately wanted him to agree. He shrugged.

"Hey, Gary and Hodge helped *me*," Jordan said. "It was kind of by accident, and what they were really trying to do was torture Jonah with my existence, but . . . maybe this time around you'll get them to do good things on purpose!"

"Let's hope so," Hadley chimed in. He looked grateful—evidently he and Angela were already thinking of the babies as their own.

"The time agency was always worried that one of the things the plane crash interrupted was my intended future as the mother of five," Angela told Jordan. "Time travel sort of already gave me two, since I took in Leonid Sednev and Maria Romanova when they escaped from 1918. I figure, we'll add these two and go from there."

"And the time agency approved my request to stay in the twenty-first century, to keep an eye on this pivotal era," Hadley added. "So . . . Angela and I are getting married next week!"

This made Mom hug Angela and Hadley—and all three babies. Jordan decided he didn't need to stay in the kitchen any longer.

But walking back out into the cluster of kids felt different now. Maybe he was seeing everyone from the perspective of being Kevin's older brother, rather than as the outsider. He knew these kids, even if they didn't really know him. He'd have to make sure nobody treated Kevin badly because of what they knew about Second. Or he'd have to make sure that they knew the good things about Second as well. Or . . .

Jordan bumped into Katherine, who was apparently back from talking to JB outside.

"Watch," Katherine whispered to him.

"Huh? Oh . . ."

He followed her gaze. She was staring at Andrea, the girl who had come in looking for Jonah. Now Jonah was standing right beside her.

"I've been trying all night to figure out how to say this," Andrea was telling Jonah. "And I kept chickening out. But I think . . . I think I've recovered. I told Aunt Patty everything, and she didn't think I was crazy, and now she's going to let my grandfather come celebrate Christmas with us. . . ."

"That's her grandfather from the sixteen hundreds!" Katherine muttered. "The one who came to live in our time because Andrea wouldn't leave the past without him."

Jordan nodded, because he knew this story as well as she did.

"But, anyhow," Andrea continued telling Jonah, "maybe I waited too long, maybe you're not interested anymore. But—"

"You're willing to be my girlfriend now?" Jonah finished for her.

Andrea nodded, and the whole roomful of kids broke out in applause.

"Um, a little privacy here?" Andrea muttered, and she and Jonah ducked into the living room by themselves.

Katherine elbowed Jordan.

"Isn't that sweet?" she said. "But don't feel like you need to keep up by getting a girlfriend too. Really, it's almost like Jonah and I are years older than you, because we traveled through time so much. . . ."

"And I at least *saw* every bit of time you traveled through," Jordan reminded her. "So maybe I'm even more mature. Anyhow, I was kind of thinking . . . Emily is really nice."

"Whoa, nothing like starting at the top," Katherine said, gaping at him. "You know she's Albert Einstein's daughter, right?"

Jordan hadn't even been thinking about that. What he'd noticed was how kindly she'd patted Kevin's head even after she knew who he really was.

"Hey, I managed to hold my own with Second and Kevin," Jordan said. "Well, sort of. I got them to trust me, anyway."

"And thanks to you, now I have a third brother!" Katherine complained jokingly.

"There are worse things," Jordan said. "You could be an only child, remember?"

He thought about how lonely she'd looked in the glimpse he'd gotten of that dimension. He could still hear Mom and Dad and Angela and Hadley exclaiming over baby Kevin in the kitchen. But he couldn't tell how Katherine really felt about getting another brother—especially one who happened to be the baby version of her former worst enemy. She and Jonah were the ones who'd been angriest with Second from the very beginning.

"I was thinking," Katherine said. "Now I know what we should get Mom and Dad for Christmas. A picture of you, me, Jonah, and Kevin. Together."

So maybe Katherine was fine with everything, after all. It was much easier to forgive a baby.

Across the room, a group of kids in Santa hats started singing "Jingle Bells." Jordan recognized Gavin and Antonio in the group, and realized it was a lot of the same kids who'd worn skull sweatshirts and acted mean in the time cave back when everything started with Chip and Jonah and Katherine. It seemed like they'd all changed a lot.

So maybe time travel really is good for some people, Jordan thought. He wondered if maybe he should go out and make this argument to JB. Jordan went over to the window and glanced out, but JB was nowhere in sight.

So that means it's all over, Jordan thought. *It's really over.*

He felt like some old person who had nothing left in his life but memories of the past. Then he heard someone behind him say, "Psst."

It was Jonah, and he was alone.

"You and Andrea broke up already?" Jordan asked.

"Very funny," Jonah said. "No—she wanted to go call her grandfather on his cell phone and let him know everything was okay."

He grinned in a goofy way that made it clear he and Andrea thought things were much better than okay.

"Some dude from the sixteen hundreds is really using a cell phone?" Jordan asked.

"I guess so," Jonah said.

Somehow this made Jordan sad. If there was no more time travel, how could fun things like that ever happen again?

Jordan saw that Jonah was motioning for somebody with his head. Katherine sidled up beside them.

"Is it time?" Katherine asked.

"I think so," Jonah said. "If we can just go somewhere private."

Katherine and Jonah led Jordan to the same spot in the dining room where Jordan had once hidden from JB.

"Now," Katherine said.

"JB wanted us to tell you that a hundred years after

people ban nuclear energy, they figure out a way to make it safe and start using it again," Jonah said.

"Okay," Jordan said. "So?"

Jonah slipped something out of the pocket of his blue jeans.

"JB also gave me this," Jonah said. "For you, me, and Katherine."

It looked like a thumb drive. But Jordan saw a little flash of light—not quite words, but the promise of words.

"Oh!" Jordan said. "It's an—"

Before he could say the word "Elucidator" Jonah and Katherine clapped their hands over his mouth.

"We have to keep it secret," Katherine said.

"And it's only for emergencies with Kevin," Jonah said. "Or . . . just times that we think are necessary."

Jordan reached out and touched the Elucidator.

"And he really trusted *us* with it, instead of Mom and Dad?" Jordan asked.

Katherine nodded. "We have the most time-travel experience," she reminded him.

Jordan pulled his hand back. It wasn't actually that he was longing to travel through time right now. Just knowing it was possible was enough.

Life right now was exactly enough for Jordan.

ACKNOWLEDGMENTS

Since this is the last book in a series that I began writing eight years ago, I feel like I have years of thank-yous to say. First of all I'd like to thank my husband and kids for putting up with me sometimes being mentally in an entirely different century. (Who would ever want to have to tell their teacher, "My mom forgot to sign that permission slip because she kind of thinks it's 1483 right now"? I don't think I was ever that bad—was I?) I owe a huge debt of gratitude to my agent, Tracey Adams, and everyone at Simon & Schuster Books for Young Readers who supported the series, especially David Gale, Navah Wolfe, and Liz Kossnar. My friends Linda Gerber, Erin MacLellan, Jenny Patton, Nancy Roe Pimm, Linda Stanek, and Amjed Qamar read portions of this and some of the earlier books and offered helpful comments. Kids, teachers, librarians, and bookstore people all over the country also often asked interesting questions that helped me see new angles to take with the books. I have particularly fond memories of a gathering of kids at a book-signing at Hicklebee's in San Jose, California, in 2010, who asked about the time travel in my books vs. Einstein's theories and string theory and all sorts of other fun physics concepts. I think they were all secretly Stanford graduate students who just happened to also be twelve-year-olds, but wow, what a fun conversation.

And, finally, I owe thanks to my friend Marcy Mermel Gessel, who made a really good suggestion five years ago when I was (already) stressing out about how I was going to end this series. Marcy, you were right—a party is always a great idea.

Reading Group Guide for
by Margaret Peterson Haddix

←——— THE MISSING: BOOK 8 ———→

REDEEMED

About the Book

Jonah's new twin must time travel and face off against his siblings' worst enemy in order to save the future—and his family—in the eighth and final book of The Missing series. After traveling through history multiple times and discovering his original identity, Jonah thought he'd fixed everything. But some of his actions left unexpected consequences. His parents—and many other adults—are still stuck as teenagers. And now Jonah has a new sibling, an identical twin brother named Jordan. As odd as all this is for Jonah, it's beyond confusing for Jordan. How does everyone in his family have memories of Jonah when he doesn't? How can his annoying kid sister, Katherine, speak so expertly about time travel—and have people from the future treating her with respect? A few rash moves by Jordan send them all into the future—and into danger. What if he's also the only one who can get them back to safety, once and for all?

Discussion Questions

The discussion questions below align with the following English Language Arts Common Core Standards: (RL.3–8.1, 2).

1. What has Jonah gained after he succeeds in saving time from collapsing?

2. What disturbing thought occurs to Jordan when he sees his identical twin?

3. What does Jordan recognize about Katherine?

4. How did Jonah and Jordan end up in different dimensions?

5. How did Sam Chase trick JB? Why did he start calling himself Second Chance?

6. What makes Mrs. Skidmore think Second Chance might be a murderer?

7. Why does Second say he is justified in breaking his promise?

8. What does the woman mean when she tells Deep Voice, "The Skidmore incident has to be the key"?

9. What did Hodge tell Jonah would be the outcome of the plane crashing?

10. Why can't the Skidmores count on the time agency for any help?

11. What is Jordan able to find out about Gary and Hodge from the Elucidator?

12. Why is the Elucidator unable to perform the invisibility function?

13. What does Deep Voice assume about the Skidmore children?

14. How does Jordan respond to Deep Voice calling them "primitives"?

15. Why doesn't Jordan trust himself to ask about his parents?

16. Who are Claude and Clyde Beckman?

17. What does Deep Voice reveal about the Elucidators?

18. What claim did Jonah make to Jordan about the disappearance of Gary and Hodge?

19. Do you agree with Jordan's accusation that Second has been "manipulating all of us all along"? If you agree, what are some examples of this manipulation?

20. What happens when Jonah and Jordan activate the Elucidators in the lab?

21. Who is Curtis Rathbone?

22. What does Jordan notice about the artwork on the walls?

23. What deal does Jonah propose to Rathbone?

24. What does Rathbone reveal about his feelings toward Gary and Hodge?

25. What is the job that Rathbone wants the Skidmores to "go back and finish"?

26. What makes Jonah wonder if Second has an identical twin?

27. Why does Deep Voice no longer trust Rathbone?

28. What sad news does Rathbone share with the Skidmores?

29. What does Second say has been the problem with everything Rathbone has done at Interchronological Rescue?

30. What crimes does Second accuse Rathbone of committing?

31. How does Jordan feel about being repeatedly mistaken for Jonah?

32. Why does Second say Jordan should trust him?

33. What does Second tell Jordan will happen if he saves his parents?

34. Why is Jordan certain Kevin can help save his mom and dad?

35. Why does Jordan tell the Elucidator to show every version of the childhoods of all three Skidmore kids?

36. How has Rathbone been using Jordan's parents as guinea pigs?

37. What is the cause of Rathbone's death?

38. What does Jordan feel bitter about?

39. Do you agree that Second was "a good guy, after all"? What does Second do that makes him a good guy?

40. Discuss possible scenarios that could require future use of the Elucidator.

Turn the page for a sneak peek at the first book in
bestselling author Margaret Peterson Haddix's new
series *Children of Exile*.

We weren't orphans after all.

That was the first surprise.

The second was that we were going home.

"Home!" my little brother, Bobo, sang as he jumped up and down on my bed, right after the Freds told us the news. "Home, home, home, home . . ."

I grabbed him mid-jump and teased, "Silly, you've never even been there before! How do you know it's worth jumping on the bed for?"

"I was born there, right?" Bobo said. "So I do know, Rosi. I *remember*."

He blinked up at me, his long, dark eyelashes sweeping his cheeks like a pair of exquisite feathers. Bobo was five; he had curls that sprang out from his head like so many exclamation points, and his big eyes always seemed to glow. If he'd known how adorable he was, he would have been dangerous.

But there was a rule in Fredtown that you couldn't tell little kids how cute they were.

It was kind of hard to obey.

"How could you remember being such a tiny baby?" I asked. "You were only a few days old when you arrived in Fredtown. *None* of us were more than a few days old, coming here."

I tried to keep my voice light and teasing. I was twelve; I should have known better than to look to a five-year-old to answer my questions.

But no one else had given me the answers I wanted. And sometimes Bobo heard things.

"Edwy says home is where we belong," Bobo said, stubbornly sticking out his lower lip. "Edwy says we should have stayed there always."

"Oh, *Edwy* says," I teased. But it was hard to keep the edge out of my voice.

Of course Edwy has an answer, I thought. *Even if he just made it up. Even if he knows it's a lie.*

Edwy was twelve, like me—we were the oldest children in Fredtown. We were born on the same day. And we were the only ones who were moved to Fredtown on the very day of our birth, instead of waiting a day or two like everyone else. The Freds always told us it had been too "dangerous" for us to stay with our parents then. For the past twelve years, they'd said it was too "dangerous" for any of us children to go home.

I was maybe three the first time I asked, *But isn't it dangerous for our parents, too? Why didn't they come to Fredtown to be safe with us?*

The Freds always said, *They are adults. You are children. Adults have to take care of themselves. It is our job to take care of you.*

I didn't think that counted as a real answer.

That was why Edwy and I had decided when we were ten—back when we still talked to each other—that we were probably orphans and the Freds just didn't want to make us sad by telling us that.

We'd argued about this a little: I said surely the newest babies of Fredtown weren't orphans. Surely *their* parents were still alive.

"But there haven't been any new babies in my family since me," Edwy said fiercely. He always got fierce when the only other choice was sounding sad. "And none in yours since Bobo."

Once he said that, I could see lots of other evidence. If our parents were still alive, wouldn't they at least send us a letter every now and then? Wouldn't they have done everything they possibly could to come get us?

Didn't they know where we were?

When I asked the Freds questions like that, they patted

me on the head and told me I was too young to understand. Or they talked about how life was made up of hard choices and, as our guardians, they had chosen what was best for all of us children. And what was best for civilization itself.

The way the Freds talked was tricky. You had to wrap your mind around their words sometimes and turn them inside out to try to figure out what they were really saying.

The way Edwy talked was tricky, too.

"Rosi!" Bobo said, squirming against my grip. "I want to jump some more!"

If any of the Freds saw us, I would be in trouble. I was twelve and Bobo was five; it was wrong for someone who was bigger and older and stronger to overpower someone smaller and younger and weaker. It was wrong to hold someone who didn't want to be held.

"Fine," I told Bobo. "But mess up your own bed, not mine."

I turned and deposited him on his own cot. I was tempted to tickle him too, to try to bring back his glee and his ear-to-ear grin. But that would have required my asking him first, *Is it all right if I tickle you?* And I didn't have the patience for that just then.

Bobo didn't spring instantly to his feet like I expected. He didn't go back to bouncing. He just sat in a heap on his own bed and asked, as if he'd just now thought of the question: "Rosi, *is* it safe to go home now? Why was it too dangerous before but safe now?"

I ruffled his hair and made my voice as light and care-free as a summer breeze.

"You know things can change, you little apple dumpling, you," I said, using the baby name our Fred-parents had given Bobo years ago. "You know the Freds wouldn't send us home if it wasn't safe."

I wasn't like Edwy. I didn't usually lie. Not on purpose.

So why did I feel like I was lying to Bobo now?

Fredtown was a simple place. If I thought way back to when I was really little, I could remember when only a handful of families lived here, in only a small cluster of buildings. Even now, there were only sixteen blocks of houses, each block a perfect square laid out in grids as precise as the graph paper Edwy and I used for geometry homework. The school, the park, the library, the town hall, and the marketplace stood in the center of the town, surrounded by all the houses.

These were the kinds of questions the little kids asked when the Freds first told us we were going home:

Can we take the park with us?

Can we take our houses?

Can we take our toys?

Who will play in the park if we're not here? Won't the playground and our houses and our toys miss us?

When they gathered us all together to tell us we were going home, the Freds seemed to want to answer *only* the little kids' questions. When Edwy or I—or any of the almost-as-old-as-us kids—raised our hands, the Freds caught our eyes and shook their heads subtly, the way they always did when they wanted to say, *Not in front of the little ones. We'll talk about your questions later.*

Later hadn't come yet.

Instead, the Fred-parents were meeting at the town hall, so all of us older kids were looking after the little girls and boys.

I was just lucky Bobo was the only little one I was in charge of today. I was lucky I hadn't been given responsibility for the ones who didn't have a brother or sister old enough to babysit, like the Calim sisters (ages four, three, two, and one) or Peki and Meki, the toddler twins next door.

But Bobo had messed up both our beds now, and was starting to fuss: "When will the Freds be back? What's for supper? I'm hungry—can I have a snack? Will there be snacks when we go home? Can I take my teddy bear? The Freds will go home with us, right? Right?"

"Let's go to the park," I said. "I'll push you on the swing."

Bobo tucked his hand into mine, and we stepped out the front door.

"Don't want to move away from Fredtown," he whispered. "Don't want to move *anywhere*. Even home."

It was like some evil fairy godmother had cast a spell on the little boy who'd so gleefully jumped up and down on his bed only moments earlier. In the blink of an eye, he'd turned into a child who might cry at the brush of dandelion fluff against his cheek; at the scrape of a shoe against his heel; at a single wrong word from me.

"Hey," I said in my strongest voice. I made myself forget for a moment that I was worried about going home too. "Hey—look at me!"

Bobo turned his head and looked. A small almost-tear trembled in his eyelashes.

"No matter what, you will have me with you, remember?" I said. "Your big sister, who's been with you always? Doesn't that matter more than where we live? People matter more than places or things. You know that."

"I know that," Bobo repeated.

The almost-tear didn't fall. But he didn't wipe it away, either.

"Okay, race you to the park!" I said, and took off, tugging on his hand.

It was perfectly safe to dash off without watching where we were going. There were stop signs at all the cross streets along the boulevard. Fredtown was designed like that, to have as many places as possible to run and play.

I told myself we were running just to get Bobo to leave his sad thoughts behind. But maybe I wanted to run away a little bit, too.

I let Bobo beat me to the park, and he was already swinging on the monkey bars by the time I got there. I pretended to huff and puff, making my final strides into huge, dramatic events, just like our Fred-daddy always did.

"Can't . . . take . . . another . . . step," I panted, totally hamming it up. "Oh, wait. . . . Almost . . . there. Almost . . ."

I made my steps gigantic and labored, as if I had only enough energy for one or two more.

Bobo giggled, just like I'd hoped.

"You're silly, Rosi," he called to me, dangling from the metal bars. "Watch!"

He kicked his legs forward, building momentum to reach for the next rung of the monkey bar. He'd just learned to swing all the way across the bars. Fred-mama, Fred-daddy, and I had all stood there and clapped for him his very first time, only last week.

And now it was my turn to have tears stinging my eyes. Those were the same monkey bars I'd first conquered when I was about Bobo's age. I could remember Fred-mama and Fred-daddy clapping for me, too, standing in the exact same spot. Every memory I had was like that—located in Fredtown. My whole life had happened here: either on the sun-splashed playground; or in the bright, open, cheery school; or in the marketplace aisles, crowded with a world of treasures; or at our house, where Fred-mama and Fred-daddy took turns tucking Bobo and me into our beds. . . .

Why didn't they just tell us to call Fredtown "home," and never make us move anywhere else? I thought rebelliously. I slashed the back of my hand against my eyes, wiping away the tears. Or at least hiding them. *Why didn't they just tell us our Fred-parents were our real parents and left it at that? Why did they even have to mention our other parents? How much could those real parents of ours actually care if they never contacted us?*

There were other little kids on the playground, other big brothers and sisters watching carefully nearby. On a normal day, I probably would have taken charge and suggested some game everyone could play; I would have gotten busy counting off teams and doling out playground balls and appointing umpires or referees. Or maybe I would have gathered the younger kids together for a giggly session of shared jokes and riddles and silly made-up stories. But I didn't like the way the eight- and nine- and ten-year-olds were watching me now—like they thought *I* had answers; like they thought I might be able to explain what it meant that we were going home.

I kept one eye on Bobo but took a step back from the playground. I pretended I was so deep in thought that it would be wrong for anyone to interrupt me. Cupping my chin in my hand, I gazed down into one of the town hall window wells—that was what we called the dug-out spaces around the basement windows. The spaces were only about two feet by two feet, just deep and wide enough to let light in. You might think the window wells would also be great places for little kids to slip down into during hide-and-seek games, but they were too obvious, the first places any seeker looked. So mostly we all just avoided them.

Only, there was a little girl hiding in this window well now.